POPULAR PUBLICATIONS   FACSIMILE EDITIONS

Famous Fantastic Mysteries #2 (November 1939)

Initially published by The Frank A. Munsey Company, *Famous Fantastic Mysteries* was dedicated to reprinting the rare science fiction and fantasy stories from the early years of *Argosy*, *The All-Story*, and *The Cavalier*. *Famous Fantastic Mysteries* is one of the most important science fiction pulps. The second issue contains classic stories by A. Merritt, Garrett P. Serviss, George Allan England, and Austin Hall, among others.

Authors:

A. Merritt, Richard Butler Glaenzer, James P. Marshall, Garrett P. Serviss, George Allan England, Austin Hall, Leslie Burton Blades

Illustrators:

Samuel Cahan, Virgil Finlay

Vol. 1   NOVEMBER, 1939   No. 2

THIS magazine is the answer to thousands of requests that we have received over a period of years, demanding a second look at famous fantasies which, since their original publication, have become accepted classics. Our choice has been dictated by *your* requests and our firm belief that these are the aces of imaginative fiction.

—*The Editors.*

THE FRANK A. MUNSEY COMPANY, Publisher, 280 Broadway, New York, N. Y.
WILLIAM T. DEWART, *President*

THE CONTINENTAL PUBLISHERS & DISTRIBUTORS, LTD.
3 La Belle Sauvage, Ludgate Hill, London, E.C., 4
Paris: HACHETTE & CIE, 111 Rue Reaumur

Make me Prove
THAT I CAN TRAIN YOU AT HOME FOR A
Good Job in Radio

I TRAINED THESE MEN

$10 TO $20 WEEK IN SPARE TIME

"I repaired many Radio sets when I was on my tenth lesson, and I have made enough money to pay for my Radio course and also my instruments. I really don't see how you can give so much for such a small amount of money. I made $600 in a year and a half, and I have made an average of $10 to $20 a week—just spare time."—JOHN JERRY, 1529 Arapahoe St., Denver, Colo.

DOUBLED SALARY IN 5 MONTHS

"Shortly after I started the N. R. I. Course I began teaching Radio classes at the Sparton School of Aeronautics. After five months I was given a chance to join the American Airlines at a salary double that which I received from the school."—A. T. BROTHERS, 1130 Ocean Park Blvd., Santa Monica, Calif.

$200 TO $300 A MONTH IN OWN BUSINESS

"For the last two years I have been in business for myself making between $200 and $300 a month. Business has steadily increased. I have N. R. I. to thank for my start in this field."—ARLIE J. FROEHNER, 300 W. Texas Ave., Goose Creek, Texas.

THIS FREE BOOK
Has Helped Hundreds of Men Make More Money

Clip the coupon and mail it. I'm certain I can train you at home in your spare time to be a Radio Technician. I will send you my first lesson free. Examine it, read it, see how clear and easy it is to understand. Judge for yourself whether my course is planned to help you get a good job in Radio, a young, growing field with a future. You don't need to give up your present job, or spend a lot of money to become a Radio Technician. I train you at home in your spare time.

Why Many Radio Technicians Make $30, $40, $50 a Week

Radio broadcasting stations employ engineers, operators, station managers. Radio manufacturers employ testers, inspectors, foremen, servicemen in good-pay jobs. Radio jobbers, dealers, employ installation and service men. Many Radio Technicians open their own Radio sales and repair businesses and make $30, $40, $50 a week. Others hold their regular jobs and make $5 to $10 a week fixing Radios in spare time. Automobile, police, aviation, commercial Radio; loudspeaker systems, electronic devices, are other fields offering opportunities for which N. R. I. gives the required knowledge of Radio. Television promises to open good jobs soon.

Many Make $5, $10 a Week Extra in Spare Time While Learning

The day you enroll, I start sending you Extra Money Job Sheets which start showing you how to do Radio repair jobs. Throughout your training I send plans and directions which have helped many make $200 to $500 a year in spare time while learning. I send special Radio equipment to conduct experiments and build circuits. The 50-50 training method make learning at home interesting, fascinating, practical. I ALSO GIVE YOU A MODERN, PROFESSIONAL ALL-WAVE, ALL-PURPOSE SET SERVICING INSTRUMENT to help you make more money fixing Radios while learning and equip you for full time work after you graduate.

Find Out What Radio Offers You

Act today. Mail the coupon for Sample Lesson and my 64-page Book, "Rich Rewards in Radio." They point out Radio's spare time and full time opportunities and those coming in Television; tell about my course in Radio and Television; show letters from men I have trained telling what they are doing and earning. Read my money back agreement. Find out what Radio offers YOU! MAIL COUPON in an envelope, or paste on a postcard—NOW!

**J. E. SMITH, President
National Radio Institute, Dept. 9MK,
Washington, D. C.**

GOOD FOR BOTH 64 PAGE BOOK SAMPLE LESSON FREE

**J. E. Smith, President, National Radio Institute
Dept. 9MK, Washington, D. C.**

Dear Mr. Smith: Send me FREE, without obligation, Sample Lesson and 64-page book "Rich Rewards in Radio" which tells about Radio's spare time and full time opportunities and how I can train at home for them. (Write Plainly).

Name..Age.......

Address...

City.............................State.............2FR

4

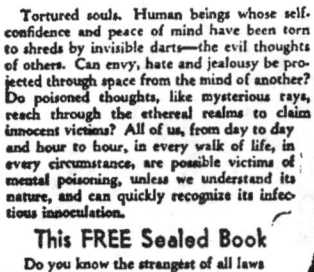

"I saw a white fire that shone like stars in a swirl of mist and I stood helpless while the sparkling devil pulled my dear ones over the ship's rail into the eerle light. I saw them a little while whirling away in the moon track behind the ship—and then they were gone!"

A Sequel to "The Moon Pool"

Through the moon door, to grapple with
the dread Dweller and wrest the six
Lost Ones from their prison of icy flame

6

The Conquest of the Moon Pool

By A. MERRITT

PART I

CHAPTER I

THE DWELLER

AS I begin this narrative, I find it necessary to refer, briefly, to my original recital which appeared under the title of "The Moon Pool," of the causes that led me into the adventure of which it is to be the history. The adventure which would forge the last links in the chain to bind the Dweller.

I have told you of that dread night on the *Southern Queen,* when the monstrous, shining Thing of living light and mingled rapture and horror embraced Throckmartin and drew him from his cabin down the moon path to its lair beneath the Moon Pool. I had promised Throckmartin to solve the mystery. But I had delayed keeping this promise for three years, believing nothing could really be done, and fearing my story would not be believed. At last, however, remorse drove me into action.

Had I set forth for that group of Southern Pacific islets called the Nan-Matal, where the Moon Pool lay hidden, a day before or after, I would not have found Olaf Huldricksson, hands lashed to the wheel of his ravished *Brunhilda,* steering it even in his sleep down the track of the Dweller. Olaf whose wife and babe the Dweller had snatched from him. Nor would I have picked up Larry O'Keefe from the wreck of his flying boat fast sinking under the long swells of the Pacific. And without O'Keefe and Huldricksson that weird and almost unthinkably fantastic drama enacted beyond the Moon Pool's gates must have had a very different curtain.

The remorse of a botanist, the burning, bitter hatred of a Norse seaman, the breaking of a wire in a flying-boat's wing —all these meeting at one fleeting moment formed the slender tripod upon which rested the fate of humanity! Could that universal irony which seems to mold our fortunes go further?

But there they were—O'Keefe and Huldricksson and I; Larry O'Keefe and Olaf Huldricksson and I, and Lakla of the flower face and wide, golden eyes. Lakla the Handmaiden of the Silent Ones, and the Three who had fashioned the Dweller from earth's secret heart—each thread in its place.

And so humanity lives!

And now let me recall to those who read my first narrative, and to make plain to those who did not, what it was that took me on my quest; that enigmatic prelude in which the Dweller first tried its growing power.

You will remember that Dr. David Throckmartin, one of America's leaders in archeological and ethnological research, had set out for the Caroline Islands, accompanied by his young wife, Edith, his equally youthful associate, Dr. Charles Stanton, and Mrs. Throckmartin's nurse from babyhood, Thora Helverson.

Their destination was that extraordinary cluster of artificially squared, basalt-walled islets off the eastern coast of Ponape, the largest Caroline Island, known as the Nan-Matal. It was Throckmartin's belief that in those prehistoric ruins lay the clue to the lost and highly civilized race which had peopled that ancient continent, which, sinking beneath the waters of the

Pacific, Atlantis-like, had left in the islands we call Polynesia only its highest peaks.

Dr. Throckmartin planned to spend a year on the Nan-Matal, hoping that within its shattered temples and terraces, its vaults and cyclopean walls, or in the maze of secret tunnels that running under the sea threaded together the isles, he would recover not only a lost page of the history of our races, but also, perhaps, a knowledge that had vanished with it.

The subsequent fate of this expedition formed what became known as the Throckmartin mystery. Three months after the little party had landed at Ponape, and had been accompanied to the ruins by a score of reluctant native workmen—reluctant because all the islanders shun the Nan-Matal as a haunted place—Dr. Throckmartin appeared alone at Port Moresby, Papua.

There he said that he was going to Melbourne to employ some white workmen to help him in his excavations, the superstitions of the natives making their usefulness negligible. He took passage on the *Southern Queen,* sailing the same day that he appeared, and three nights later he vanished utterly from that vessel.

It was officially reported that he had either fallen from the ship or had thrown himself overboard. A relief party sent to the Nan-Matal for the others in his party found no trace of his wife, of Stanton, or of Thora Helverson. The native workmen, questioned, said that on the nights of the full moon the *ani* or spirits of the ruins had great power. That on these nights no Ponapean would go within sight or sound of them, and that by agreement with Throckmartin they had been allowed to return to their homes on these nights, leaving the expedition "to face the spirits alone."

AFTER the full of the moon on the third month of the expedition's stay, the natives had returned to the Throckmartin camp only to find it deserted. And then, "knowing that the *ani* had been stronger," they had fled.

I had been a passenger with Throckmartin on the *Southern Queen.* I had been with him when that wondrous horror which had followed him down the moon path after it had set its unholy seal upon him had snatched him from the vessel. He had told me his story, and I had promised, Heaven forgive me, that if the Dweller took him as it had taken his wife and Stanton and Thora, I would follow.

He had told me his story, and I knew that story was true—for twice I had seen the inexplicable power which Throckmartin, discovering, had loosed upon himself and those who loved him. That unearthly Thing which left on the faces of its prey soul-deep lines of mingled agony and rapture, of joy celestial and misery infernal, side by side, as though the hand of God and the hand of Satan working in harmony had etched them!

I first beheld the Dweller on that first night out from Papua when it came racing over the horizon to claim Throckmartin.

We two were on the upper deck. He had not yet summoned the courage to tell me of what had befallen him. Storm threatened but suddenly, far to the north, the clouds parted, and upon the waters far away the moon shone.

Swiftly the break in the high-flung canopies advanced toward us and the silver rapids of the moon stream between them came racing down toward the *Southern Queen* like a gigantic, shining serpent writhing over the rim of the world. And down its shimmering length a pillared radiance sped. It reached the barrier of blackness that still held between the ship and the head of the moon stream and beat against it with a swirling of shimmering misty plumes, throbbing lacy opalescences and vaporous spiralings of living light.

Then, as the protecting shadow grew less, I saw that within the pillar was a core, a nucleus of intense light—veined, opalescent, vital. And through gusts of tinkling music came a murmuring cry as of a calling from another sphere, making soul and body shrink from it irresistibly and reach toward it with an infinite longing. "Av-o-lo-ha! Av-o-lo-ha!" it sighed.

Straight toward the radiant vision walked Throckmartin, his face transformed from all human semblance by unholy blending of agony and rapture that had fallen over it like a mask. And then—the clouds closed, the moon path was blotted out, and where the shining Thing had been was—nothing!

What had been there was the Dweller!

It was after I had beheld that apparition that Throckmartin told me what would have been, save for what my own eyes had seen, his incredible story. How, upon a first night of the full moon, camping on another shore, they had seen lights moving on the outer bulwarks of that islet of the Nan-Matal, called Nan-Tanach, the "place of frowning walls," and faintly to them over the waters had crept the crystalline music, while far beneath, as though from vast distant caverns, a mighty muffled chanting had risen. How, on going to Nan-Tanach next day, they had found set within the inner of its three titanic terraces, a slab of stone, gray and cold and strangely repellent to the touch. Above it and on each side was a rounded breast of basalt in each of which were seven little circles that gave to the hand that same alien shock, "as of frozen electricity," that contact with the gray slab gave.

And that night, when sleep had seemed to drop down upon them from the moon, but before the sleep had conquered him, he had seen the court of the gray rock curdle with light. Into it had walked Thora, bathed and filled with a pulsing effulgence beside which all earthly light was shadow!

He told me of their search for Thora at dawn, when the slumber had fallen from their eyes, and of their discovery of her kerchief caught beneath the lintel of the gray slab, betraying that it had opened, and opening, closed upon her. Of their efforts to force it, and of the vigil that night when Stanton was taken and walked "like a corpse in which flamed a god and a devil" in the embrace of the Dweller

upon the shattered walls of Tanach, vanishing at last through the moon door, even as had Thora. And the muffled, distant, mighty chanting as of a multitude that hailed his passage.

After that, of the third night, when his wife and he watched despairingly beside the moon door, waiting for it to open, hoping to surprise the shining Thing that came through it, and surprising, conquer it. Of their wait until the moon swam up and its full light shone upon the terrace. Of the sudden gleaming out of the little circles under its rays and of the sighing murmur of the moon door, swinging open as its hidden mechanism responded to the force of the light falling on the circles. And of his mad rush down the glimmering passage beyond the moon-door portal to the threshold of the wondrous chamber of the Moon Pool.

ABSORBED, silent, marveling, I listened as he described that place of mystery—a vaulted arch that seemed to open into space; a space filled with lambent, coruscating, many-colored mist whose brightness grew even as he watched; before him an awesome pool, circular, perhaps twenty feet wide. Around it a low, softly curving lip of glimmering, silvery stone. The pool's water was palest blue. Within its silvery rim it was like a great, blue eye staring upward.

Upon it streamed seven shafts of radiance. They poured down upon it like torrents; they were like shining pillars of light rising from a sapphire floor. One was the tender pink of the pearl; one of the aurora's green; a third a deathly white; the fourth the blue in mother-of-pearl; a shimmering column of pale amber, a beam of amethyst; a shaft of molten silver. The pool drank them!

And even as Throckmartin gazed, he saw run through the blue water tiny gleams of phosphorescence, sparkles and coruscations of pale incandescence, and far, far down in its depths he sensed a movement, a shifting gleam as of some radiant body slowly rising.

Mists then began to float up from the surface, tiny swirls that held and hung in the splendor of the seven shafts, absorbing their glory and at last coalescing into the shape I had seen and that he called the Dweller.

He had raised his pistol and sent bullet after bullet into it. And as he did so, out from it swept a gleaming tentacle. It caught him above the heart; wrapped itself round him. Over him rushed a mingled ecstasy and horror. It was, he said, as though the cold soul of evil and the burning soul of good had stepped together within him.

He saw that the shining nucleus of that which he had watched shape itself from vapors and light had form—but a form that eyes and brain could not define; as though a being of another world should assume what it might of human semblance, but could not hide that what human eyes saw was still only a part of it. It was neither man nor woman; it was unearthly and androgynous and even as he found its human semblance, that semblance changed, while all the while every atom of him thrilled with interwoven rapture and terror.

Behind him he had heard the swift feet of his wife, racing to his aid. Love gave him power, and he wrested himself from the Dweller. Even as he did so he fell, and saw her rush straight into the radiant glory! Saw, too, the Dweller swiftly wrap its shining mists around her and drew her over the lip of the pool; dragged himself to the verge and watched her sink in its embrace, down, down through the depths— "a shining, many-colored, nebulous cloud, and in it Edith's face, disappearing, her eyes staring up at me filled with ecstasy supernal and infernal horror—and—vanished!"

Then, far below, again the triumphant chanting!

There had come to Throckmartin madness. He had memory of running wildly through glimmering passages; then blackness and oblivion until he found himself far out at sea in the little boat they had used to cruise around the lagoons of the

Nan-Matal. He had bribed the half-caste captain of a ship that picked him up to take him to Port Moresby, from whence he intended to go to Melbourne, hoping to find some who would return with him, force the haunted chamber, and battle with him against the Dweller.

And on that third night I cowered in the corner of his cabin and saw the Dweller take him!

For three years I was silent, and then, obeying a sudden, irresistible impulse, I started, alone, for the Nan-Matal to make reparation. For Throckmartin had not entirely believed that his wife was dead, nor Stanton nor Thora; rather he thought that they might be held in some unearthly bondage.

And he had, too, a vague belief that the deep, underground chantings that had accompanied the disappearance of the Dweller with its victims, pointing clearly as they did to the existence of other beings or powers in its mysterious den, held a vast threat against humanity. How true was his scientific clairvoyance, and yet how far from the amazing, unthinkable truth, you are to learn. It was my own conviction that in both he had been right; and it was this conviction which now forced me onward at all speed toward the Carolines.

I delayed my departure from America only long enough to get certain instruments and apparatus that long brooding over the phenomena had suggested might be useful in coping with them.

Nine weeks later, with my paraphernalia, I was northward bound from Port Moresby on the *Suwarna*, a swift little copra sloop with a fifty-horse-power motor auxiliary, and heading for Ponape—for the Nan-Matal and the Chamber of the Moon Pool and all that it held for me of soul-shaking awe and peril.

CHAPTER II

"THE SPARKLING DEVIL TOOK THEM!"

WE sighted the *Brunhilda* some five hundred miles south of Ponape. Soon after we had left Port Moresby the wind had fallen, but the *Suwarna*, although

!ar from being as fragrant as the Javan flower for which she was named, could do her twelve knots an hour. Da Costa, the captain, was a garrulous Portuguese. The crew were six huge, chattering Tonga boys.

The *Suwarna* had cut through Finschafen Huon Gulf to the protection of the Bismarcks, and we were rolling over the thousand-mile stretch of open ocean with New Hanover far behind us and our boat's bow pointed straight toward Nukuor of the Monte Verdes. After we had rounded Nukuor we should, barring accident, reach Ponape in not more than sixty hours.

Beneath us the slow, prodigious swells of the Pacific lifted us in gentle, giant hands and sent us as gently down the long, blue wave slopes to the next broad, upward slope. There was a spell of peace over the ocean that was semihypnotic, stilling even the Portuguese captain who stood dreamily at the wheel, slowly swaying to the rhythmic lift and fall of the sloop.

There came a whining hail from the Tonga boy lookout draped lazily over the bow.

"Sail he b'long port side!"

Da Costa straightened and gazed while I raised my glass. The vessel was a scant mile away, and must have been visible long before the sleepy watcher had seen her. She was a sloop about the size of the *Suwarna*, without power. All sails set, even to a spinnaker she carried, she was making the best of the little breeze. I tried to read her name, but the vessel jibed sharply as though the hands of the man at the wheel had suddenly dropped the helm—and then with equal abruptness swung back to her course. The stern came in sight, and on it I read *Brunhilda*.

I shifted my glasses to the figure at the wheel. It came to me that there was something odd about him. He was crouching down over the spokes in a helpless, huddled sort of way, and even as I looked the vessel veered again, abruptly as before. I saw the helmsman straighten up and bring the wheel about with a vicious jerk.

He stood so for a moment, looking straight ahead, entirely oblivious of us,

and then seemed again to sink down within himself. It came to me that his was the action of a man striving against a weariness unutterable. I swept the deck with my glasses. There was no other sign of life. I turned to find the Portuguese staring intently and with puzzled air at the sloop, now separated from us by a scant half mile.

"Something veree wrong I think there, sair," he said in his curious English. "The man on deck I know. He is captain and owner of the *Br-rwun'ild*. His name Olaf Huldricksson, what you say—Norwegian. He is eithair veree sick or veree tired, but I do not understand where is the crew and the starb'd boat is gone."

As he spoke I clearly saw the arms at the wheel of the *Brunhilda* relax, the wheel spin and the vessel lurch about to swell and wind and saw again the helmsman stiffen like a man awakened violently from deep sleep; saw his arms tighten spasmodically and bring the ship once more to her course.

"Veree sick or somet-ing veree wrong," Da Costa repeated. "I t'ink I better go close and see if he need help, sair?"

It was the right thing to do. I nodded acquiescence. He shouted an order to the engineer and as he did so the faint breeze died utterly and the sails of the *Brunhilda* flapped down inert. I saw the helmsman glare about him and thought I heard him curse. But we were now nearly abreast and a scant five hundred yards away. The engine of the *Suwarna* died and the Tonga boys leaped to one of the boats.

"You Olaf Huldricksson!" shouted Da Costa. "What's a matter wit' you?"

The man at the wheel turned toward us. As his body lifted I saw that he was a giant of a man: his shoulders enormous; thick chested, strength in every line of him, he towered like a Viking of old at the rudder bar of his sharp ship.

I raised the glass again; his face sprang into the lens as though he himself had leaped from his deck and was staring at me; and never have I seen a face that was lined and marked as though by ages of unsleeping misery as was that of Olaf Huldricksson! The bloodshot eyes peered into mine with a look in their depths that might have been in the eyes of a mummy.

THE glasses dropped from my shaking hand. The two Tonga boys had the boat alongside and were waiting at the oars. The little captain was dropping into it.

"Wait!" I cried. I ran into my cabin, grasped my emergency medical kit and climbed down the rope ladder. The two Tonga boys bent to the oars. We reached the side and Da Costa and I each seized a lanyard dangling from the stays and swung ourselves swiftly on board. Da Costa approached Huldricksson softly.

"What's the matter, Olaf?" he began and then was silent, looking down at the wheel. My gaze followed his and we shrank together involuntarily. For the hands of Huldricksson were lashed fast to the spokes of the wheel by thongs of thin, strong cord. They had been bound so tightly that they were swollen and black. The thongs had bitten so into the sinewy wrists that they were hidden in the outraged flesh, cutting so deeply that blood fell, slow drop by drop, at his feet. We sprang toward him, reaching out hands to his fetters to loose them. Even as we touched them, Huldricksson grew rigid with anger that had in it something diabolic. He aimed a vicious kick at me and then another at Da Costa which sent the Portuguese tumbling into the scuppers.

"Let be!" croaked Huldricksson; his voice was as thick and lifeless as though forced from a dead throat, and I saw that his lips were cracked and dry and his parched tongue was black. "Let be! Go! Let be!" The words beat upon the ears heavily, painfully. It was the dead alive and speaking!

The Portuguese had picked himself up, whimpering with rage and knife in hand, but as Huldricksson's voice reached him he stopped. Amazement crept into his eyes and as he thrust the blade back into his belt they softened with pity.

"Something veree wrong wit' Olaf," he murmured to me. "I think he crazee!"

And then Olaf Huldricksson began to curse us. He did not speak—he howled from that hideously dry mouth his imprecations and I think I never heard such hate and bitterness issue from any man's lips. He cursed us by everything in heaven and earth and hell—yes, and he cursed earth, hell and heaven as well. And all the time his bloodshot eyes roamed the seas and his hands, clenched and rigid on the wheel, dropped blood.

"I go below," said Da Costa nervously. "His wife, his little Freda, they are always wit' him. You wait." He darted down the companionway and was gone. Huldricksson suddenly was silent, slumping down over the wheel, forgetting us.

Da Costa's head appeared at the top of the companion steps.

"There is nobody, nobody," he said. "I do not understan'."

Then Olaf Huldricksson opened his dry lips again and as he spoke a thrill ran through me, stopping my heart.

"The sparkling devil took them!" croaked Olaf Huldricksson. "The sparkling devil took them! Took my Helma and my little Freda! The sparkling devil came down from the moon and took them!"

He swayed and two great tears ran down his cheeks. Da Costa moved toward him again, and again Huldricksson watched him, once more alertly, wickedly, from his reddened eyes.

I took a hypodermic syringe from my case and filled it with morphin. I drew Da Costa to me.

"Get to the side of him," I whispered, "talk to him." He saw the little syringe in my hand and nodded. He moved over toward the wheel.

"Where is your Helma and Freda, Olaf?" he said.

Huldricksson turned his head toward him. "The shining devil took them," he repeated. "The moon devil."

A yell broke from him. I had thrust the needle into his arm just above one swollen wrist and had quickly shot the drug through. He struggled to release himself and then began to rock drunkenly side by side. The morphin, taking him in his weakness, worked quickly. Soon over his face we saw a peace descend. The pupils of the staring eyes contracted. Once, twice, he swayed and then his bleeding, prisoned hands held high and still gripping the wheel, he dropped to the deck.

It was with utmost difficulty that we loosed the thongs, but at last it was done. We rigged a little swing and the Tonga boys slung the great inert body over the side into the dory. Soon we had Huldricksson in my bunk. Da Costa sent half his crew over to the sloop in charge of the Cantonese. They took in all sail, stripping Huldricksson's boat to the masts and then with the *Brunhilda* nosing quietly along after us at the end of a long hawser, one of the Tonga boys at her wheel, we resumed our way.

I had cleansed and bandaged the drugged Norseman's lacerated wrists and was sponging the blackened, parched mouth with warm water and a mild antiseptic when the Portuguese softly entered the cabin. I did not hear him until he spoke, so engrossed was I in my thoughts of this mystery of the *Brunhilda*. At first, when Huldricksson had spoken of a "sparkling devil from the moon" I had felt a shock of apprehension. Could it be that on the very threshold of my quest the Dweller had come out to meet me?

But in the light of Huldricksson's fettering this thought had vanished. There had probably occurred on the *Brunhilda* one of those swift, devilish tragedies of the South Seas that ever and anon flare up like lightning out of hell. A mutiny of the only half tamed crew, a treacherous blow from behind that had felled the Norseman to the deck, a mordant humor or obscure superstition that had left him to awaken fettered to the wheel of his ravished vessel, a carrying away of mother and child to some unspeakable death.

SUCH a story is a commonplace in those vast reaches of sea and sea-hidden lairs of cruel and savage tribes. And yet there was no mark or blow upon the captain's head. Suddenly I was aware of Da Costa's presence and turned. His unease was manifest and held, it seemed to me, a queer, furtive anxiety.

"What you think of Olaf, sair?" he asked. I shrugged my shoulders. "You think he killed his woman and his babee?" He went on. "You think he crazee and killed all?"

"Nonsense, Da Costa," I answered. "You saw the boat was gone. His crew mutinied and tied him up the way you saw."

Da Costa shook his head slowly. "No," he said. "No. The crew did not. Nobody there on board when Olaf was tied."

"What!" I cried, startled. "What do you mean?"

"I mean," he said slowly, "that Olaf tie himself!"

"Wait!" he went on at my incredulous gesture of dissent. "Wait, I show you." He had been standing with hands behind his back and now I saw that he held in them the same thongs that had bound Huldricksson. They were bloodstained and each ended in a broad leather tip skillfully spliced into the cord. "Look!" he said, pointing to these leather ends. I looked and saw in them deep indentations as of teeth. I snatched one of the thongs and opened the mouth of the unconscious man on the bunk. Carefully I placed the leather within it and gently forced the jaws shut on it. It was true. Those marks were where Olaf Huldricksson's teeth had gripped! Dazed, I turned to Da Costa.

"Wait!" he said again. "I show you." He took the cords and rested his hands on the supports of a chair back. Rapidly he twisted one of the thongs around his left hand, drew a loose knot, shifted the cord up toward his elbow. This left wrist and hand still free and with them he twisted the other cord around the right wrist; drew a similar knot. His hands were now in the exact position that Huldricksson's had been on the *Brunhilda* but with cords and knots hanging loose. Then Da Costa reached down his head, took a leather end in his teeth and with a jerk drew the end of the thong that noosed his left hand tight; similarly he drew tight the second.

And then he stood and strained at his fetters. There before my eyes he had pinioned himself so that without aid he could not release himself. And he was exactly as Huldricksson had been!

"You will have to cut me loose, sair," he said. "I cannot move them. It is an old trick on these seas. Sometimes it is necessary that a man stand at the wheel many hours, without help, and he does this so that if he sleep the wheel wake him, yes, sair."

I looked from him to the man on the bed.

"But why, sair," said Da Costa slowly, "did Olaf have to tie his hands?"

I had no answer.

"We'll have to wait till he awakens, captain," I said. He nodded acquiescence and was silent for a time. "What did you think, sair, of what he said of sparkling devils?" he asked at last. And as he spoke I knew that this was what had been on his mind all along. Clearly he knew something, had heard something, that gave the words I had dismissed an unquieting significance. I looked at him closely.

"I don't know," I said. "Do you?"

He fidgeted, avoided my eyes, and then surreptitiously crossed himself.

"No," he replied. "I know nothing. Some things I have heard, but they tell many tales on these seas."

He turned, almost abruptly, and started for the door. Before he reached it he turned again. "But this I do know," he half whispered, "I do know I am glad there is no full moon tonight." He passed out, leaving me staring after him in amazement. What did the Portuguese know?

I bent over the sleeper. On his face was no trace of that unholy mingling of opposites, of mingled joy and fear, that the Dweller stamped upon its victims. But with Da Costa's revelations the security I had felt in my theory of the prisoned wrists crumbled. Huldricksson's words came back to me—"The sparkling devil took them!" Nay, they had been even more explicit—"The sparkling devil that came down from the moon!"

They sank upon my heart like weights, carrying subconscious conviction that resisted all my efforts to dismiss. I lifted the sheet from Huldricksson and went over his body minutely, turning it from side to side. The Norseman was, as I have said, a giant, and his mighty, muscled form was clean and white as a girl's. Nowhere was there a trace of that cold, white stain which was the mark of the touch of the Dweller and that had been, on Throckmartin, a shining cincture girdling the body just below the heart.

Throckmartin had believed, and I had believed with him, that the thing I had gone forth to find had no power outside the islet of the moon door and that it was only by virtue of that mark it had been enabled to follow him. But was this true? Huldricksson had been steering straight for Ponape, not away from it—and there was no trace of the Nan-Matal's dread mystery upon him.

Had the Dweller swept down unheralded and unknown upon the *Brunhilda*, drawing down the moon path Olaf Huldricksson's wife and babe even as it had drawn Throckmartin? But if this were so then I must revise much of what I thought I knew of its action, for the ravishing of the *Brunhilda* could mean only one of two things: we had been wrong in our theory that the Dweller's power was limited by place, or else in the years that had passed its power had overcome that limitation.

As I sat thinking, the cabin grew suddenly dark, and from above came a shouting and patter of feet. Down upon us swept one of the abrupt, violent squalls that are met with in those latitudes. I lashed Huldricksson fast in the berth and ran up on deck.

A HALF hour passed. Then the squall died as quickly as it had arisen. The sea quieted. Over in the west, from beneath the tattered, flying edge of the storm, dropped the setting sun.

I watched it, and rubbed my eyes and stared again. For over its flaming portal something huge and black moved, like a gigantic beckoning finger!

Da Costa had seen it, too, and he turned the *Suwarna* straight toward the descending orb and its strange shadows. As we approached we saw it was a little mass of wreckage and that the beckoning finger was a wing of canvas, sticking up and swaying with the motion of the waves. On the highest point of the wreckage sat a tall figure calmly smoking a cigarette.

We brought the *Suwarna* to, dropped a boat, and with myself as coxswain pulled toward what I knew now was a wrecked hydroplane. Its occupant took a long puff at his cigarette, waved a cheerful hand, and shouted a reassuring greeting. And just as he did so a great wave raised itself up behind him, took the wreckage, tossed it high in a swelter of foam, and passed on. When we had steadied our boat, where wreck and man had been was—nothing.

I scanned the water with anxious eyes. Who had been this debonair castaway, and from whence in these far seas had dropped his plane? There came a tug at the side of our boat, two muscular brown hands gripped it close to my left, and a sleek, black, wet head showed its top between them. Two bright blue eyes that held deep within them a laughing deviltry looked into mine, and a long, lithe body drew itself gently over the thwart and seated its dripping self at my feet.

"Much obliged," said this man from the sea. "I knew somebody was sure to come along when the O'Keefe banshee didn't show up."

"The what?" I asked in amazement.

"The O'Keefe banshee. Oh, yes, pardon me, I'm Larry O'Keefe. It's a far way from Ireland, but not too far for the O'Keefe banshee to travel if the O'Keefe was going to kick in."

I looked again at my astonishing rescue. He seemed perfectly serious, and later I was to know how exasperatingly, naïvely, and entirely serious he was on that subject.

"Have you a cigarette?" said Larry O'Keefe. "Mine went out," he added with a grin, as he reached a moist hand out for the little cylinder, took it, lighted it on the match I struck for him, and then

gazed at me frankly and with manifest curiosity. I returned the gaze as frankly.

I saw a lean, intelligent face whose fighting jaw was softened by the wistfulness of the clean-cut lips and the roguishness that lay side by side with the deviltry in the laughing blue eyes. Nose of a thoroughbred with the suspicion of a tilt. A long, well-knit, slender figure that I knew must have all the strength of fine steel; the uniform of a lieutenant in the Royal Flying Corps of Britain's navy.

He laughed, stretched out a firm hand, and gripped mine.

"Thank you really ever so much, old man," he said.

I liked Larry O'Keefe from the beginning, but I did not dream how that liking was to be forged into man's strong love for man by fires which souls such as his and mine—and yours who read this—could never dream.

Larry! Larry O'Keefe, where are you now with your leprechawns and banshee, your heart of a child, your laughing blue eyes, and your fearless soul? Shall I ever see you again, Larry O'Keefe, dear to me as some best-beloved younger brother? Larry!

CHAPTER III

LARRY O'KEEFE

PRESSING back the questions I longed to ask, I introduced myself.

A second later we touched the side of the *Suwarna*, and I was forced to curb my curiosity until we reached the deck. Da Costa greeted us eagerly, and was plainly gratified by the military salute which O'Keefe bestowed upon him.

"You haven't seen a German boat called the *Wolf* about, have you?" he asked with a grin, after he had elaborately thanked the bowing little Portuguese skipper for his rescue. "That thing you saw me sitting on was all that was left of one of His Majesty's best little hydroplanes after that cyclone threw it off as excess baggage. And by the way, about where are we?"

Da Costa gave him our approximate position from the noon reckoning.

O'Keefe whistled. "A good three hundred miles from where I left the H. M. S. *Dolphin* about four hours ago," he said. "That squall I rode in on was some whizzer!

"About an hour ago I thought I saw a chance to dig up and out of it. I turned, and blick went my upper right wing, and down I dropped. Engine began to work loose, and just as I knew something had to come along quick or the banshee of the O'Keefes was due for a long, swift trip from Ireland, I sighted you.

"And here I am, and again I say I'm much obliged to you," finished Larry O'Keefe. "And I'll take another cigarette, if you don't mind."

"I don't know how we can notify your ship, Lieutenant O'Keefe," I said. "We have no wireless."

"Doctair Goodwin," said Da Costa, "we could change our course, sair—perhaps—"

"Thanks, but not a bit of it," broke in O'Keefe. "Lord alone knows where the *Dolphin* is now. Anyway, the *Dolphin* is just as apt to run into you as you into her. Maybe we'll strike something with a wireless, and I'll trouble you to put me aboard." He hesitated. "Where are you bound, by the way?" he asked.

"For Ponape," I answered.

"No wireless there," mused O'Keefe. "Beastly hole. Stopped a week ago for fruit. Natives seemed scared to death at us—or something. What are you going there for?"

I saw Da Costa dart a furtive glance at me. It troubled me. I had, of course, told him nothing of the real reasons for my journey, stating simply, when I had employed him, that I wished to go to Ponape where the scientific work I had planned might keep me many weeks. What did the man know, I wondered, and what was the explanation of his remarks in the cabin and of his manifest unease? O'Keefe's sharp eyes had noted the glance and, misinterpreting it and my consequent hesitation, flushed in embarrassment.

"Oh, I beg your pardon," he said. "Maybe I oughtn't to have asked that?"

"It's no secret, lieutenant," I replied, somewhat testily. "I'm about to undertake some exploration work there. A little digging among the ruins on the Nan-Matal."

I looked at the Portuguese sharply as I named the place. I distinctly saw a pallor creep under his skin and again he made swiftly the sign of the cross, glancing as he did so uneasily to the north. I made up my mind then to question him when opportunity came. He turned from his quick scrutiny of the sea and addressed O'Keefe.

"There's nothing on board to fit you, lieutenant," he said, looking over the tall figure before him. "But perhaps we can find something while your clothes dry. Will you come to my cabin?"

"Oh, just give me a sheet to throw around me, captain," said O'Keefe, following him. Darkness had fallen, and as the two disappeared I softly opened the door of my own cabin and listened. I could hear Huldricksson breathing deeply.

I drew my electric flash, and shielding its rays from my face, looked at him. His sleeping was changing from the heavy stupor of the drug into one that was at least on the borderland of the normal. Satisfied as to his condition, I returned to deck.

O'KEEFE was there on deck, looking like a specter in the cotton sheet he had wrapped about him. A deck table had been cleated down and one of the Tonga boys was setting it for our dinner. Soon the very creditable larder of the *Suwarna* dressed the board, and O'Keefe, Da Costa and I attacked it. The night had grown close and oppressive. Behind us the forward light of the *Brunhilda* glided and the binnacle lamp threw up a faint glow in which her black helmsman's face stood out mistily. O'Keefe had looked curiously a number of times at our tow, but had asked no questions.

"You're not the only passenger we picked up today," I told him. "We found the captain of that sloop, lashed to his wheel, nearly dead with exhaustion, and his boat deserted by every one except himself."

"What was the matter?" asked O'Keefe in astonishment.

"We don't know," I answered. "He fought us, and I had to drug him before we could get him loose from his lashings. He's sleeping down in my berth now. His wife and little girl ought to have been on board, the captain here says, but— they weren't."

"Any signs of a fight?" asked O'Keefe.

I shook my head, and again I saw Da Costa swiftly cross himself. "We'll have to wait until he wakes up to get the story," I concluded.

"Wife and child gone!" said O'Keefe. "And you saw nothing?"

"From the condition of his mouth he must have been alone at the wheel and without water at least two days and nights before we found him," I replied. "And as for looking for anyone on these waters after such a time, it's hopeless."

"That's true," said O'Keefe. "But his wife and baby! Poor, poor devil!"

I watched O'Keefe as he talked, feeling my liking for him steadily increasing. If I could but have a man like this beside me on the path of unknown peril upon which I had set my feet, I thought wistfully. We sat and smoked a bit, sipping the coffee the Portuguese made so well.

Da Costa at last relieved the Cantonese at the wheel. O'Keefe and I drew chairs up to the rail. The brighter stars shone out dimly through a hazy sky. Gleams of phosphorescence tipped the crests of the waves and sparkled with an almost angry brilliance as the bow of the *Suwarna* tossed them aside. Far to the east a faint silver glow heralded the rising moon. O'Keefe pulled contentedly at a cigarette. The glowing spark lighted the keen, boyish face and the blue eyes, now black and brooding under the spell of the tropic night.

"Are you American or Irish, O'Keefe?" I asked suddenly.

"Why?" he laughed.

"Because," I answered, "from your name and your service I would suppose you Irish, but your command of pure Americanese makes me doubtful."

He grinned amiably.

"I'll tell you how that is," he said. "My mother is an American—a Grace, of Virginia. My father was O'Keefe, of Coleraine. And these two loved each other só well that the heart they gave me is half Irish and half American. My father died when I was sixteen. I used to go to the States with my mother every other year for a month or two. But after my father died we used to go to Ireland every other year. And there you are. I'm as American as I am Irish.

"When I'm in love, or excited, or dreaming, or mad I have the brogue. But for the every-day purposes of life I like the United States talk, and I know Broadway as well as I do Binevenagh Lane, and the Sound as well as St. Patrick's Channel. Educated a bit at Eton, a bit at Oxford, a bit at Harvard. Always too much O'Keefe with Grace money to have to make any. In love lots of times, and never a heartache after that wasn't a pleasant one, and never a real purpose in life until I took the king's shilling and earned my wings; always ready for adventure—Larry O'Keefe."

"But it was the Irish O'Keefe who sat out there waiting for the banshee," I laughed.

"It was that," he said somberly, and I heard the brogue creep over his voice like velvet and his eyes grew brooding again. "There's never an O'Keefe for these thousand years that has passed without his warning. An' twice have I heard the banshee calling—once it was when my younger brother died an' once when my father lay waiting to be carried out on the ebb tide."

He mused a moment, then went on: "An' once I saw an Annir Choille, a girl of the green people, flit like a shadow of green fire through the Carntogher woods, an' once at Dunchraig I slept where the ashes of the Dun of Cormac MacConcobar are mixed with those of Cormac an' Eilidh the Fair, all burned in the nine flames that sprang from the harping of Cravetheen, an' I heard the echo of his dead harp-ings—"

He paused again, then, softly, with

that curiously sweet, high voice that only the Irish seem to have, he sang:

"Woman of the white breasts, Eilidh;
  Woman of the gold-brown hair, and lips
    of the red, red rowan,
  Where is the swan that is whiter, with
    breast more soft,
  Or the wave on the sea that moves as thou
    movest, Eilidh?"

CHAPTER IV

OLAF'S STORY

THERE was a little silence. I looked upon him with wonder. Clearly he was in deepest earnest. I know the psychology of the Gael is a curious one and that deep in all their hearts their ancient traditions and beliefs have strong and living roots.

Here was this soldier, facing war and all its ugly realities open-eyed and fearless, picking, indeed, the most dangerous branch of service for his own, a modern if ever there was one, appreciative of most unmystical Broadway and yet soberly and earnestly attesting to his belief in banshee, in shadowy people of the woods and phantom harpers! I wondered what he would think if he could see the Dweller and then, with a pang, that perhaps his superstitions might make him an easy prey.

For how then was I to have known that Larry O'Keefe's childlike faith in the existence of these fantasies of the Gaelic imagination was to prove not his weakness but his strong buckler against creatures that not even the imagination of his race could conceive?

I looked eastward where the moon, now nearly a week past the full, was mounting.

"You can't make me see what you've seen, lieutenant," I laughed. "But you can make me hear. I've always wondered what kind of a noise a disembodied spirit could possibly make without any vocal cords or breath or any other earthly sound-producing mechanism. How does the banshee sound?"

O'Keefe did not laugh. Instead, he looked at me seriously.

"All right," he said. "I'll show you."

From deep down in his throat came first a low, weird sobbing that mounted steadily into a keening whose mournfulness made my skin creep. And then O'Keefe's hand shot out and gripped my shoulder, and I stiffened like stone in my chair—for from behind us, like an echo, and then taking up the cry, swelled a wail that seemed to hold within it a sublimation of the sorrows of centuries! It gathered itself into one heartbroken, sobbing note and died away! O'Keefe's grip loosened, and he rose swiftly to his feet.

"It's all right, Goodwin," he said. "It's for me. It found me, all this way from Ireland."

There was no trace of fear in face or voice. "Buck up, professor," laughed O'Keefe. "There's nothing for you to be afraid of. And never yet was there an O'Keefe who feared the kind spirit that carries the warnin'."

Again the silence was rent by the cry. But now I had located it. It came from my room, and it could mean only one thing. Huldricksson had wakened.

"Forget your banshee!" I gasped, and made a jump for the cabin.

Out of the corner of my eye I noted a look of half-sheepish relief flit over O'Keefe's face, and then he was beside me. Da Costa shouted an order from the wheel, the Cantonese ran up and took it from his hands and the little Portuguese pattered down toward us. My hand on the door, ready to throw it open, I stopped. What if the Dweller were within? What if the new power I feared it had attained had made it not only independent of place but independent of that full flood of moon ray which Throckmartin had thought essential to draw it from the blue pool!

The Portuguese had paused, too, and looking at him I saw my own cravenness reflected. Now, from within, the sobbing wail began once more to rise. O'Keefe pushed me aside and with one quick motion threw open the door and crouched low within it. I saw an automatic flash dully in his hand; saw it cover the cabin from side to side, following the swift sweep of his eyes around it. Then he straightened and his face, turned toward the berth, was filled with wondering pity.

Da Costa and I had stepped in behind him. Through the window streamed a shaft of the moonlight. It fell upon Huldricksson's staring eyes; in them great tears slowly gathered and rolled down his cheeks; from his opened mouth came the woe-laden wailing. I ran to the port and drew the curtains. Da Costa snapped the lights.

The Norseman's dolorous crying stopped as abruptly as though cut. His gaze rolled toward us. And then his whole body reddened with a shock of rage, and at one bound he broke through the strong leashes I had buckled round him and faced us, a giant, naked figure tense with wrath, his eyes glaring, his yellow hair almost erect with the force of the passion visibly surging through him. Da Costa shrunk behind me. O'Keefe, coolly watchful, took a quick step that brought him in front of me.

"Where do you take me?" said Huldricksson, and his voice was thick as the growl of a beast. "Where is my boat?"

I touched O'Keefe gently and stood in front of the giant. He glared at me, and I saw the muscles of the gigantic arms flex and the hands below the bandaged wrist clench. He was berserk—mad!

"Listen, Olaf Huldricksson," I said. "We take you to where the sparkling devil took your Helma and your Freda. We follow the sparkling devil that came down from the moon. Do you hear me?" I spoke slowly, distinctly, striving to pierce the mists that I knew swirled around the strained brain. And the words did pierce. He stared at me for a moment. I heard O'Keefe murmur: "Good stuff! That's the idea. Humor him." Huldricksson stared at me and thrust out a shaking hand. As I gripped it I saw his madness fade, while his great chest heaved and fell. "You say you follow?" he asked falteringly. "You know where to follow? Where it took my Helma and my little Freda?"

"Just that, Olaf Huldricksson," I answered. "Just that! I pledge you my life that I know."

Da Costa stepped forward. "He speaks true, Olaf," he said. "Dr. Goodwin here he follow as he say. You go faster on the *Suwarna* than on the *Br-rw-un'ilda*, Olaf, yes."

The giant Norseman, still gripping my hand, looked at him. "I know you Da Costa," he said. "You are all right. Ja! You are a fair man. Where is the *Brunhilda?*"

"She follow be'ind on a big rope, Olaf," soothed the Portuguese. "Soon you see her. But now lie down an' tell us, if you can, why you tie yourself to your wheel an' what it is that happen, Olaf."

"If you'll tell us how the sparkling devil came it will help us all when we get to where it is, Huldricksson," I said.

On O'Keefe's face there was an expression of well-nigh ludicrous doubt and amazement. He glanced from one to the other. The giant shifted his own tense look from me to the Irishman. I saw a gleam of approval in his eyes. He loosed me, and gripped O'Keefe's arm. "*Staerk!*" he said. "*Ja*—strong and with a strong heart. A man—*ja!* He comes, too—we shall need him—*ja?*" He turned toward me. I looked toward O'Keefe and saw his doubt deepen.

"He comes," I said, "if he can."

ONCE more Huldricksson searched me with his glance; once more turned and absorbed O'Keefe in the icy blue of his eyes.

"A man, *ja,*" he repeated. He pointed to me. "And you—a man, *ja!* But not the same as him—and me."

"I tell," he said, and seated himself on the side of the bunk. "It was four nights ago. My Freda"—his voice shook—"Mine Yndling! She loved the moonlight. I was at the wheel and my Freda and my Helma they were behind me. The moon was behind us and the *Brunhilda* was like a swanboat sailing down with the moonlight sending her, *ja.*

"I heard my Freda say: 'I see a nisse coming down the track of the moon.' And I hear her mother laugh, low, like a mother does when her Yndling dreams. I was happy, that night, with my Helma and my Freda, and the *Brunhilda* sailing like a swan-boat, *ja*. I heard the child say, 'The nisse comes fast!' And then I heard a scream from my Helma, a great scream—like a mare when her foal is torn from her. I spun round fast, *ja!* I dropped the wheel and spun fast! I saw—" He covered his eyes with his hands.

The Portuguese had crept close to me, and I heard him panting like a frightened dog. O'Keefe, immobile, watched the Norseman narrowly. His hand fell and hate crept into his eyes; a bitter hate; that winged and white-hot hate that makes even the gods tremble.

"I saw a white fire spring over the rail," whispered Olaf Huldricksson. "It whirled round and round, and it shone like—like stars in a whirlwind mist. There was a noise in my ears. It sounded like bells—little bells, *ja!* Like the music you make when you run your finger round goblets. It made me sick and dizzy, the bells' noise.

"My Helma was—*indeholde*—what you say—in the middle of the white fire. She turned her face to me and she turned it on the child, and my Helma's face burned into my heart. Because it was full of fear, and it was full of happiness—of *glyaede*. I tell you that the fear in my Helma's face made me ice here"—he beat his breast with clenched hand—"but the happiness in it burned on me like fire. And I could not move.

"I said in here"—he touched his head—"I said, 'It is Loki come out of Helvede. But he cannot take my Helma, for Christ lives and Loki has no power to hurt my Helma or my Frede! Christ lives! Christ lives!' I said. But the sparkling devil did not let my Helma go. It drew her to the rail; half over it. I saw her eyes upon the child and a little she broke away and reached to it. And my Freda jumped into her arms. And the fire wrapped them both and they were gone! A little I saw them whirling on the moon track behind the *Brunhilda*, and they were gone!

"The sparkling devil took them! Loki was loosed, and he had power. I turned the *Brunhilda*, and I followed where my Helma and mine Yndling had gone. My boys crept up and asked me to turn again. But I would not. They dropped a boat and left me. I steered straight on the path. I lashed my hands to the wheel that sleep might not loose them. I steered on and on and on—

"Where was the God I prayed when my wife and child were taken?" cried Olaf Huldricksson—and it was as though I heard Throckmartin three years before asking that same bitter question. "I have left Him as He left me, *ja!* I pray now to Thor and to Odin, who can fetter Loki!" He sank back, covering again his eyes.

"Olaf," I said, "what you have called the sparkling devil has taken ones dear to me. I, too, was following it when we found you. You shall go with me to its home, and there we will try to take from it your wife and child and my friends as well. But now that you may be strong for what is before us, you must sleep again."

"You speak the truth!" he said at last slowly. "I will do what you say!"

He stretched out an arm at my bidding. I gave him a second injection. He lay back and soon he was sleeping. I turned toward Da Costa. His face was livid and sweating, and he was trembling pitifully. O'Keefe stirred.

"You did that mighty well, Dr. Goodwin," he said. "So well that I almost believed you myself."

"What did you think of his story, Mr. O'Keefe?" I asked.

His answer was almost pitifully brief and colloquial.

"Nuts!" he said. I was a little shocked, I admit. "I think he's crazy, Dr. Goodwin," he corrected himself, quickly. "What else could I think?"

I turned to the little Portuguese without answering.

"There's no need for any anxiety tonight, captain," I said. "Take my word for it. You need some rest yourself. Shall I give you a sleeping draft?"

"I do wish you would, Dr. Goodwin, sair," he answered gratefully. "Tomorrow, when I feel bettair, I would have a talk with you."

I nodded. He had known something then! I mixed him an opiate of considerable strength. He bowed and went to his own cabin.

I locked the door behind him and then, sitting beside the sleeping Norseman, I told O'Keefe my story from end to end. He asked few questions as I spoke; only watched me with a somewhat disconcerting intensity. In the main his inquiries dealt with the sound phenomena accompanying the apparition of the Dweller. He made a few somewhat startling interruptions dealing with Throckmartin's psychology. And after I had finished he cross-examined me rather minutely upon my recollections of the radiant phases upon each appearance, checking these with Throckmartin's observations of the same activities in the Chamber of the Moon Pool.

"And now what do you think of it all?" I asked.

He sat silent for a while.

"Not what you seem to think, Dr. Goodwin," he answered at last, gravely. "Let me sleep over it and, like the captain, I'll tell you tomorrow. One thing of course is certain—you and your friend Throckmartin and this man here saw—something. But"—he was silent again and then continued with a kindness that I found vaguely irritating—"but I've noticed that when a scientist gets superstitious it—er—takes very hard!

"Here's a few things I can tell you now, though," went on O'Keefe, while I struggled to speak. "I pray in my heart that the old *Dolphin* is so busy she'll forget me for a while and that we won't meet anything with wireless on board her going up. Because, Dr. Goodwin, I'd dearly love to take a crack at your Dweller.

"And another thing," said Larry O'Keefe. "After this cut out the trimmings, Doc, and call me plain Larry, for whether I think you're crazy or whether I don't you're there with the nerve, professor, and I'm for you.

"Good night!" said Larry O'Keefe and took himself out to the deck hammock he had insisted upon having slung for him, refusing the captain's importunities to use his own cabin.

And it was with extremely mixed emotions as to his compliment that I watched him go. Superstitious! I, whose pride was my scientific devotion to fact and fact alone! Superstitious—and this from a man who believed in banshees and ghostly harpers and Irish wood nymphs and no doubt in leprechawns and all their tribe!

Half laughing, half irritated and wholly happy in even the part promise of Larry O'Keefe's comradeship on my venture, I arranged a couple of pillows, stretched myself out on two chairs and took up my vigil beside Olaf Huldricksson.

CHAPTER V

A LOST PAGE OF EARTH

WHEN I awakened the sun was streaming through the cabin porthole. Outside a fresh voice lilted. I lay on my two chairs and listened. The song was one with the wholesome sunshine and the breeze blowing stiffly and whipping the curtains. It was Larry O'Keefe at his matins.

I opened my door. O'Keefe stood outside laughing. Behind him the Tonga boys clustered, wide-toothed and adoring. Even the Cantonese mate had something on his face that served for a grin and Da Costa was beaming. I closed the door behind me.

The *Suwarna*, her engines silent, was making fine headway under all sail, the *Brunhilda* skipping in her wake cheerfully with half her canvas up.

The sea was crisping and dimpling under the wind. Blue and white was the world as far as the eye could reach. Schools of little silvery green flying fish broke through the water rushing on each side of us; flashed for an instant and were gone. Behind us gulls hovered and dipped. The shadow of mystery had retreated far over the rim of this wide awake and beautiful world. And if, subconsciously, I knew that somewhere it was brooding and waiting, for a little while at least I was consciously free of its oppression.

"How's the patient?" asked O'Keefe.

He was answered by Huldricksson himself, who must have risen just as I left the cabin. The great Norseman had slipped on a pair of pajamas and, giant torso naked under the sun, he strode out upon us. We all of us looked at him a trifle anxiously. But Olaf's madness had left him. His face was still drawn and in his eyes was much sorrow, but the berserk rage had vanished. He stretched out a hand to us in turn.

"This is Dr. Goodwin, Olaf," said Da Costa. "An' this is Lieutenant O'Keefe of the English Navy."

Huldricksson bowed, with a touch of grace that revealed him not all rough seaman—and indeed, as I was later to find, the Norwegian had been given gentle upbringing and a fair education before the wanderlust of his race had swept him into these far seas.

He addressed himself straight to me: "You said last night we follow?"

I nodded.

"It is where?" he asked again.

"We go first to Ponape and from there to Metalanim Harbor—to the Nan-Matal. You know the place?"

Huldricksson bowed, a white gleam as of ice showing in his blue eyes.

"It is there?" he asked.

"It is there that we must first search," I answered.

"Good!" said Olaf Huldricksson. "It is good!"

He looked at Da Costa inquiringly and the little Portuguese, following his thought answered his unspoken question.

"We should be at Ponape tomorrow morning early, Olaf."

"Good!" repeated the Norseman. He looked away, his eyes tear filled.

A restraint fell upon us; the embarrassment all men experience when they feel a great sympathy and a great pity, neither of which they quite know how to give expression. By silent consent we discussed at breakfast only the most casual topics.

When the meal was over Huldricksson expressed a desire to go aboard the *Brunhilda*.

The *Suwarna* hove to and Da Costa and he dropped into the small boat. When they reached the *Brunhilda's* deck I saw Olaf take the wheel and the two fall into earnest talk. I beckoned to O'Keefe and we stretched ourselves out on the bow hatch under cover of the foresail. He lighted a cigarette, took a couple of leisurely puffs, and looked at me expectantly.

"Well," I asked, "and what do you think of it now?"

"Well," said O'Keefe, "suppose you tell me what you think, and then I'll proceed to point out your scientific errors." His eyes twinkled mischievously.

"I THINK," I said, "it is possible that some members of that race peopling the ancient continent which we know existed here in the Pacific and which was destroyed by a comparatively gradual subsidence, have survived. We know that many of these islands are honey-combed with caverns and vast subterranean spaces too great to be so called. These are literally underground lands, running in many cases far out beneath the ocean floor. It is possible that for some reason the survivors of this race of which I speak sought refuge in these abysmal spaces, one of whose entrances is on the island where Throckmartin's party met its end.

"As for their persistence in these caverns, we know the lost people possessed a high science. This is indisputable. It may be that they had gone far in their mastery of certain universal forms of energy. They may have discovered the secret of that form of magnetic etheric vibration we call light. If so, they would have had no difficulty in maintaining life down there, and, indeed, shielded by earth's crust from the natural forces which always have surface man more or less at their mercy, they may have developed a civilization and extended a science immensely more advanced than ours. And unless they have also developed a complete indifference to conquest and an inflexible determination never to come forth from their world, they must always continue to be a potential menace to our world."

I paused. His keen face was now all eager attention.

"Have you ever heard of the Chamats?" I asked him. He shook his head.

"In Papua," I explained, "there is a widespread and immeasurably old tradition that 'imprisoned under the hills' is a race of giants who once ruled this region 'when it stretched from sun to sun' and 'before the moon god drew the waters over it'—I quote from the legend. Not only in Papua but in Borneo and Java and in fact throughout Malaysia you find this story. And, so the tradition runs, these people—the Chamats—will one day break through the hills and rule the world; 'make over the world' is the literal translation of the constant phrase in the tale. Does this convey anything to you, Larry?"

"Something," he nodded. "Go on."

"It conveys something to me," I said, "especially in the light of what Throckmartin heard and saw and what Huldricksson and I witnessed.

"It is possible that these survivors are experimenting with their science, and that what I call 'the Dweller' is one of their results. Or it may be that the phenomenon is something that they created long ago and control of which they may have lost. Or again it may be some unknown energy that they found when they entered their subterranean realm and which they have learned to control or which controls them.

"This much is sure—the moon door, which is clearly operated by the action of moonlight upon some unknown element or combination in much the same way that the metal selenium functions under sun rays or the electric light, and the crystals through which the moon rays pour down upon the pool their prismatic columns, are humanly made mechanisms.

"Set within the ruins they would seem to argue for the ancientness of the work. But who can tell when moon door and moon lights were set in their places? Nevertheless, so long as they are humanly made, and so long as it is this flood of moonlight from which the Dweller draws its power of materialization, the Dweller itself, if not the product of the human mind is at least dependent upon the product of the human mind for its appearance."

My pride in this analysis was short lived.

"Wait a minute, Goodwin," said O'Keefe. "Do you mean to say you think that this thing is made of—well, of moonshine?"

"Moonlight," I replied, "is, of course, reflected sunlight. But the rays which pass back to earth after their impact on the moon's surface are profoundly changed. The spectroscope shows that they lose practically all the slower vibrations we call red and infra-red, while the extremely rapid vibrations we call the violet and ultra-violet are accelerated and altered. Many scientists hold that there is an unknown element in the moon—perhaps that which makes the gigantic luminous trails that radiate in all directions from the lunar crater Tycho—whose energies are absorbed by and carried on the moon rays.

"At any rate, whether by the loss of the vibrations of the red or by the addition of this mysterious force, the light of the moon becomes something entirely different from mere modified sunlight—just as the addition or subtraction of one other chemical in a compound of several makes the product a substance with entirely different energies and potentialities.

"Now these rays are given perhaps still another mysterious activity by the transparent globes through which Throckmartin told me they passed in the Chamber of the Moon Pool and whose colors they take. The result is the necessary factor in the formation of the Dweller. There would be nothing scientifically improbable in such a process, Larry.

"We know the extraordinary effect of the Finsen rays, which are only the concentration of the chemical energies in the green and blue of the spectrum, upon malignant cell growths in the human body; and we know that the X-ray can dissolve the normal barrier of matter for us, making the solid transparent. We do not begin to know how to harness the potentialities of light. This hidden race may have learned; and learning, may have created forms with powers undreamed by us."

"LISTEN, Doc," said Larry earnestly, "I'll take everything you say about this lost continent, the people who used to live on it, and their caverns, for granted. But by the sword of Brian Boru, you'll never get me to fall for the idea that a bunch of moonshine can handle a big woman such as you say Throckmartin's Thora was, nor a two-fisted man such as you say Throckmartin was. You'll never get me to believe that any bunch of concentrated moonshine could handle them and take them waltzing off along a moonbeam back to wherever it goes. No Doc, not on your life."

"I've told you that what you call moonshine is an aggregate of vibrations with immense potential power, Larry," I answered, considerably irritated. "What we call matter is nothing but a collection of infinitely small particles of electricity—electrons; and the way the electrons are grouped makes of matter man or wood or metal or stone. Light is a magnetic vibration of the ether and is probably composed of similar particles of electricity but functioning in another way from the particles that make matter. Learn the secret of making light and you come close to learning the secret of matter.

"Why, if you could take all the energy out of the sunshine that in one minute covers one square foot of earth, you could blast all of earth to bits. And your wonderful radio is nothing but vibrations, yet it carries words around the world with almost the speed of light itself—"

"No," he interrupted. "You're wrong."

"All right O'Keefe," I answered, now very much irritated indeed. "What's your theory?" And I could not resist adding: "Fairies?"

"Professor," he grinned, "if it's a fairy it's Irish and when it sees me it'll be so glad there'll be nothing to it. 'I was lost, strayed or stolen, Larry avick,' it'll say, 'an' I was so homesick for the old sod I was desp'rit,' it'll say, 'an' take me back quick before I do any more har-rm!' It'll tell me—an' that's the truth."

I forgot my chagrin in our laughter.

"But I'll tell you what I think," he said soberly. "Back at the first battle of the Marne there were any number of Englishmen who thought they saw the old archers of Crecy and Agincourt, dead these half dozen centuries, twanging phantom bows and shooting down the enemy by the hundred. And you can find thousands of Frenchmen who saw Joan of Arc and Napoleon regularly. It's what the doctors call collective hallucination. Somebody sees something a little queer; his imagination gets to work hard because his nerves are pretty well strained anyway, he says to the next fellow: 'Don't you see it?' and the next fellow says, 'Sure I see it, too!' And there you are—bowmen of Mons, St. George on his white horse, Joan in armor, and all the rest of it."

"If you think that explains Throckmartin and myself, how do you explain Huldricksson, who never saw Throckmartin and didn't see me before the Thing came to the *Brunhilda?*" I asked with, I admit, some heat.

"Now don't get me wrong," replied Larry. "I believe you all saw something all right. But what I think you saw was some kind of gas. All this region is volcanic and islands and things are constantly poking up from the sea. It's probably gas; a volcanic emanation; something new to us and that drives you crazy—lots of kinds of gas do that.

"It hit the Throckmartin party on that island and they probably were all more or less delirious all the time; thought they saw things; talked it over and—collective hallucination. When they got it bad they most likely jumped overboard one by one. Huldricksson sails into a place where it is and it hits his wife. She grabs the child and jumps overboard. Maybe the moon rays make it luminous."

"But that doesn't explain the moon door and the phenomena of the lights in the Chamber of the Pool," I said at last.

"You haven't seen them, have you?" asked Larry. "And Throckmartin admitted he was pretty nearly crazy when he thought he did. Well!"

For a time I was silent.

"Larry," I said at last, "whether you are right or I am right, I must go to the Nan-Matal. Will you go with me, Larry?"

"Goodwin," he replied, "I surely will. I'm as interested as you are. If I'm reported dead for a while, there's nobody to care. So that's all right. Only, old man, be reasonable. You've thought over this so long, you're going bugs, honestly you are."

And again, the gladness that I might have Larry O'Keefe with me, was so great that I forgot to be angry.

CHAPTER VI

THE MOON DOOR OPENS—AND SHUTS

DA COSTA, who had come aboard unnoticed by either of us, now tapped me on the arm.

"Doctair Goodwin," he said, "can I see you in my cabin, sair?"

At last, then, he was going to speak. I followed him.

"Doctair," he said, when we had entered, "this is a veree strange thing that has happened to Olaf. Veree strange. An' the natives of Ponape, they have been very much excite' lately. An' none go near the Nan-Matal now, for they say the spirits have got great power and are angree because of that othair partee which they take.

"Of what they fear I know nothing, nothing!" Again that quick, furtive crossing of himself. "But this I have to tell you. There came to me from Ranaloa last month a man, a German, a doctair, like you. His name it was Von Hetzdorp. I take him to Ponape an' the natives there, they will not take him to the Nan-Matal, where he wish to go. So I take him. We leave in a boat, with much instrument carefully tied up. I leave him there wit' the boat an' the food. He tell me to tell no one an' pay me not to. But you are a friend an' Olaf he depend much upon you an' so I tell you, sair."

"You know nothing more than this, Da Costa?" I asked. "You're sure?"

"Nothing! Nothing more!" he answered. But I was not so sure. Later I told O'Keefe.

The next morning we raised Ponape, without further incident, and before noon the *Suwarna* and the *Brunhilda* had dropped anchor in the harbor. Upon the excitement and manifest dread of the natives, when we sought among them for carriers and workmen to accompany us, I will not dwell. No payment we offered would induce a single one of them to go to the Nan-Matal. Nor would they say why.

They were sullen and panicky, and I think the most disconcerting thing of all in their attitude, was the open relief they showed when they learned that a British warship might steam in, seeking O'Keefe. It indicated that their fear was deep-rooted and real, indeed.

We piled the longboat up with my instruments and food and camping equipment. The *Suwarna* took us around to Metalanim Harbor, and there, with the tops of ancient sea walls deep in the blue water beneath us, and the ruins looming up out of the mangroves, a scant mile from us, left us.

Da Costa's anxiety and uneasiness were almost pitiful. There were tears in the eyes of the little Portuguese when he bade us farewell, invoking all the saints to stand by and protect us; and the sorrow in his face and the fervor of his parting grip were eloquent of his conviction that never again would he behold us.

Then, with Huldricksson manipulating our small sail and Larry at the rudder, we rounded the titanic wall that swept down into the depths, passed monoliths, standing like gigantic sentinels upon its shattered verge. We turned at last into the canal that Throckmartin, on his map, had marked as the passage which led straight to that place of ancient mysteries where the moon door is portal of that dread chamber wherein the Dweller made itself manifest.

And as we entered that channel we were enveloped by a silence; a silence so intense, so weighted, that it seemed to have substance; an alien silence that clung and stifled and still stood aloof from us, the living.

Standing down in the chambered depths of the Great Pyramid I had known something of such silence, but never such intensity as this. Larry felt it and I saw him look at me askance. If Olaf, sitting in the bow, felt it, too, he gave no sign. His blue eyes, with again the glint of ice within them watched the channel before us.

As we passed, there arose upon our left sheer walls of black basalt blocks, cyclopean, towering fifty feet or more, broken here and there by the sinking of their deep foundations. And only where they had so broken, had the hand of time been able to crumble them. From these dark ramparts the silence seemed to ooze, and my skin crept as though from hidden places in them scores of eyes, ages dead, peered out at us, like ghosts of a lost Atlantis.

In front of us the mangroves widened out and filled the canal. On our right the lesser walls of Tau, somber blocks smoothed and squared and set with a cold, mathematical nicety, that filled me with vague awe, slipped by. Through breaks I caught glimpses of dark ruins and of great fallen stones that seemed to crouch and menace us as we passed. Somewhere there, hidden, were the seven globes that poured the moon fire down upon the Moon Pool.

Now we were among the mangroves and, sail down, the three of us pushed and pulled the boat through their tangled roots and branches. The noise of our passing split the silence, like a profanation, and from the ancient bastions came murmurs —forbidding, strangely sinister. And now

we were through, floating on a little open space of shadow-filled water. Before us lifted the gateway of Nan-Tanach, gigantic, broken, incredibly old. Shattered portals through which had passed men and women of earth's dawn; old with a weight of years that pressed leadenly upon the eyes that looked upon it, and yet in some curious, indefinable way—menacingly defiant.

Beyond the gate, back from the portals, stretched a flight of enormous basalt slabs, a giant's stairway indeed; and from each side of it marched the high walls that were the Dweller's pathway. None of us spoke as we grounded the boat and dragged it up upon a half-submerged pier.

"What next?" whispered Larry, at last.

"I think we ought to take a look around," I replied in the same low tones. "We'll climb the wall here and take a flash about. The whole place ought to be plain as day from that height."

Huldricksson, his blue eyes alert, nodded. With the greatest of difficulty we clambered up the broken blocks, the giant Norseman at times lifting me like a child, and stood at last upon the broad top. From this vantage-point, not only the whole of Nan-Tanach, but all of the Nan-Matal lay at our feet.

TO THE east and south of us, set like children's blocks in the midst of the sapphire sea, were dozens of islets, none of them covering more than two square miles of surface; each of them a perfect square or oblong within its protecting walls. Behind these walls were grouped ruins—houses, temples, palaces, all the varying abodes of men. On none was there sign of life, save for a few great birds that hovered here and there and gulls dipping in the blue waves beyond.

We turned our gaze down upon the island on which we stood. It was, I estimated, about three-quarters of a mile square. The sea wall enclosed it like the sides of a gigantic box. It was really an enormous basalt-sided open cube, and within it two other open cubes. The enclosure between the first and second wall was stone paved, with here and there a broken pillar and long stone benches.

The hibiscus, the aloe-tree and a number of small shrubs had found place, but seemed only to intensify its stark loneliness. It came to me that this had been the assembling place of those who, thousands upon thousands of years ago, had gathered within this citadel of mystery. Beyond the wall that was its farther boundary was a second enclosure, littered with broken pillars, fragments of stone and numerous small structures; and the second enclosure's limit was the third wall, a terrace not more than twenty feet high. Within it was what had been without doubt the heart of Nan-Tanach—an open space three hundred feet square; at each of its corners a temple.

Directly before us, black and staring like an eyeless socket, was the entrance to the "treasure-house of Chau-ta-Leur" the sun king. The blocks that had formed its doors lay shattered beside it. And opposite it should be, if Throckmartin's story had not been a dream, the gray slab he had named the moon door.

"Wonder where the German fellow can be?" asked Larry.

I shook my head. There was no sign of life here. Had Von Hetzdorp gone, or had the Dweller taken him, too? Whatever had happened, there was no trace of him below us or on any of the islets within our range of vision. We scrambled down the side of the gateway. Olaf looked at me wistfully.

"We start the search now, Olaf," I said. "And first, O'Keefe, let us see whether the gray stone is really here. After that we will set up camp, and while I unpack, you and Olaf search the island. It won't take long."

Larry gave a look at his service automatic and grinned. We made our way up the steps, through the outer enclosures and into the central square. I confess to a fire of scientific curiosity and eagerness tinged with a dread that O'Keefe's analysis might be true. Would we find the moving slab and, if so, would it be as Throckmartin had described? It so, then even Larry would have to admit that here was something that theories of gases and luminous emanations would not explain; and the first test of the whole amazing story would be passed. But if not—

And there before us, the faintest tinge of gray setting it apart from its neighboring blocks of basalt, was the moon door!

There was no mistaking it. This was, in very deed, the portal through which Dr. Throckmartin had seen pass that gloriously dreadful apparition he called the Dweller; through it the Dweller had borne in an embrace of living light first Thora, Mrs. Throckmartin's maid, and then Dr. Stanton, his youthful colleague. And through it at last had gone Throckmartin, down the shining tunnel beyond, whose luminous lure led to that enchanted chamber into which streamed the seven moon torrents that drew the Dweller from the wondrous pool that was its lair.

Across its threshold had raced Edith Throckmartin, my lost friend's young bride, fearlessly flying down that haunted passage to aid her husband in his fruitless fight against the Thing—and out of it he himself had rushed, a merciful darkness shrouding consciousness and sight, after he had watched her sink, slowly sink, down through the blue waters of the moon pool, wrapped in the Dweller's coruscating folds, to—what?

And then there seemed to drift out through the stone to face me that inexplicable being of swirling, spiraling plumes and jets of sparkling opalescence, of crystal sweet chimings, of murmuring sighings that Throckmartin had told me stamped upon the faces of its prey wedded anguish and rapture, terror and ecstasy commingled, joy of heaven and agony of hell, the seal of God and devil monstrously mated. The Thing that my own eyes had seen clasp Throckmartin in our cabin of the *Southern Queen* and draw him swiftly down the moon path.

What was that portal, more enigmatic

than was ever sphinx? And what lay beyond it? What did that smooth stone, whose wan deadness whispered of ages old corridors of time opening out into alien, unimaginable vistas, hide? It had cost the world of science Throckmartin's great brain, as it had cost Throckmartin those he loved. It had drawn me to it in search of Throckmartin, and its shadow had fallen upon the soul of Olaf the Norseman; and upon what thousands upon thousands more, I wondered, since the brains that had conceived it had vanished?

Did the Dweller lurk behind it in wait for us? When we found its open-sesame would we find within truths of our world's youth to which the riches of Ali Baba's cave were but dross? Was there that within which would force science to recast its hard won theories of humanity, of its evolution, of its painful progress from brute to what we call man? Or would we loose upon the world some nameless, blasting evil, some survival of our planet's nightmare hours, some supernormal, inhuman thing spawned by unthinkable travail in a hidden cavern of mother earth?

A barrier of unknown stone—fifteen feet high and ten feet wide; and yet it might bar the way to a lost paradise or hold back a hell undreamed by even cruelest brains! What lay beyond it?

SWIFTLY the thoughts raced through my mind as I stood staring at the gray slab and then through me passed a wave of weakness. And not until then did I realize the intense, subconscious anxiety that had possessed me.

I stretched out a shaking hand and touched the surface of the slab. A faint thrill passed through my hand and arm, oddly unfamiliar and as oddly pleasant; as of electric contact holding the very essence of cold. O'Keefe, watching, imitated my action. As his fingers rested on the stone his face filled with astonishment. In Huldricksson's eyes was mingled hope and despair. I beckoned him; he laid a hand on the slab and swiftly withdrew it. But I saw the despair die from his face,

leaving only eagerness, a sudden hope.

"It is the door!" he said. I nodded. There was a low whistle of astonishment from O'Keefe and he pointed up toward the top of the gray stone. I followed the gesture and saw, above the moon door and on each side of it, two gently curving bosses of rock, perhaps a foot in diameter.

"The moon door's keys," I said.

"It begins to look so," answered Larry. "If we can find them," he added.

"There's nothing we can do till moonrise," I replied. "And we've none too much time to prepare as it is. Come!"

But stark lonely as was that place, I felt, as we passed out, as though eyes were upon me, watching with an intensity of malevolence, a bitter hatred. Olaf must have felt it, too, for I saw him glance sharply around and his face hardened. I said nothing, however, nor did he; and a little later we were beside our boat. We lightered it, set up the tent, and as it was now but a short hour to sundown I told them to leave me and make their search. They went off together, and I busied myself with opening some of the paraphernalia I had brought with me.

First of all I took out two Becquerel ray-condensers that I had bought in New York. Their lenses would collect and intensify to the fullest extent any light directed upon them. I had found them most useful in making spectroscopic analysis of luminous vapors, and I knew that at Yerkes Observatory splendid results had been obtained from them in collecting the diffused radiance of the negulae for the same purpose.

It was my theory that the mechanism operating the moon door responded only to the force of the full light of the moon shining through the seven little circles which Throckmartin had discovered set within each of the bosses above it; just as the Dweller could materialize only under the same full-moon force shining through the varicolored lights. Obviously the time, then, of the door's opening and the phenomenon's materialization must coincide.

With the moon only a few days past

its full, it was practically certain that by setting the Becquerel condensers above the bosses I could concentrate enough light upon the circles to set the opening mechanism in motion. And as the ray stream from the waning moon was insufficient to energize the pool, we could enter the chamber free from any fear of encountering its tenant, make our preliminary observations and go forth before the satellite had dropped so far that the concentration in the condensers would fall below that necessary to keep the slab from closing.

I took out also a small spectroscope, easily carried and a few other small instruments for the analysis of certain light manifestations and the testing of metal and liquid. Finally, I put aside my emergency medical kit.

I had hardly finished examining and adjusting these before O'Keefe and Huldricksson returned. They reported signs of a camp at least ten days old beside the northern wall of the outer court, but beyond that no evidence of others beyond ourselves on Nan-Tanach. Moonrise would not occur until nine-thirty, and until then there was no use of attacking the moon door.

We prepared supper, ate and talked a little, but for the most part were silent. Even Larry's high spirits were not in evidence; half a dozen times I saw him take out his automatic and look it over. He was more thoughtful than I had ever seen him. Once he went into the tent, rummaged about a bit and brought out an-

other revolver which, he said, he had got from Da Costa, and a half-dozen clips of cartridges. He passed the gun to Olaf.

At last a glow in the southeast heralded the rising moon. I picked up my instruments and the medical kit; Larry and Olaf shouldered each a short ladder that was part of my equipment. With our electric flashes pointing the way, we walked up the great stairs, through the enclosures, and straight to the gray stone.

By this time the moon had risen and its clipped light shone full upon the slab. I saw faint gleams pass over it as of fleeting phosphorescence, but so faint were they that I could not be sure of the truth of my observation. The base of the gray stone bisected a curious cuplike depression whose perfectly rounded sides were as smooth as though they had been polished by a jeweler. This half cup was, at its deepest, two and a half feet, and its lip joined the basalt pavement four feet from the barrier of the great slab.

WE SET the ladders in place. Olaf I assigned to stand before the door and watch for the first signs of its opening—if open it should—and the big sailor accepted the post eagerly, thinking, I suppose, that it would bring him nearer the loved ones he now was sure were within. The Becquerals were set within three-inch tripods, whose feet I had equipped with vacuum rings to enable them to hold fast to the rock.

I scaled one ladder and fastened a condenser over the boss; descended; sent Larry up to watch it, and, ascending the second ladder, rapidly fixed the other in its place. Then, with O'Keefe watchful on his perch, I on mine and Olaf's eyes fixed upon the moon door, we began our vigil. Suddenly there was an exclamation from Larry.

"Seven little lights are beginning to glow on this stone, Goodwin!" he cried.

But I had already seen those beneath my lens begin to gleam out with a silvery luster. Swiftly the rays within the condenser began to thicken and increase, and as they did so the seven small circles waxed like stars growing out of the dusk, and with a queer—curdled is the best word I can find to define it—luster entirely strange to me.

I placed a finger upon one of them and received a shock such as I had felt on touching the moon door, only greatly intensified. Clearly a current of some kind was set up within the substance when the moonlight fell upon it. And now the lights were glowing steadily. Beneath me I heard a faint, sighing murmur and then the voice of Huldricksson:

"It opens—the stone turns—"

I began to climb down the ladder. Again came Olaf's voice:

"The stone—it is open—" And then a shriek that came from the very core of his heart; a wail of blended anguish and pity, of rage and despair—and the sound of swift footsteps racing through the wall beneath me!

I dropped to the ground. The moon door was wide open, and through it I caught a glimpse of a corridor filled with a faint, pearly vaporous light like earliest misty dawn. But of Olaf I could see nothing! And even as I stood, gaping, from behind me came the sharp crack of a rifle. I saw the glass of the condenser at Larry's side flash and fly into fragments; saw him drop swiftly to the ground and the automatic in his hand flash once, twice, into the darkness.

Saw, too, the moon door begin to pivot slowly, slowly back into its place!

I rushed toward the turning stone with the wild idea of holding it open. As I thrust my hands against it there came at my back a snarl and an oath and Larry staggered under the impact of a body that had flung itself straight at his throat. He reeled at the lip of the shallow cup at the base of the slab, slipped upon its polished curve, fell and rolled with that which had attacked him, kicking and writhing, straight through the narrowing portal into the mistily luminous passage!

Forgetting all else, I sprang with a cry to his aid. And as I leaped I felt the closing edge of the moon door graze my side. And then, as Larry raised a fist, brought it down upon the temple of the man who had grappled with him and rose from the twitching body unsteadily to his feet, I heard shuddering past me a mournful whisper; spun about as though some giant hand had whirled me—and stood so, rigid, appalled!

For the end of the corridor no longer opened out into the moonlit square of ruined Nan-Tanach. It was barred by a solid mass of glimmering stone. The moon door had closed!

And where was Olaf Huldricksson? And who was the man at our feet who had brought this calamity down upon us? And what were we to do, prisoned, and my bewildered brain told me, hopelessly prisoned, without food, in the very lair of the Dweller itself?

TO BE CONTINUED IN THE NEXT ISSUE

In the next issue:

THE LORD OF DEATH
A Complete Novelet
By HOMER EON FLINT

Golden Atlantis

By RICHARD BUTLER GLAENZER

ATLANTIS is no fable. I have heard
   The murmur of its bells on golden nights.
And in the wailing of the tropic bird
   The memory of ancient homing flights
   To a tall island where the humblest rights—
Those of a bird as well as man—were held
   Sacred since inborn, safe from jealous spites.
Atlantis was a land where freedom dwelled.

They were not truly sages who averred
   That the great eastern Atlantean bights
Lav close to Egypt, and that from them purred
   The sphinx-prowed galleys, spreading dark delights
   Along the Nile, creating appetites
Brazen as Moloch's. Could the golden-belled
   Have chimed with slavers of Israelites?
Atlantis was a land where freedom dwelled.

This I know best—down in my heart has stirred,
   In answer to the Pool of Malachites,
Still bubbling fathoms deep, the living word—
   A word so healing that it cured all blights
   A word so kindly that it checked all slights,
A word from which all loving-kindness welled.
   The word that follows, in the tongue of sprites:
"Atlantis was a land where freedom dwelled!"

ENVOI

Prince of the world, Maker of blacks and whites,
   Of red men, yellow, man however spelled,
Giver whose hand, disdained as empty, smites,
   Atlantis *was*, a land where freedom dwelled!

The World in the Balance

By J. P. MARSHALL

From Saturn they came, and gave the world a three-day ultimatum

UPPER BROADWAY drowsed lazily through the heat of the July afternoon. A policeman, taking advantage of a momentary lull in the rush of traffic, paused to mop his forehead and scan the blue sky above him.

High up over the roofs of the buildings floated a toy balloon, its bright green color plainly seen even at that height. The officer grinned as he speculated over the mental anguish of the child who must have lost it.

The whirl of traffic closed in again, and for two hours the officer guided cars and pedestrians. Then came another break, and as before he brushed his handkerchief across his forehead and scanned the heavens.

Two hours! And yet the balloon was still there, holding the same relative position, except that it was nearer, bigger, out of all proportion to the size of the ordinary toy type. The officer let several cars pass unheeded while he tried to discover how a balloon could float freely and still beat up against the wind, for certainly it was moving toward him in spite of the breeze at his back.

The officer was not the only person in New York who was puzzled by the actions of the green sphere. From all parts of the city people watched, wondering what sort of an advertising project they were witnessing.

Evening came on, and still that gayly colored globe hung over the city, motion-

No further warning
was needed

less now. Night—and it stood outlined against the sky like a phosphorescent moon, lighted by some sort of shifting fitful flame that seemed to come from within and swirl up over its surface.

From the harbor a brilliant pencil of light shot out, circled around and then up, coming to rest on the strange object. Then New York fairly rubbed its eyes!

It was gone! The beam from the searchlight swept here and there, trying to point it out again, but to no avail.

Suddenly from far above came an answering beam; a thin thread-like stream of green. In eerie fashion the beam shortened and lengthened, swept around in a wide arc, and then pointed straight down at the figure of Liberty.

A slight greenish glow surrounded the upper part of the statue.

The harbor searchlight circled to bear on the figure, and the watchers gasped. Liberty was broken! The entire head and half the torso had disappeared, the remaining part standing there with the searchlight playing up and down its shortened length.

There had been no noise, no crash.

Half the Statue of Liberty had simply vanished.

Up to that point curiosity had held the city in its grip. Now fear took its place.

Telephone and telegraph lines hummed with the news of the vandalism. And out over the harbor that phosphorescent globe suddenly became visible again.

An hour—two hours passed. From Mineola two huge armored bombers took off into the air and winged toward the scene of the disturbance. By the noise of the motors and the flare of the exhausts the populace followed the flight of the airplanes over the city, out over the harbor, straight toward that shining globe.

The bombers cut a wide circle around their objective; and then the roar of the motors became interspersed with the rattle of machine gun fire.

The globe moved; dropped swiftly until it rode just over the crests of the waves, then shot straight up with bewildering

The green globe rose high over the harbor and the city held its breath

speed. From the bottom of the craft crept a short green ray that grew and lengthened, whipping here and there until it found its mark.

The same greenish glow that had surrounded the statue enveloped one of the bombers. Its motor became silent.

It was gone! The other gave a final burst from its machine gun and fled.

The globe did not pursue; there was no need. That green ray flashed around toward the machine, hesitated, came to rest and then lengthened. Its tip touched the airplane, and like its mate it vanished, with that same greenish haze as the only sign of its passing!

THE sun rose over a disorganized city. People half-heartedly started toward their work. Some of the more hardy souls carried on as before, but the great majority were held by the fear of the unknown.

The happenings of the previous night seemed like some fantastic nightmare visited on the entire populace. But there in the harbor stood the wrecked body of Liberty as a grim reminder of the reality of things, and above, so high as to be just visible, rested that green agent of destruction.

At noon it began to grow larger as it

descended. Straight as a falling stone it fell toward the heart of the city, checked its·rush just over the tops of the sky-scrapers, then floated down to rest in the center of Times Square.

In appearance the object was a wonderfully smooth green sphere about a hundred and fifty feet in diameter, with no apparent opening of any kind.

For an hour it rested there, motionless, while the crowds gathered and the traffic of the city became paralyzed. Squad after squad of police arrived to form a circle around the sphere. Four machine gun crews hastily set up their weapons to command it from any point; and still nothing happened.

One officer, bolder or more foolhardy than the rest, slowly approached the bulky object. Foot by foot he cut down the intervening distance until he stood only an arm's length away.

He reached out a hand, touched it gingerly and hastily backed away several steps. Gaining courage he approached again and drummed lustily on the smooth surface with his club.

The sphere gave out a hollow metallic ring, that was all. Again he reached out a hand to touch the hammered surface; and as his fingers met it he promptly turned a back somersault.

The bewildered expression on his face as he scrambled to his feet would have been ludicrous at any other time. Now it was anything but funny to the watching crowds.

"It's charged," he yelled. "Electricity! My arm is numb!"

A sharp clang came from the interior of the sphere as a small section slid away, leaving an opening framing a hideous face when viewed from earthly standards. Another clang, and another section opened, leaving a space large enough for the creature's body to emerge.

Short of stature, and powerful of physique, with that ugly head surmounting the body, the stranger was far from prepossessing in appearance.

He beckoned to the stunned officer, and that person, as if hypnotized, drew toward him with lagging feet.

The strange one uttered several guttural sounds and raised his brows as if in question. The officer shook his head. The other whipped out a pad and stylus, scratched rapidly and handed the result to the officer. Again the latter shook his head.

Impatiently the stranger beckoned him closer, and reaching out placed a huge powerful hand over the officer's temples, while he gazed steadily into his eyes. The policeman gave a yelp of astonishment and turned to his fellow officers.

"He says he wants to see the commander of this planet!" he gasped.

"Commander of the planet? There isn't any!"

The officer looked helplessly at the stranger, at a loss to know how to convey the information. The other solved his problem by placing one of the officer's hands over each of his own temples and again looking him in the eyes.

The officer was intelligent. Weird as it seemed, he realized that the other had the power to communicate by telepathy.

He gazed back steadily at his questioner and concentrated on the words of his answer. The stranger showed surprise and raised his hands again.

"He wants the ruler of the country then," announced the officer.

"He'll have to go to Washington."

The last answer being relayed, the stranger showed signs of impatience again.

"He says he wants to see someone in authority!"

The police commissioner stepped forward.

"I'll talk to him," he answered.

For half an hour the commissioner and the strange visitor carried on a silent conversation. Suddenly the stranger raised his hand with an unmistakable gesture of finality, and turning about, stepped back into his sphere.

A moment he stood there, then the section clanged back into place and the globe lifted. As if in a trance, the commissioner stood watching, his face drawn with the horror of some knowledge he had just gained. The spell broke; the commissioner spun on his heel and barked a command:

"Quick! The machine guns! Don't let him get away."

The four guns rose and spat their leaden hail against the surface of the sphere. That terrible green ray, visible even in bright sunlight suddenly shone from a small aperture near the bottom.

The gunners were doomed, and they knew it. With blanched faces they stuck to their weapons and rained bullets at the rising craft.

The globe turned slowly, the ray swinging with it. A flare of green struck a gun squad and passed on. Machine gun, crew—all disintegrated before the eyes of the crowd. Even the pavement below was badly scarred.

In the center of the spot where the gun crew had been were only several small shining objects.

Unmindful of his own danger, the commissioner leaped to the spot and fell on his knees.

"By the Eternal!" he muttered again, as he picked up the glittering objects. There were two gold watches; one, an open-faced model, was merely an empty case, the other, a hunting-case type, was unharmed.

Near the watches were two gold rings; the first a wedding ring, the second a diamond setting from which the stone had vanished.

The commissioner's voice was hoarse with concentrated hate and horror. "If I live," he exclaimed, "I will make you pay for the murder of these boys!"

He shook his fist at the fast ascending globe, and ran for his car.

A SOLEMN-FACED group of men sat around the table in the commissioner's office the following afternoon.

Next to the commissioner was a stern-looking naval commander, in charge of the dreadnaught in the harbor. Beside the commander sat a small elderly man, the country's greatest astronomer.

Across from the latter, drumming his fingers nervously on the polished table top, was a younger man, his keen eyes darting from one to another of the group. He was a scientist, one of those men to whom civilization owes its greatest progress.

A major, commanding the available land forces, completed the group.

The fleet was away, but steaming at full speed for New York. The military forces of the nation were being entrained from all points toward the city. But it was all useless, and those around the table knew it.

"Tell us, commissioner"—the major tugged at his mustache thoughtfully—"tell us, please, just what passed in that mental conversation."

"We have three days!" The commissioner's voice was dull with the agony of despair. "He gave us three days to surrender the entire country. Saturday he will come again, to Times Square, and we must meet him and tell him our decision.

"What can we do? How can we fight such an enemy? That devilish globe will simply hang up there out of range, loose that ray, and wipe us out! It can conquer the world. Its commander knows it. We know it! And yet—to give up without a blow—"

"You, major, and you, commander, you are the professional fighting men. What do you say?"

The major met the glance of the commander, and both winced. They knew their limitations, yet each was prepared to take up the hopeless fight. The major spoke:

"We hold the fate of the world in our hands, gentlemen. It is not America alone, it is the world! Washington has instructed us to hold out as best we can until other forces arrive, but Washington does not know— One must have been here to realize the terror of the thing.

"Heaven knows how many warriors that globe carries, what other weapons it conceals. It must be prevented from landing here, but how? Commissioner"—a sudden thought seemed to strike the major—"did you find out where it came from?"

"I asked. Tl e stranger answered with some name that was meaningless to me, but into my mind flashed a picture of a globe whirling in space, while around it spun an outer ring like this." The commissioner grasped a pencil and sketched his thought.

The astronomer reached over and pulled the sheet toward him.

"A globe—an outer ring. It must be Saturn! But we always supposed that it was unlivable for humans!"

"We have the proof! Here! Now!"

"What a chance!" The astronomer was thinking aloud. "What a chance! If we could but capture the thing with its crew alive. The things they could tell—" His eyes were dreamy, his mind far away, wandering through the solar system; the scientist always seeking knowledge.

"No!" It was the naval commander who spoke. "We cannot risk it. Destroy the thing. We must bend all our efforts to that result. We cannot, must not risk the chance of its escape. We must destroy it now!"

"Yes." The scientist nodded. "Destroy it! I can quite understand the professor's feeling. If we merely succeed in driving it away, what then? It would return to its planet and bring others next time. Beyond a doubt the craft is experimental in its nature. If it returns, others will follow. If it is destroyed the others will not come because of its supposed failure. It may be years before another attempt will be made, and in that time we will have been able to prepare for such a possibility. The question is: How are we to destroy this present menace?"

"Mine the Square." The major offered the suggestion with almost an air of apology. "Mine the whole of Times Square, and when it lands—"

"No." The scientist shook his head. "They will be wary. They have an intelligence of a higher degree than ours. It may hurt to admit it, but we must deal with facts. They will not blunder into a trap. What can you offer, commander?"

The commander shook his head.

"I can only stand to my guns," he answered, snapping his jaws together. "It is hopeless, but I cannot surrender. When it comes I shall open fire with the ship's anti-aircraft guns—and pray."

"You, commissioner?" The scientist had quite easily assumed command. "What do you propose?"

The commissioner opened his lips to speak, and shook his head.

"I tried before," he almost whispered, "and you know the result."

"Then listen to me." The scientist leaned forward, his eyes snapping, his words crackling through the room like electric sparks. "You have all admitted your inability to contend with the enemy. Guns, ships, men, everything is useless! Everything withers before that baleful ray except one thing—and there lies our defense, and our weapon!"

He leaned over and picked up the watch cases and rings that the commissioner had brought from the scene of the tragedy of the previous day.

"Are you mad? Several bits of damaged jewelry to fight with!" The major glared accusingly at the scientist. "You cannot be making sport at such a time."

"No. Here." The scientist leaned forward again. "See this case? It was open faced, and the ray destroyed the works. This other watch has a hunting case, and it is unharmed. The ray does not consume gold, nor material that is protected by a gold covering. Listen, and then tell me if I am mad!"

HALF an hour later the five men sat leaning back in their chairs. Eyes that had been dull with the knowledge of defeat were now bright with the hope of victory.

"Hurry." The scientist turned to the commissioner. "You have the men trained for the work. Send them out. Tell them to bring every metalsmith they can find, even if they have to carry them. Take over the jewelers' factories; they have the machinery and the tools. Gather gold, gold, gold—from anywhere and everywhere. Do not stop to bargain. Confiscate in the name of the government. You have force; if the need comes use it! And in the museum you will find models—get them."

All that night, through all of Thursday and all of Friday, the jewelers' shops hummed with activity. Near midnight of Friday the whine of machinery began to decrease; by two o'clock Saturday morning the last shop became dark and silent.

Trucks sped to police headquarters carrying the handiwork of the metal-smiths: twenty-five shining suits of armor of pure beaten gold, twenty-five ridiculous little round gold shields, their face burnished so that they shone and sparkled with each little bit of light that touched them.

The scientist viewed the collection.

"It is all we can do." He turned to the commissioner. "Camouflage the suits with black paint. There is no need to show our enemy the nature of our defense. Pick me twenty-four men who aren't afraid to die, and send them to me. I am going to wear one suit myself."

"Twenty-three," the commissioner replied quietly. "I need pick only twenty-three. One suit is for me. I am thinking of those dead gunners of mine."

"As you will," the scientist nodded. "If we fail, it will not matter much which of us are among the living and which are dead!"

SATURDAY dawned clear, with the whole populace watching the sky. News was abroad! The green globe had been seen in Europe, Asia, all over the world, and at each place of call it had left the same trail of destruction and the same ultimatum: three days to surrender!

This was to be the day of America's answer—and the whole world was watching, waiting for the news that would mean victory and safety, or defeat and chaos.

At ten o'clock the globe appeared, looking no bigger than a marble when first sighted. Down it drifted until it hung fairly low over the harbor, less than two miles up.

From the ground a flock of airplanes sprang, to swiftly form into battle formation and speed toward the enemy.

The air battle was soon over. The machine guns on the planes had hardly become warm before the green ray appeared, at first only one, then as the planes drew nearer the whole globe fairly bristled with rays darting here and there in every direction.

Before that deadly barrage of light the planes disappeared. One after another they dropped from existence until but a scant half dozen were left. These last turned and streaked back toward the landing field, beaten.

Behind them the rays lengthened and sped to catch up with them. There were four—two—one! The lone survivor circled, dipped, and straightened out for the landing; but the wheels never touched the ground. Less than a hundred feet up it became—nothing!

A series of heavy reports from the harbor marked the entry into the fray of the anti-aircraft guns on the dreadnaught. The globe shot straight up so swiftly that the watchers' necks all jerked back in unison in an attempt to follow that flight. Safely out of range, the globe floated quietly again.

A bundle of green threads grew down toward the dreadnaught. Standing on the bridge, the commander saw, and knew his fate.

"Cease firing! Overboard! Every man jack that can get over—go!"

The order was passed along, and the surface of the harbor became dotted with bobbing heads.

Alone on the bridge, the commander gripped the rail until the knuckles of his hands stood out white. His upturned eyes followed the approach of the rays. The enemy was slow, maliciously letting the victims taste the full dregs of death. At last they struck!

The huge dreadnaught melted from sight instantly. A rushing, whirling maelstrom grew on the spot as the surrounding waves rushed in to fill up the gap left by the disintegrating waters. And the commander had gone down with his ship.

In a side street off Times Square twenty-five heavily moving men stirred uneasily. The golden armor bore down on them, and the strain of waiting was beginning to wear on taut nerves.

Fortunately for their peace of mind, they had been unable to see the drama that had been enacted in and over the harbor, but they had no illusions concerning their own part that was yet to be played. They knew that it would be either victory or death.

The globe descended again, circled the city, and stopped high up over the square.

"Scatter!" The scientist gave his gold-muffled order. "Circle the square and come out when you hear the siren. You know your stations; you know what you have to do. Remember, on our success or failure hangs the fate of the nation, and it may well be the fate of the world."

He spoke to the men within the gold-armored truck that carried the huge siren:

"Watch me, and when I raise my arm sound the signal."

The globe dropped slowly, warily, suspecting a possible trap. A volley of rays reached down to the square and its environs.

The pavement in the center of the square vanished, leaving a huge shallow crater. The scientist was right; it would have been useless to mine the square. The tall, proud structure of the Times Building disappeared, the Paramount and others followed one by one, until in the center of New York there was a huge circle of barrenness, with only a light green haze drifting across the space where Times Square had been.

Nearer dropped the globe, and again it stopped, barely a hundred feet up.

The scientist raised his arm. The huge siren screeched out its signal, the sound echoing back and forth from the walls of the buildings yet standing.

The men of the gold armor appeared, walking slowly, heavily over the edge of the crater, each swinging his burnished shield. Slowly they drew toward each other until they had formed a rough circle about three hundred feet across.

The globe hung quietly, then, as if in question, a slim green ray crept down and touched one of the armored men. As by magic, the black paint covering the armor disappeared, leaving a brilliant golden figure standing out in the full afternoon light.

The globe shot up a few hundred feet, hesitated, then drifted down to its former level. Twenty-five rays gleamed out from its polished surface; the entire band of armored men suddenly shone as had the first.

The scientist waved his arm and swung his shield before him. The others followed suit. Again following his lead, they all faced their shields upward. Those green rays, impotently playing over the golden figures, were caught on the polished surfaces of the shields. A moment of wavering, and then the reflected rays shot back toward their projector. Too late the commander of that weird craft must have realized the meaning of those shields—golden mirrors, each sending back at him the terrible ray of death that was his own weapon.

Like a toy balloon drawn over a gas flame, the globe itself disintegrated. A ball of greenish mist hung motionless overhead—then only the clear blue of the sky could be seen.

In the center of the square two golden figures clasped each other clumsily and attempted to shake hands.

"Thank Heaven, we've won!" The scientist jerked up his gold visor and peered at the commissioner.

"Yes." The commissioner's reply was blurred by a choking sob. "America—the world—is safe. And those dead heroes—they will rest happily now!"

The DECEMBER ISSUE ON SALE NOVEMBER EIGHTH

The Editors' Page

THE first issue of FAMOUS FANTAS-TIC MYSTERIES seems to have gone over with a bang. Readers were delighted with the book. Many had suggestions for changes.

Some of those letters—all that we have had room for—are published in the "Readers' Viewpoint" department beginning on page 125 of this issue.

———— • ————

We are really pleased to tell you, that as a result of the spontaneous response and acceptance of the first issue, which was indicated as a bi-monthly, we are encouraged to publish the magazine monthly hereafter. The readers have actually demanded it. They have demanded the long classics of science-fiction in serial form. We begin to give them to you in this issue.

———— • ————

Many of our readers seemed to have been under the impression that the complete novelettes "The Moon Pool" and "The Girl in the Golden Atom" were condensed versions of the complete stories. This is not quite a fact. It happens that in each case the two stories above referred to had originally been published far in advance of the long novels entitled "The Conquest of the Moon Pool" and "The People of the Golden Atom", which are respectively sequels to the two stories published in our first issue.

These sequels are now prepared for republication, the first part of "The Conquest of the Moon Pool" being presented to you in this issue.

———— • ————

The polls of the readers are interesting. A strong demand for Ralph Milne Farley's "The Radio Man" indicates that that serial will be started next month. Homer Eon Flint's unforgettable "The Lord of Death", R. F. Starzl's "The Red Germ of Courage", Edison Marshall's "Who Is Charles Avison?"—these and many more too numerous to mention are musts.

However, the biggest "must" of all is the Austin Hall—Homer Eon Flint "The Blind Spot." That story, we are happy to tell you, is now in preparation and we expect to be able to give it to you soon.

———— • ————

The readers' letters show that they are well informed on the whole field of science fiction. Many of them can list most of the important stories with their publication dates, and rate them according to their merits as classics.

Well, it's *your* magazine.

———— • ————

No coupon this month; readers prefer to express their viewpoints in letters.

And how we want those letters!

Some of the readers have already done this, as you will see by turning to the department which we have devoted to letters. We shall want to get your reaction to this issue, also. You do not have to know the names of stories to do this, but you can tell us how you like them.

We want to be guided by your criticism and compliments. This is your chance to read the greatest science-fiction classics of all time.

Guide us in selecting our table of contents for you.

—The Editors

There came a blinding flash from the roof of Dr. Syx's mill

The Moon Metal

By GARRETT P. SERVISS
Author of "The Second Deluge," "Conquest of Mars," etc.

Who was Dr. Syx, and whence came the metal that made him dictator of the whole world?

CHAPTER I

SOUTH POLAR GOLD

WHEN the news came of the discovery of gold at the South Pole in 1949, nobody suspected that the beginning had been reached of a new era in the world's history. The newsboys cried "Extra!" as they had done a thousand times for murders, battles, fires, and Wall Street panics, but nobody was excited. In fact, the reports at first seemed so exaggerated and improbable that hardly anybody believed a word of them. Who could have been expected to credit a despatch, forwarded by cable from New Zealand, and signed by an unknown name, which contained such a statement as this?

"A seam of gold which can be cut with a knife has been found within ten miles of the South Pole."

In a little while several additional reports came, some via New Zealand, others via South America, and all confirming in every respect what had been sent before. Then a New York newspaper sent a swift steamer to the Antarctic, and when this enterprising journal published a four-page cable describing the discoveries in detail, all doubt vanished and the rush began.

For many years silver had been absent from the coinage of the world. Its increasing abundance rendered it unsuitable for money, especially when contrasted with gold.

The common monetary system prevailing in every land fostered trade and facilitated the exchange of products. Travelers never had to bother their heads about the currency of money; any coin that passed in New York would pass for its face value in London, Paris, Berlin, Rome, Madrid. Or in Leningrad. Constantinople, Cairo, Khartoum, Jerusalem, Peking, or Yeddo. It was indeed the "Golden Age," and the world had never been so free from financial storms.

UPON this peaceful scene the south polar gold discoveries burst like an unheralded tempest.

I happened to be in the company of a famous bank president when the confirmation of those discoveries suddenly filled the streets with yelling newsboys.

"Get me one of those 'extras'!" he said, and an office-boy ran out to obey him. As he perused the sheet his face darkened.

"I'm afraid it's too true," he said at length. "Yes, there seems to be no getting around it. Gold is going to be as plentiful as iron. If there were not such a flood of it, we might manage, but when they begin to make trousers buttons out of the same metal that is now locked and guarded in steel vaults, where will be our standard of worth? My dear fellow," he continued, impulsively laying his hand on my arm, "I would as willingly face the end of the world as this that's coming!"

"You think it so bad, then?" I asked. "But most people will not agree with you. They will regard it as very good news."

"How can it be good?" he burst out. "What have we got to take the place of gold? Can we go back to the age of barter? Can we substitute cattle-pens and wheat-bins for the strong boxes of the Treasury? Can commerce exist with no common measure of exchange?"

His premonitions of disaster turned out

Reprinted from the May, 1905, All-Story Magazine. (Originally copyrighted, 1900, by Garrett P. Serviss.)

to be but too well grounded. The deposits of gold at the South Pole were richer than the wildest reports had represented them. The shipments of the precious metal to America and Europe soon became enormous—so enormous that the metal was no longer precious.

The price of gold dropped like a falling stone, with accelerated velocity, and within a year every money center in the world had been swept by a panic. Gold was more common than iron. Every government was compelled to demonetize it, for when once gold had fallen into contempt it was less valuable in the eyes of the public than stamped paper. For once the world had thoroughly learned the lesson that too much of a good thing is worse than none of it.

Then somebody found a new use for gold by inventing a process by which it could be hardened and tempered, assuming a wonderful toughness and elasticity without losing its non-corrosive property, and in this form it rapidly took the place of steel.

In the meantime, every effort was made to bolster up credit. Endless were the attempts to find a substitute for gold. The chemists sought it in their laboratories and the mineralogists in the mountains and deserts. Platinum might have served, but it, too, had become a drug in the market through the discovery of immense deposits. Out of the twenty odd elements which had been rarer and more valuable than gold, such as uranium, gallium, etc., not one was found to answer the purpose. In short, it was evident that since both gold and silver had become too abundant to serve any longer for a money standard, the planet held no metal suitable to take their place.

The entire monetary system of the world must be readjusted, but in the readjustment it was certain to fall to pieces. In fact, it had already fallen to pieces; the only recourse was to paper money, but whether this was based upon agriculture or mining or manufacture, it gave varying standards, not only among the differ-ent nations, but in successive years in the same country. Exports and imports practically ceased. Credit was discredited, commerce perished, and the world, at a bound, seemed to have gone back, financially and industrially, to the dark ages.

One final effort was made. A great financial congress was assembled at New York. Representatives of all the nations took part in it. The ablest financiers of Europe and America united the efforts of their genius and the results of their experience to solve the great problem. The various governments all solemnly stipulated to abide by the decision of the congress.

But, after spending months in hard but fruitless labor, that body was no nearer the end of its undertaking than when it first assembled. The entire world awaited its decision with bated breath, and yet the decision was not formed.

At this paralyzing crisis a most unexpected event suddenly opened the way.

CHAPTER II

THE MAGICIAN OF SCIENCE

AN ATTENDANT entered the room where the perplexed financiers were in session and presented a peculiar-looking card to the president, Mr. Boon. The president took the card in his hand and so complete was his absorption that Herr Finster, the celebrated Berlin banker, who had been addressing the chair for the last two hours from the opposite end of the long table, got confused, entirely lost track of his verb, and suddenly dropped into his seat, very red in the face and wearing a most injured expression.

But President Boon paid no attention except to the singular card, which he continued to turn over and over, balancing it on his fingers and holding it now at arm's-length and then near his nose, with one eye squinted as if he were trying to look through a hole in the card.

At length this odd conduct of the presiding officer drew all eyes upon the card, and then everybody shared the interest of Mr. Boon. In shape and size the card was not extraordinary, but it was composed of metal. What metal? Plainly it was not tin, brass, copper, bronze, silver, aluminum—although its lightness might have suggested that metal—nor even base gold.

The president, although a skilled metallurgist, confessed his inability to say what it was. So intent had he become in examining the curious bit of metal that he forgot it was a visitor's card of introduction, and did not even look for the name which it presumably bore.

As he held the card up to get a better light upon it, a stray sunbeam from the window fell across the metal, and instantly it bloomed with exquisite colors! The president's chair being in the darker end of the room, the radiant card suffused the atmosphere about him with a faint rose tint, playing with surprising liveliness into alternate canary color and violet.

The effect upon the company of clear-headed financiers was extremely remarkable. The unknown metal appeared to exercise a kind of mesmeric influence, its soft hues blending together in a chromatic harmony which captivated the sense of vision as the ears are charmed by a perfectly rendered song. Gradually all gathered in an eager group around the president's chair.

"What can it be?" was repeated from lip to lip.

"Did you ever see anything like it?" asked Mr. Boon for the twentieth time.

None of them had ever seen the like of it. A spell fell upon the assemblage. For five minutes no one spoke, while Mr. Boon continued to chase the flickering sunbeam with the wonderful card. Suddenly the silence was broken by a voice which had a touch of awe in it:

"It must be the metal!"

The speaker was an English financier, First Lord of the Treasury, Hon. James Hampton-Jones, K. C. B. Immediately everybody echoed his remark, and the strain being thus relieved, the spell dropped from them and several laughed loudly over their momentary aberration.

PRESIDENT BOON recollected himself, and, coloring slightly, placed the card flat on the table, in order more clearly to see the name. In plain red letters it stood forth with such surprising distinctness that Mr. Boon wondered why he had so long overlooked it.

Dr. MAX SYX

"Tell the gentleman to come in," said the president, and thereupon the attendant threw open the door.

The owner of the mysterious card fixed every eye as he entered. He was several inches more than six feet in height. His complexion was very dark, his eyes were intensely black, bright, and deep-set, his eyebrows were bushy and up-curled at the ends, his sable hair was close-trimmed, and his ears were narrow, pointed at the top, and prominent. He wore black mustaches, covering only half the width of his lip and drawn into projecting needles on each side, while a spiked black beard adorned the middle of his chin.

He smiled as he stepped confidently forward, with a courtly bow, but it was a very disconcerting smile, because it more than half resembled a sneer. This uncommon person did not wait to be addressed.

"I have come to solve your problem," he said, facing President Boon, who had swung round on his pivoted chair.

"The metal!" exclaimed everybody in a breath, and with a unanimity and excitement which would have astonished them if they had been spectators instead of actors of the scene. The tall stranger bowed and smiled again.

"Just so," he said. "What do you think of it?"

"It is beautiful!"

The mesmeric spell seemed once more to fall upon the assemblage, for the financiers noticed nothing remarkable in the next act of the stranger, which was to take a chair, uninvited, at the table, and the moment he sat down he became the presiding officer as naturally as if he had just been elected to the post. They all waited for him to speak, and when he opened his mouth they listened with breathless attention.

His words were of the best English, but there was some peculiarity, which they had already noticed, either in his voice or his manner of enunciation, which struck all of the listeners as denoting a foreigner. But none of them could satisfactorily place him. Neither the Americans, the Englishmen, the Germans, the Frenchmen, the Russians, the Austrians, the Italians, the Spaniards, the Turks, the Japanese, or the Chinese at the board could decide to what race he belonged.

"This metal," he began, "I have discovered and named. I call it 'artemisium.' I can produce it, in the pure form, abundantly enough to replace gold, giving it the same relative value that gold possessed when it was the universal standard."

As Dr. Syx spoke, he snapped the card with his thumb-nail, and it fluttered with quivering hues like a humming-bird hovering over a flower. He seemed to await a reply, and President Boon asked:

"What guarantee can you give that the supply would be adequate and continuous?"

"I will conduct a committee of this congress to my mine in the Rocky Mountains, where, in anticipation of the event, I have accumulated enough refined artemisium to provide every civilized land with an amount of coin equivalent to that which is formerly held in gold. I can there satisfy you of my ablity to maintain the production."

"But how do we know that this metal of yours will answer the purpose?"

"Try it," was the laconic reply.

"There is another difficulty," pursued the president. "People will not accept a new metal in place of gold unless they are convinced that it possesses equal intrinsic value. They must first become familiar with it, and it must be abundant enough and desirable enough to be used sparingly in the arts, just as gold was."

"I have provided for all that," said the stranger, with one of his disconcerting smiles. "I assure you that there will be no trouble with the people. They will be only too eager to get and to use the metal. Let me show you."

He stepped to the door, and immediately returned with two black attendants bearing a large tray filled with articles shaped from the same metal as that of which the card was composed. The financiers all jumped to their feet with exclamations of surprise and admiration, and gathered around the tray, whose dazzling contents lighted up the corner of the room where it had been placed as if the moon were shining there.

There were elegantly formed vases, adorned with artistic figures, embossed and incised, and glowing with delicate colors which shimmered in tiny waves with the slightest motion of the tray. Cups, pins, finger-rings, earrings, watch-chains, combs, studs, lockets, medals, tableware, models of coins—in brief almost every article in the fabrication of which precious metals have been employed was to be seen there in profusion, and all composed of the strange new metal which everybody on the spot declared was far more splendid than gold.

"Do you think it will answer?" asked Dr. Syx.

"We do," was the unanimous reply.

ALL then resumed their seats at the table, the tray with its magnificent array having been placed in the center of the board. This display had a remarkable influence. Confidence awoke in the breasts of the financiers. The dark clouds that had oppressed them rolled off, and the prospect grew decidedly brighter.

"What terms do you demand?" at length asked Mr. Boon, cheerfully rubbing his hands.

"I must have military protection for my mine and reducing works," replied Dr. Syx. "Then I shall ask the return of one per cent on the circulating medium, together with the privilege of disposing of a certain amount of the metal—to be limited by agreement—to the public for use in the arts. Of the proceeds of this sale I will pay ten per cent to the government in consideration of its protection."

"But," exclaimed President Boon, "that will make you the richest man who ever lived!"

"Undoubtedly," was the reply.

"Why," added Mr. Boon, opening his eyes wider as the facts continued to dawn upon him, "you will become the financial dictator of the whole earth!"

"Undoubtedly," again responded Dr. Syx unmoved. "That is what I purpose to become. My discovery entitles me to no less. But, remember, I place myself under government inspection and restriction. I should not be allowed to flood the market, even if I were disposed to do so. But my own interest would restrain me. It is to my advantage that artemisium, once adopted, shall remain stable in value."

A shadow of doubt suddenly crossed the president's face.

"Suppose your secret is discovered," he said. "Surely your mine will not remain the only one. If you, in so short a time, have been able to accumulate an immense quantity of the new metal, it must be extremely abundant. Others will discover it, and then where shall we be?"

While Mr. Boon uttered these words, those who were watching Dr. Syx (as the president was not) resembled persons whose startled eyes are fixed upon a wild beast preparing to spring. As Mr. Boon ceased speaking he turned toward the visitor, and instantly his lips fell apart and his face paled.

Dr. Syx had drawn himself up to his full stature, and his features were distorted with that peculiar mocking smile which had now returned with a concentrated expression of mingled self-confidence and disdain.

"Will you have relief or not?" he asked in a dry, hard voice. "What can you do? I alone possess the secret which can re-

store industry and commerce. If you reject my offer, do you think a second one will come?"

President Boon found voice to reply, stammeringly:

"I did not mean to suggest a rejection of the offer. I only wished to inquire if you thought it probable that there would be no repetition of what occurred after gold was found at the South Pole?"

"The earth may be full of my metal," returned Dr. Syx, almost fiercely, "but so long as I alone possess the knowledge how to extract it, is it of any more worth than common dirt? But come," he added after a pause, and softening his manner, "I have other schemes. Will you, as representatives of the leading nations, undertake the introduction of artemisium as a substitute for gold, or will you not?"

"Can we not have time for deliberation?" asked President Boon.

"Yes; one hour. Within that time I shall return to learn your decision," replied Dr. Syx, rising and preparing to depart. "I leave these things"—pointing to the tray—"in your keeping, and"—significantly—"I trust your decision will be a wise one."

His curious smile again curved his lips and shot the ends of his mustache upward, and the influence of that smile remained in the room when he had closed the door behind him. The financiers gazed at one another for several minutes in silence, then they turned toward the coruscating metal that filled the tray.

CHAPTER III

THE GRAND TETON MINE

AWAY on the western border of Wyoming, in the all but inaccessible heart of the Rocky Mountains, three mighty brothers, "the Big Tetons," look perpendicularly into the blue eye of Jenny's Lake, lying at the bottom of the profound depression among the mountains called Jackson's Hole. Bracing against one another for support, these remarkable peaks lift their granite spires nearly fourteen thousand feet into the blue dome that arches the crest of the continent. Their sides, and especially those of their chief, the Grand Teton, are streaked with glaciers, which shine like silver trappings when the morning sun comes up above the wilderness of mountains stretching away eastward from the hole.

When the first white men penetrated this wonderful region, and one of them bestowed his wife's name upon Jenny's Lake, they were intimidated by the Grand Teton. It made their flesh creep, accustomed though they were to rough scrambling among mountain gorges and on the brows of immense precipices, when they glanced up the face of the peak, where the cliffs fall, one below another, in a series of breathless descents, and imagined themselves clinging for dear life to those skyey battlements.

But when, in 1872, Messrs. Stevenson and Langford finally reached the top of the Grand Teton—the only successful members of a party of nine practised climbers who had started together from the bottom—they found there a little rectangular inclosure, made by piling up rocks, six or seven feet across and three feet in height, bearing evidences of great age, and indicating that the red Indians had, for some unknown purpose, resorted to the summit of this tremendous peak long before the white men invaded their mountains. Yet neither the Indians nor the whites ever really conquered the Teton, for above the highest point that they attained rises a granite buttress, whose smooth vertical sides seemed to them to defy everything but wings.

On a July morning, about a month after the visit of Dr. Max Syx to the assembled financiers in New York, a party of twenty horsemen, following a mountain trail, arrived on the eastern margin of Jackson's Hole, and pausing upon a commanding eminence, with exclamations of wonder, glanced across the great depression, where lay the shining coils of the Snake River, at the towering forms of the Tetons, whose ice-striped cliffs flashed lightnings in the sunshine. Curling above one of the wild gorges that cut the lower slopes of the Tetons was a thick black smoke, which, when lifted by a passing breeze, obscured the precipices half-way to the summit of the peak.

Had the Grand Teton become a volcano? Certainly no hunting or exploring party could make a smoke like that. But a word from the leader of the party of horsemen explained the mystery.

"There is my mill, and the mine is underneath it."

The speaker was Dr. Syx, and his companions were members of the financial congress. When he quitted their presence in New York, with the promise to return within an hour for their reply, he had no doubt in his own mind what that reply would be. He knew they would accept his proposition, and they did. No time was then lost in communicating with the various governments, and arrangements were quickly perfected whereby, in case the inspection of Dr. Syx's mine and its resources proved satisfactory, America and Europe should unite in adopting the new metal as the basis of their coinage. As soon as this stage in the negotiations was reached, it only remained to send a committee of financiers and metallurgists, in company with Dr. Syx, to the Rocky Mountains.

"An inspection of the records at Washington," Dr. Syx continued, addressing the horsemen, "will show that I have filed a claim covering ten acres of ground around the mouth of my mine. This was done as soon as I had discovered the metal. The filing of the claim and the subsequent proceedings which perfected my ownership attracted no attention, because everybody was thinking of the South Pole and its gold-fields."

THE party gathered closer around Dr. Syx and listened to his words with silent attention, while their horses rubbed noses and jingled their gold-mounted trappings.

"As soon as I had legally protected myself," he continued, "I employed a force of men, transported my machinery and material across the mountains, erected my furnaces, and opened the mine. I was safe from intrusion, and even from idle curiosity, for the reason I have just mentioned. In fact, so exclusive was the attraction of the new gold-fields that I had difficulty in obtaining workmen, and finally I sent to Africa and engaged negroes, whom I placed in charge of trustworthy foremen."

"And with their aid you have mined enough metal to supply the mints of the world?" asked President Boon.

"Exactly so," was the reply. "But I no longer employ the large force which I needed at first.

"I shall show you to-day," said Dr. Syx, with his curious smile, "twenty-five thousand tons of refined artemisium, stacked in rock-cut vaults under the Grand Teton."

"And you have dared to collect such inconceivable wealth in one place?"

"You forget that it is not wealth until the people have learned to value it, and the governments have put their stamp upon it."

The party did not wait for further explanations. They were eager to see the wonderful mine and the store of treasure. Spurs were applied, and they galloped down the steep trail, forded the Snake River, and, skirting the shore of Jenny's Lake, soon found themselves gazing up the headlong slopes and dizzy parapets of the Grand Teton. Dr. Syx led them by a steep ascent to the mouth of the canyon, above one of whose walls stood his mill, and where the "champ, champ" of a powerful engine saluted their ears.

CHAPTER IV

THE WEALTH OF THE WORLD

AN ELECTRIC light shot its penetrating rays into a gallery cut through virgin rock and running straight toward the heart of the Teton. The center of the gallery was occupied by a nar-row railway, on which a few flat cars, propelled by electric power, passed to and fro. Black-skinned and silent workmen rode on the cars, both when they came laden wth broken masses of rock from the farther end of the tunnel and when they returned empty.

Suddenly, to an eye situated a little way within the gallery, appeared at the entrance the dark face of Dr. Syx, wearing its most discomposing smile, and a moment later the broader countenance of President Boon loomed in the electric glare beside the doctor's black framework of eyebrows and mustache. Behind them were grouped the other visiting financiers.

"This tunnel," said Dr. Syx, "leads to the mine head, where the ore-bearing rock is blasted."

As he spoke a hollow roar issued from the depths of the mountain, followed in a short time by a gust of foul air.

"You probably will not care to go in there," said the doctor, "and, in fact, it is very uncomfortable. But we shall follow the next car-load to the smelter, and you can witness the reduction of the ore."

Accordingly, when another car came rumbling out of the tunnel with its load of cracked rock, they all accompanied it into an adjoining apartment, where it was cast into a metallic shute, through which, they were informed, it reached the furnace.

"While it is melting," explained Dr. Syx, "certain elements, the nature of which I must beg to keep secret, are mixed with the ore, causing chemical action which results in the extraction of the metal. Now let me show you pure artemisium issuing from the furnace."

He led the visitors through two apartments into a third, one side of which was walled by the front of a furnace. From this projected two or three small spouts, and iridescent streams of molten metal fell from the spouts into earthen receptacles, from which the blazing liquid was led, like flowing iron, into a system of molds, where it was allowed to cool and harden.

The financiers looked on wonderingly and their astonishment grew when they were conducted into the rock-cut storerooms beneath, where they saw metallic ingots glowing like gigantic opals in the light which Dr. Syx turned on. They were piled in rows along the walls as high as a man could reach. A very brief inspection sufficed to convince the visitors that Dr. Syx was able to perform all that he promised. Although they had not penetrated the secret of his process of reducing the ore, yet they had seen the metal flowing from the furnace, and the piles of ingots proved conclusively that he had uttered no vain boast when he said he could give the world a new coinage.

But President Boon, being himself a metallurgist, desired to inspect the mysterious ore a little more closely. Possibly he was thinking that if another mine was destined to be discovered he might as well be the discoverer as anybody. Dr. Syx attempted no concealment, but his smile became more than usually scornful as he stopped a laden car and invited the visitors to help themselves.

"I think," he said, "that I have struck the only lode of this ore in the Teton, or possibly in this part of the world, but I don't know for certain. There may be plenty of it only waiting to be found. That, however, doesn't trouble me. The great point is that nobody except myself knows how to extract the metal."

Mr. Boon closely examined the chunk of rock which he had taken from the car. Then he pulled a lens from his pocket, with a deprecatory glance at Dr. Syx.

"Oh, that's all right," said the latter, with a laugh, the first that these gentlemen had ever heard from his lips, and it almost made them shudder; "put it to every test, examine it with the microscope, with fire, with electricity, with the spectroscope—in every way you can think of! I assure you it is worth your while!"

Again Dr. Syx uttered his freezing laugh, passing into the familiar smile, which had now become an undisguised mock.

"Upon my word," said Mr. Boon, taking his eye from the lens, "I see no sign of any metal here!"

"Look at the green specks!" cried the doctor, snatching the specimen from the president's hand. "That's it! That's artemisium! But it's of no use unless you can get it out and purify it, which is my secret!"

For the third time Dr. Syx laughed, and his merriment affected the visitors so disagreeably that they showed impatience to be gone. Immediately he changed his manner.

"Come into my office," he said, with a return to the graciousness which had characterized him ever since the party started from New York.

WHEN they were all seated, and the doctor had handed round a box of cigars, he resumed the conversation in his most amiable manner.

"You see, gentlemen," he said, turning a piece of ore in his fingers, "artemisium is like aluminum. It can only be obtained in the metallic form by a special process. While these greenish particles, which you may perhaps mistake for chrysolite or some similar unisilicate, really contain the precious metal, they are not entirely composed of it. The process by which I separate out the metallic element while the ore is passing through the furnace is, in truth, quite simple, and its very simplicity guards my secret. Make your minds easy as to over-production. A man is as likely to jump over the moon as to find me out.

"But," he continued, again changing his manner, "we have had business enough for one day; now for a little recreation."

While speaking, the doctor pressed a button on his desk, and the room, which was illuminated by electric lamps—for there were no windows in the building—became dark, except part of one wall, where a broad area of light appeared.

Dr. Syx's voice had become very soothing when next he spoke:

"I am fond of amusing myself with a

peculiar form of motion picture projector, which I invented some years ago, and which I have never exhibited except for the entertainment of my friends.

He had hardly ceased speaking when the illuminated space seemed to melt away, leaving a great opening through which the spectators looked as if into another world on the opposite side of the wall. For a minute or two they could not clearly discern what was presented; then, gradually, the flitting scenes and figures became more distinct until the lifelikeness of the spectacle absorbed their whole attention.

Before them passed, in panoramic review, a sunny land, filled with brilliant-hued vegetation, and dotted with villages and cities which were bright with light-colored buildings. People appeared moving through the scenes, as in a movie show, but with infinitely more semblance of reality. In fact, the pictures, blending one into another, seemed to be life itself. Yet it was not an earth-like scene. The colors of the passing landscape were such as no man in the room had ever beheld; and the people, tall, round-limbed, with florid complexion, golden hair, and brilliant eyes and lips, were indescribably beautiful and graceful in all their movements.

FROM the land the view passed out to sea, and bright blue waves, edged with creaming foam, ran swiftly under the spectator's eyes, and occasionally, driven before light winds, appeared fleets of daintily shaped vessels, which reminded the beholder, by their flashing wings, of the feigned "ship of pearl."

After the fairy ships and breezy sea views came a long, curving line of coast, brilliant with coral sands, and indented by frequent bays, along whose enchanting shore. lay pleasant towns, the landscapes behind them splendid with groves, meadows, and streams.

Presently the shifting photographic film, or whatever the mechanism may have been, appeared to have settled upon a chosen scene, and there it rested. A broad

champaign reached away to distant sapphire mountains, while the foreground was occupied by a magnificent house, resembling a large country villa, fronted with a garden, shaded by bowers and festoons of huge, brilliant flowers. Birds of radiant plumage flitted among the trees and blossoms, and then appeared a company of gayly attired people, including many young girls, who joined hands and danced in a ring, apparently with shouts of laughter, while a group of musicians standing near thrummed and blew upon curiously shaped instruments.

Suddenly the shadow of a dense cloud flitted across the scene; whereupon the brilliant birds flew away with screams of terror. An expression of horror came over the faces of the people. The children broke from their merry circle and ran for protection to their elders. The utmost confusing and whelming terror were evinced for a moment—then the ground split asunder, and the house and the garden, with all their living occupants, were swallowed by an awful chasm which opened just where they had stood. The great rent ran in a widening line across the sunlit landscape until it reached the horizon, when the distant mountains crumbled, clouds poured in from all sides at once, and billows of flame burst through them as they veiled the scene.

But in another instant the commotion was over, and the world whose curious spectacles had been enacted as if on the other side of a window, seemed to retreat swiftly into space, until at last, emerging from a fleecy cloud, it reappeared in the form of the full moon hanging in the sky, but larger than is its wont, with its dry ocean-beds, its keen-spired peaks, its ragged mountain ranges, its gaping chasms, its immense crater rings, and Tycho, the chief of them all, shooting ray-like streaks across the scarred face of the abandoned lunar globe.

The show was ended, and Dr. Syx, turning on only a partial illumination in the room, rose slowly to his feet, his tall form appearing strangely magnified in the gloom, and invited his bewildered guests to accompany him to his house, outside the mill, where he said dinner awaited them. As they emerged into daylight they acted like persons just aroused from an opiate dream.

CHAPTER V

WONDERS OF THE NEW METAL

WITHIN a twelvemonth after the visit of President Boon and his fellow-financiers to the mine in the Grand Teton, a railway had been constructed from Jackson's Hole, connecting with one of the Pacific lines, and the distribution of the new metal was begun. All of Dr. Syx's terms had been accepted. United States troops occupied a permanent encampment on the upper waters of the Snake River, to afford protection, and as the consignments of precious ingots were hurried east and west on guarded trains, the mints all over the world resumed their activity. Once more a common monetary standard prevailed, and commerce revived as if touched by a magic wand.

Artemisium quickly won its way in popular favor. Its matchless beauty alone was enough. Not only was it gladly accepted in the form of money, but its success was instantaneous in the arts. Dr. Syx and the inspectors representing the various nations found it difficult to limit the output to the agreed-upon amount. The demand was incessant.

Goldsmiths and jewelers continually discovered new excellences in the wonderful metal. Its properties of translucence and refraction enabled skilful artists to perform marvels. By suitable management a chain of artemisium could be made to resemble a string of vari-colored gems, each separate link having a tint of its own, while, as the wearer moved, delicate complementary colors chased one another in rapid undulation from end to end.

A fresh charm was added by the new metal to the personal adornment of women, and an enhanced splendor to the pageants of society. Gold in its palmiest days had never enjoyed such a vogue. A crowded reception-room or a dinner-party where artemisium abounded possessed an indescribable atmosphere of luxury and richness, refined in quality, yet captivating to every sense. Imaginative persons went so far as to aver that the sight and presence of the metal exercised a strangely soothing and dreamy power over the mind, like the influence of moonlight streaming through the tree-tops on a still, balmy night.

The public curiosity in regard to the origin of artemisium was boundless. The various nations published official bulletins in which the general facts omitting, of course, such incidents as the singular exhibition seen by the visiting financiers on the wall of Dr. Syx's office—were detailed to gratify the universal desire for information.

President Boon not only submitted the specimens of ore-bearing rock which he had brought from the mine to careful analysis, but also appealed to several of the greatest living chemists and mineralogists to aid him; but they were all equally mystified. The green substance contained in the ore, although differing slightly from ordinary chrysolite, answered all the known tests of that mineral. It was remembered, however, that Dr. Syx had said that they would be likely to mistake the substance for chrysolite, and the result of their experiments justified his prediction. Evidently the doctor had gone a stone's-cast beyond the chemistry of the day, and, just as evidently, he did not mean to reveal his discovery for the benefit of science, nor for the benefit of any pockets except his own.

Notwithstanding the failure of the chemists to extract anything from Dr. Syx's ore, the public at large never doubted that the secret would be discovered in good time, and thousands of prospectors flocked to the Teton Mountains in search of the ore. And without much difficulty they found it. Evidently the doctor had been mistaken in thinking that his mine might be the only one. The new miners hurried specimens of the green-speckled rock to the chemical laboratories for experimentation, and meanwhile began to lay up stores of the ore in anticipation of the time when the proper way to extract the metal should be discovered.

But, alas! that time did not come. The fresh ore proved to be as refractory as that which had been obtained from Dr. Syx. But in the midst of the universal disappointment there came a new sensation.

ONE morning the newspapers glared with a despatch from Grand Teton station announcing that the metal itself had been discovered by prospectors on the eastern slope of the main peak.

"It outcrops in many places," ran the despatch, "and many small nuggets have been picked out of crevices in the rocks."

The excitement produced by this news was even greater than when gold was discovered at the South Pole. Again a mad rush was made for the Tetons. The heights around Jackson's Hole and the shores of Jackson's and Jenny's lakes were quickly dotted with camps, and the military force had to be doubled to keep off the curious, and occasionally menacing, crowds which gathered in the vicinity and seemed bent on unearthing the great secret locked behind the windowless walls of the mill. There, the column of black smoke and the roar of the engine served as reminders of the incredible wealth which the sole possessor of that secret was rolling up.

This time no mistake had been made. It was a fact that the metal, in virgin purity, had been discovered scattered in various places on the ledges of the Grand Teton. In a little while thousands had obtained specimens with their own hands. The quantity was distressingly small, considering the number and the eagerness of the seekers, but that it was genuine artemisium not even Dr. Syx could have denied. He, however, made no attempt to deny it.

"Yes," he said when questioned, "I find that I have been deceived. At first I

thought the metal existed only in the form of the green ore, but of late I have come upon veins of pure artemisium in my mine. I am glad for your sakes, but sorry for my own. Still, it may turn out that there is no great amount of free artemisium, after all."

While the doctor talked in this manner, close observers detected a lurking sneer which his acquaintances had not noticed since artemisium was first adopted as the money basis of the world.

The crowd that swarmed upon the mountain quickly exhausted all of the visible supply of the metal. Sometimes they found it in a thin stratum at the bottom of crevices, where it could be detached in opalescent plates and leaves of the thickness of paper. These superficial deposits evidently might have been formed from water holding the metal in solution. Occasionally, deep cracks contained nuggets and wiry masses which looked as if they had run together when they were molten.

The most promising spots were soon staked out in miners' claims, machinery was procured, stock companies were formed, and borings were begun. The enthusiasm arising from the earlier finds and the flattering surface indications caused everybody to work with feverish haste and energy, and within two months one hundred tunnels were piercing the mountain.

For a long time nobody was willing to admit the truth which gradually forced itself upon the attention of the miners. The deeper they went the scarcer became the indications of artemisium! In fact, such deposits as were found were confined to fissures near the surface. But Dr. Syx continued to report a surprising increase in the amount of free metal in his mine, and this encouraged all who had not exhausted their capital to push on their tunnels in the hope of finally striking a vein. At length, however, the smaller operators gave up in despair, until only one heavily capitalized company still remained working.

CHAPTER VI

A STRANGE DISCOVERY

"IT IS my belief that Dr. Max Syx is a deceiver."

The person who uttered this opinion was a young engineer, Andrew Hall, who had charge of the operations of one of the mining companies which were driving tunnels into the Grand Teton.

"What do you mean by that?" asked President Boon, who was the principal backer of the enterprise.

"I mean," replied Hall, "that there is no free metal in this mountain, and Dr. Syx knows there is none."

"But he is getting it himself from his mine," retorted President Boon.

"So he says, but who has seen it? No one is admitted into the Syx mine, his foremen are forbidden to talk, and his workmen are specially imported negroes who do not understand English."

"But," persisted Mr. Boon, "how, then, do you account for the nuggets scattered over the mountain? And, besides, what object could Dr. Syx have in pretending that there is free metal to be had for the digging?"

"He may have salted the mountain, for all I know," said Hall. "As for his object, I confess I am entirely in the dark; but, for all that, I am convinced that we shall find no more metal if we dig ten miles for it."

"Nonsense," said the president; "if we keep on we shall strike. Did not Dr. Syx himself admit that he found no free artemisium until his tunnel had reached the core of the peak? We must go as deep as he has gone before we give up."

"I fear the depths he attains are beyond most people's reach," was Hall's answer, while a thoughtful look crossed his clear-cut brow, "but since you desire it, of course the work shall go on. I shall like, however, to change the direction of the tunnel."

"Certainly," replied Mr. Boon; "bore in whatever direction you think proper, only don't despair."

ABOUT a month after this conversation, Andrew Hall, with whom a community of tastes in many things had made me intimately acquainted, asked me one morning to accompany him into his tunnel.

"I want to have a trusty friend at my elbow," he said, "for, unless I am a dreamer, something remarkable will happen within the next hour, and two witnesses are better than one."

When we arrived at the head of the tunnel I was surprised at finding no workmen there.

"I stopped blasting some time ago,' said Hall in explanation, "for a reason which, I hope, will become evident to you very slowly, and yesterday I paid off the men and dismissed them with the announcement, which, I am confident, President Boon will sanction after he hears my report of this morning's work, that the tunnel is abandoned. You see, I am now using a drill which I can manage without assistance. I believe the work is almost completed, and I want you to witness the end of it."

He then carefully applied the drill, which noiselessly screwed its nose into the rock. When it had sunk to a depth of a few inches he withdrew it, and, taking a hand-drill capable of making a hole not more than an eighth of an inch in diameter, cautiously began boring in the center of the larger cavity. He had made hardly a hundred turns of the handle when the drill shot through the rock! A gratified smile illuminated his features, and he said in a suppressed voice:

"Don't be alarmed; I'm going to put out the light."

Instantly we were in complete darkness, but being close at Hall's side I could detect his movements. He pulled out the drill, and for half a minute remained motionless as if listening. There was no sound.

"I must enlarge the opening," he whispered, and immediately the faint grating of a sharp tool cutting through the rock informed me of his progress.

"There," at last he said. "I think that will do; now for a look."

I could tell that he had placed his eye at the hole and was gazing with breathless attention. Presently he pulled my sleeve.

"Put your eye here," he whispered, pushing me into the proper position for looking through the hole.

At first I could discern nothing except a smoky blue glow. But soon my vision cleared a little, and then I perceived that I was gazing into a narrow tunnel which met ours directly end to end. Glancing along the axis of this gallery, I saw, some two hundred yards away, a faint light which evidently indicated the mouth of the tunnel.

At the end where we had met it the mysterious tunnel was considerably widened at one side, as if the excavators had started to change direction and then abandoned the work, and in this elbow I could just see the outlines of two or three flat cars loaded with broken stone, while a heap of the same material lay near them. Through the center of the tunnel ran a railway track.

"DO YOU know what you are looking at?" asked Hall in my ear.

"I begin to suspect," I replied, "that you have accidentally run into Dr. Syx's mine."

"If Dr. Syx had been on his guard this accident wouldn't have happened," replied Hall, with a low chuckle.

"I heard you remark a month ago," I said, "that you were changing the direction of your tunnel. Has this been the aim of your labors ever since?"

"You have hit it," he replied. "Long ago I became convinced that my company was throwing away its money in a vain attempt to strike a lode of pure artemisium. But President Boon has great faith in Dr. Syx, and would not give up the work. So I adopted what I regarded as the only practicable method of proving the truth of my opinion and saving the company's funds.

"An electric indicator, of my invention, enabled me to locate the Syx tunnel when I got near it, and I have met it end on, and opened this peephole in order to observe the doctor's operations. I feel that such spying is entirely justified in the circumstances. Although I cannot yet explain just how or why, I feel sure that Dr. Syx was the cause of the sudden discovery of the surface nuggets, and that he has encouraged the miners for his own ends, until he has brought ruin to thousands who have spent their last cent in driving useless tunnels into this mountain. It is a righteous thing to expose him."

"But," I interposed, "I do not see that you have exposed anything yet except the interior of a tunnel."

"You will see more clearly after a while," was the reply.

Hall now placed his eye again at the aperture, and was unable entirely to repress the exclamation that rose to his lips. He remained staring through the hole for several minutes without uttering a word. Presently I noticed that the lenses of his eye were illuminated by a ray of light coming through the hole, but he did not stir.

After a long inspection he suddenly applied his ear to the hole and listened intently for at least five minutes. Not a sound was audible to me, but, by an occasional pressure of the hand, Hall signified that some important disclosure was reaching his sense of hearing. At length he removed his ear.

"Pardon me," he whispered, "for keeping you so long in waiting, but what I have just seen and overheard was of a nature to admit of no interruption. He is still talking, and by pressing your ear against the hole you may be able to catch what he says."

"Who is 'he'?"

"Look for yourself."

I placed my eye at the aperture, and almost recoiled with the violence of my surprise. The tunnel before me was brilliantly illuminated, and within three feet of the wall of rock behind which we crouched stood Dr. Syx, his dark profile looking almost satanic in the sharp contrast of light and shadow. He was talking to one of his foremen, and the two were the only visible occupants of the tunnel. Putting my ear to the little opening, I heard his words distinctly:

"——end of their rope. Well, they've spent a pretty lot of money for their experience, and I rather think we shall not be troubled again by artemisium-seekers for some time to come."

The doctor's voice ceased, and instantly I clapped my eye to the hole. He had changed his position so that his black eyes now looked straight at the aperture. My heart was in my mouth, for at first I believed from his expression that he had detected the gleam of my eyeball. But if so, he probably mistook it for a bit of mica in the rock, and paid no further attention. Then his lips moved, and I put my ear again to the hole. He seemed to be replying to a question the foreman had asked.

"If they do," he said, "they will never guess the real secret."

Thereupon he turned on his heel, kicked a bit of rock off the track, and strode away toward the entrance. The foreman paused long enough to turn out the electric lamp, and then followed the doctor.

"Well," asked Hall, "what have you heard?"

I told him everything.

"It fully corroborates the evidence of my own eyes and ears," he remarked, "and we may count ourselves extremely lucky. It is not likely that Dr. Syx will be heard a second time proclaiming his deception with his own lips. It is plain that he was led to talk as he did to the foreman on account of the latter's having informed him of the sudden discharge of my men this morning. Their presence within earshot of our hiding-place during their conversation was, of course, pure accident, and so you can see how kind fortune has been to us. I expected to have to watch and listen and form deductions for a week, at least, before getting the information which five lucky minutes have given us."

While he was speaking my companion busied himself in carefully plugging up the hole in the rock. When it was closed to his satisfaction he turned on the light in our tunnel.

"Did you observe," he asked, "that there was a second tunnel?"

"What do you say?"

"When the light was on in there I saw the mouth of a smaller tunnel entering the main one behind the cars on the right. Did you notice it?"

"Oh, yes," I replied. "I did observe some kind of a dark hole there, but I paid no attention to it because I was so absorbed in the doctor."

"Well," rejoined Hall, smiling, "it was worth considerably more than a glance. As a matter of thought I find it even more absorbing than Dr. Syx. Did you see the track in it?"

"No," I had to acknowledge, "I did not notice that. But," I continued, a little piqued by his manner, "being a branch of the main tunnel, I don't see anything remarkable in its having a track also."

"It was rather dim in that hole," said Hall, still smiling in a somewhat provoking way, "but the railroad track was there plain enough. And, whether you think it remarkable or not, I should like to lay you a wager that that track leads to a secret worth a dozen of the one we have just overheard."

CHAPTER VII

A MYSTERY INDEED!

WHEN President Boon had heard our story he promptly approved Hall's dismissal of the men. He expressed great surprise that Dr. Syx should have resorted to a deception which had been so disastrous to innocent people, and at first he talked of legal proceedings. But after thinking the matter over he concluded that Syx was too powerful to be attacked with success. Especially when the only evidence against him was that he had claimed to find artemisium in his mine at a time when, as everybody knew, artemisium actually was found outside the mine. There was no apparent motive for the deception, and no proof of malicious intent. In short, Mr. Boon decided that the best thing for him and his stockholders to do was to keep silent about their losses and await events. And, at Hall's suggestion, he also determined to say nothing to anybody about the discovery we had made.

"It could do no good," said Hall, in making the suggestion, "and it might spoil a plan I have in mind."

"What plan?" asked the president.

"I prefer not to tell just yet," was the reply.

A few days afterward I received an invitation from Hall to accompany him once more into the abandoned tunnel.

"I have found out what that side-track means," he said, "and it has plunged me into another mystery so dark and profound that I cannot see my way through it. I must beg you to say no word to any one concerning what I show you."

I gave the required promise, and we entered the tunnel, which nobody had visited since our former adventure. Having extinguished our lamp, my companion opened the peep-hole, and a thin ray of light streamed through from the tunnel on the opposite side of the wall. He applied his eye to the hole.

"Yes," he said, quickly stepping back and pushing me into his place, "they are still at it. Look and tell me what you see."

"I see," I replied, after placing my eye at the aperture, "a gang of men unloading a car which has just come out of the side tunnel, and putting its contents upon another car standing on the track of the main tunnel."

"Yes, and what are they handling?"

"Why, ore, of course."

"And do you see nothing significant in that?"

"To be sure!" I exclaimed. "The ore may have come back from the furnace-room, because the side tunnel turns off so as to run parallel with the other."

"It not only may have come back, it actually has come back," said Hall.

"How can you be sure?"

"Because I have been over the track, and know that it leads to a secret apartment directly under the furnace in which Dr. Syx pretends to melt the ore!"

FOR a minute after hearing this avowal I was speechless.

"Are you serious?" I asked at length.

"Perfectly serious. Run your finger along the rock here. Do you perceive a seam? Two days ago, after seeing what you have just witnessed in the Syx tunnel, I carefully cut out a section of the wall, making an aperture large enough to crawl through, and, when I knew the workmen were asleep, I crept in there and examined both tunnels from end to end. But in solving one mystery I have run myself into another infinitely more perplexing."

"How is that?"

"Why does Dr. Syx take such elaborate pains to deceive his visitors, and also the government officers? It is now plain that he conducts no mining operations whatever. This mine of his is a gigantic blind. Whenever inspectors or scientific curiosity seekers visit his mill his mute workmen assume the air of being very busy. The cars laden with his so-called 'ore' rumble out of the tunnel and their contents are ostentatiously poured into the furnace, or appear to be poured into it, really dropping into a receptacle beneath, to be carried back into the mine again. And then the doctor leads his gulled visitors around to the other side of the furnace and shows them the molten metal coming out in streams.

"Now, what does it all mean? That's what I'd like to find out. What's his game? For, mark you, if he doesn't get artemisium from this pretended ore, he gets it from some other source, and right on this spot, too. There is no doubt about that. The whole world is supplied by Syx's furnace with something that comes from his ten acres of Grand Teton rock. What is that something? How does he get it, and where does he hide it? These are the things I should like to find out."

"What will you do?" I asked.

"I don't know exactly what. But I've got a dim idea which may take shape after a while."

Hall was silent for some time; then he suddenly asked:

"Did you ever hear of that queer show with which Dr. Syx entertained the members of the financial commission?"

"Yes, I've heard the story, but I don't think it was ever made public."

"No, I believe not. Odd thing, wasn't it, making a feature of the moon?"

"Why, yes, very odd, but just like the doctor's eccentric ways, though. He's always doing something to astonish somebody, without any apparent earthly reason. But what put you in mind of that?"

"Free artemisium put me in mind of it," replied Hall quizzically.

"I don't see the connection."

"I'm not sure that I do either, but when dealing with Dr. Syx nothing is too improbable to be thought of."

CHAPTER VIII

MORE OF DR. SYX'S MAGIC

IMPORTANT business called me East soon after the meeting with Hall described in the foregoing chapter, and before I again saw the Grand Teton very stirring events had taken place.

After the failure of the mining operations there was a moderate revival of the efforts to reduce the Teton ore, but no success cheered the experimenters. Prospectors also wandered all over the earth looking for pure artemisium, but in vain. The general public, knowing nothing of what Hall had discovered, and still believing Syx's story that he also had found pure artemisium in his mine, accounted for the failure of the tunneling operations on the supposition that the metal, in a free state, was excessively rare, and that Dr. Syx had had the luck to strike the only vein of it that the Grand Teton contained. As if to give countenance to this opinion, Dr. Syx now announced, in the most public manner, that he had been deceived again, and that

the vein of free metal he had struck being exhausted, no other had appeared. Accordingly, he said, he must henceforth rely exclusively, as in the beginning, upon reduction of the ore.

Artemisium had proved itself an immense boon to mankind, and the new era of commercial prosperity which it had ushered in already exceeded everything that the world had known in the past. School-children learned that human civilization had taken five great strides, known respectively, beginning at the bottom, as the "age of stone," the "age of bronze," the "age of iron," the "age of gold," and the "age of artemisium."

Nevertheless, sources of dissatisfaction finally began to appear, and, after the nature of such things, they developed with marvelous rapidity. People began to grumble about "contraction of the currency." In every country there arose a party which demanded "free money." Demagogues pointed to the brief reign of paper money after the demonetization of gold as a happy period, when the people had enjoyed their rights, and the "money barons" were kept at bay.

Then came denunciations of the international commission for restricting the coinage. Dr. Syx was described as "a devil-fish sucking the veins of the planet and holding it helpless in the grasp of his tentacular billions." In the United States, meetings of agitators passed furious resolutions, denouncing the government, assailing the rich, cursing Dr. Syx, and calling upon "the oppressed" to rise and "take their own." The final outcome was, of course, violence. Mobs had to be suppressed by military force. But the most dramatic scene in the tragedy occurred at the Grand Teton. Excited by inflammatory speeches and printed documents, several thousand armed men assembled in the neighborhood of Jenny's Lake and prepared to attack the Syx mine. For some reason the military guard had been depleted, and the mob, under the leadership of a man named Bings, who showed no little talent as a commander and strategist, surprised the small force of soldiers and locked them up in their own guard-house.

Telegraphic communication having been cut off by Bings, a fierce attack was made on the mine. The assailants swarmed up the sides of the canyon, and attempted to break in through the foundation of the buildings. But the masonry was stronger than they had anticipated, and the attack failed. Sharp-shooters then climbed the neighboring heights, and kept up an incessant peppering of the walls.

No reply came from the gloomy structure. The huge column of black smoke rose uninterruptedly into the sky, and the noise of the great engine never ceased for an instant. The mob gathered closer on all sides and redoubled the fire of the rifles, to which was now added the belching of several machine-guns. Ragged holes began to appear in the walls, and at the sight of these the assailants yelled with delight. It was evident that the mill could not long withstand so destructive a bombardment.

SUDDENLY it became evident that the besieged were about to take a hand in the fight. Thus far they had not shown themselves or fired a shot, but now a movement was perceived on the roof, and the projecting arms of some kind of machinery became visible. Many marksmen concentrated their fire upon the mysterious objects, but apparently with little effect. Bings, mounted on a rock, so as to command a clear view of the field, was on the point of ordering a party to rush forward with axes and beat down the formidable doors, when there came a blinding flash from the roof, something swished through the air, and a gust of heat met the assailants in the face. Bings dropped dead from his perch, and then, as if the scythe of the Destroyer had swung downward, and to the right and left in quick succession, the close-packed mob was leveled, rank after rank, until the few survivors crept behind rocks for refuge.

Instantly the atmospheric broom swept up and down the canyon and across the mountain's flanks, and the marksmen fell in bunches like shaken grapes. Nine-tenths of the besiegers were destroyed within ten minutes after the first movement had been noticed on the roof. Those who survived owed their escape to the rocks which concealed them, and they lost no time in crawling off into neighboring chasms, and. as soon as they were beyond eye-shot from the mill, they fled with panic speed.

THEN the towering form of Dr. Syx appeared at the door. Emerging without sign of fear or excitement, he picked his way among his fallen enemies, and, approaching the military guard-house, undid the fastening and set the imprisoned soldiers free.

"I think I am paying rather dear for my whistle," he said, with a characteristic sneer, to Captain Carter, the commander of the troop. "It seems that I must not only defend my own people and property when attacked by mob force, but must also come to the rescue of the soldiers whose pay-rolls are met from my pocket."

The captain made no reply, and Dr. Syx strode back to the works. When the released soldiers saw what had occurred their amazement had no bounds. It was necessary at once to dispose of the dead, and this was no easy undertaking for their small force. However, they accomplished it, and at the beginning of their work made a most surprising discovery.

"How's this, Jim?" said one of the men to his comrade, as they stooped to lift the nearest victim of Dr. Syx's withering fire. "What's this fellow got all over him?"

"Artemisium, 'pon my soul!" responded "Jim," staring at the body. "He's all coated over with it."

Immediately from all sides came similar exclamations. Every man who had fallen was covered with a film of the precious metal, as if he had been dipped into an electrolytic bath. Clothing seemed to have been charred, and the metallic atoms had penetrated the flesh of the victims. The rocks all around the battle-field were similarly veneered.

"It looks to me," said Captain Carter, "as if old Syx had turned one of his spouts of artemisium into a hose-pipe and soaked 'em with it."

"That's it," chimed in a lieutenant; "that's exactly what he's done."

"Well," returned the captain, "if he can do that, I don't see what use he's got for us here."

"Probably he don't want to waste the stuff," said the lieutenant. "It must have cost him plenty to plate this crowd!"

The story of the marvelous way in which Dr. Syx defended his mill became the sensation of the world for many days. The hose-pipe theory, struck off on the spot by Captain Carter, seized the popular fancy, and was generally accepted without further question. Moreover, no one could deny that Dr. Syx was well within his rights in defending himself by any means when so savagely attacked, and his triumphant success, no less than the ingenuity which was supposed to underlie it, placed him in an heroic light which he had not hitherto enjoyed.

As to the demagogues who were responsible for the outbreak and its terrible consequences, they slunk out of the public eye, and the result of the battle at the mine seemed to have been a clearing up of the atmosphere, such as a thunderstorm effects at the close of a season of foul weather.

But now, little as men guessed it, the beginning of the end was close at hand.

CHAPTER IX

THE DETECTIVE OF SCIENCE

THE morning of my arrival at Grand Teton station, on my return from the East, Andrew Hall met me with a warm greeting.

"I have been anxiously expecting you," he said, "for I have made some progress toward solving the great mystery. I have not yet reached a conclusion, but I hope soon to let you into the entire secret. In the meantime you can aid me with your companionship, if in no other way, for,

since the defeat of the mob, this place has been mighty lonesome. I am on speaking terms with Dr. Syx, and occasionally, when there is a party to be shown around, I visit his works, and make the best possible use of my eyes. Captain Carter of the military is a capital fellow, but I want somebody to whom I can occasionally confide things, and so you are as welcome as moonlight in harvest-time."

"Tell me something about that wonderful fight with the mob. Did you see it?"

"I did. I had got wind of what Bings intended to do while I was down at Pocotello, and I hurried up here to warn the soldiers, but unfortunately I came too late. Finding the military cooped up in the guard-house and the mob masters of the situation, I kept out of sight on the side of the Teton, and watched the siege with my binocular."

"What of the mysterious force that the doctor employed to sweep off the assailants?"

"Of course Captain Carter's suggestion that Syx turned molten artemisium from his furnace into a hose-pipe and sprayed the enemy with it is ridiculous. But it is much easier to dismiss Carter's theory than to substitute a better one. I saw the doctor on the roof with a gang of black workmen, and I noticed the flash of polished metal turned rapidly this way and that, but there was some intervening obstacle which prevented me from getting a good view of the mechanism employed. It certainly bore no resemblance to a hose-pipe, or anything of that kind. No emanation was visible from the machine, but it was stupefying to see the mob melt down."

"How about the coating of the bodies with artemisium?"

"There you are back on the hose-pipe again," laughed Hall. "But, to tell you the truth, I'd rather be excused from expressing an opinion on that operation in wholesale electro-plating just at present. I've the ghost of an idea what it means, but let me test my theory a little before I formulate it. In the meanwhile, won't you take a stroll with me?"

"Certainly; nothing could please me better," I replied. "Which way shall we go?"

"To the top of the Grand Teton."

"What, are you seized with the mountain-climbing fever?"

"Not exactly, but I have a particular reason for wishing to take a look from that pinnacle."

"I suppose you know the real apex of the peak has never been trodden by man?"

"I do know it, but it is just that apex that I am determined to have under my feet for ten minutes. The failure of others is no argument for us."

"Just as you say," I rejoined. "But I suppose there is no indiscretion in asking whether this little climb has any relation to the mystery?"

"If it didn't have an important relation to the clearing up of that dark thing I wouldn't risk my neck in such an undertaking," was the reply.

ACCORDINGLY, the next morning we set out for the peak. All previous climbers, as we were aware, had attacked it from the west. That seemed the obvious thing to do, because the westward slopes of the mountain, while very steep, are less abrupt than those which face the rising sun. In fact, the eastern side of the Grand Teton appears to be absolutely unclimbable. But both Hall and I had had experience with rock-climbing in the Alps and the Dolomites, and we knew that what look like the hardest places sometimes turn out to be next to the easiest. Accordingly we decided—the more particularly because it would save time, but also because we yielded to the common desire to outdo our predecessors—to try to scale the giant right up his face.

We carried a very light but exceedingly strong rope about five hundred feet long, wore nail-shod shoes and had each a metal-pointed staff and a small hatchet in lieu of the regular mountaineer's ax. Advancing at first along the broken ridge between two gorges, we gradually approached the steeper part of the Teton where the cliffs looked so sheer and smooth that it seemed no wonder that nobody had ever tried to scale them. The air was deliciously clear and the sky wonderfully blue above the mountains, and the moon, a few days past its last quarter, was visible in the southwest, its pale crescent face slightly blued by the atmosphere, as it always appears when seen in daylight.

Slow westering, a phantom sail—
The lonely soul of yesterday.

BEHIND us, somewhat north of east, lay the Syx works, with their black smoke rising almost vertically in the still air. Suddenly, as we stumbled along on the rough surface, something whizzed past my face and fell on the rock at my feet. I looked at the strange missile that had come like a meteor out of open space with astonishment.

It was a bird. It lay motionless, its outstretched wings having a curious shriveled aspect, while the flaming color of the breast was half obliterated with smutty patches. Stooping to pick it up, I noticed a slight bronzing, which instantly recalled to my mind the peculiar appearance of the victims of the attack on the mine.

"Look here!" I called to Hall, who was several yards in advance. He turned, and I held up the bird by a wing.

"Where did you get that?" he asked.

"It fell at my feet a moment ago."

Hall glanced in a startled manner at the sky, and then down the slope of the mountain.

"Did you notice in what direction it was flying?" he asked.

"No; it dropped so close that it almost grazed my nose. I saw nothing of it until it made me blink."

"I have been heedless," muttered Hall under his breath. At the time I did not notice the singularity of his remark, my attention being absorbed in contemplating the unfortunate tanager.

"Look how its feathers are scorched," I said.

"I know it," Hall replied, without glancing at the bird.

"And it is covered with a film of artemisium," I added, a little piqued by his abstraction.

"I know that, too."

"See here, Hall," I exclaimed, "are you trying to make game of me?"

"Not at all, my dear fellow," he replied, dropping his cogitation. "Pray forgive me. But this is no new phenomenon to me. I have picked up birds in that condition on this mountain before. There is a terrible mystery here, but I am slowly letting light into it, and if we succeed in reaching the top of the peak I have good hope that the illumination will increase.

"Here, now," he added a moment later, sitting down upon a rock and thrusting the blade of his penknife into a crevice, "what do you think of this?"

He held up a little nugget of pure artemisium, and then went on:

"You know that all this slope was swept as clean as a Dutch housewife's kitchen floor by the thousands of miners and prospectors who swarmed over it a year or two ago, and do you suppose they would have missed such a tidbit if it had been here then?"

"Dr. Syx must have been salting the mountain again," I suggested.

"Well," replied Hall, with a significant smile, "if the doctor hasn't salted it somebody else has, that's plain enough. But perhaps you would like to know precisely what I expect to find out when we get on the topknot of the Teton."

"I should certainly be delighted to learn the object of our journey," I said assuringly.

"It is of supreme importance to the success of my plans. In a word, I hope to be able to look down into a part of Dr. Syx's mill, which, if I am not mistaken, no human eye except his and those of his most trustworthy helpers has ever been permitted to see. And if I see there what I fully expect to see, I shall have got a long step nearer to a great fortune."

"Good!" I cried. *"En avant,* then! We are losing time."

CHAPTER X

THE TOP OF THE GRAND TETON

THE climbing soon became difficult, until at length we were going up hand over hand, taking advantage of crevices and knobs which an inexperienced eye would have regarded as incapable of affording a grip for the fingers or a support for the toes. Presently we arrived at the foot of a stupendous precipice, which was absolutely insurmountable by any ordinary method of ascent. Parts of it overhung, and everywhere the face of the rock was too free from irregularities to afford footing except to a fly.

"Now, to borrow the expression of old Bunyan, we are hard put to it," I remarked. "If you will go to the left I will take the right and see if there is any chance of getting up."

"I don't believe we could find any place easier than this," Hall replied, "and so up we go where we are."

"Have you a pair of wings concealed about you?" I asked, laughing at his folly.

"Well, something nearly as good," he responded, unstrapping his knapsack. He produced a silken bag, which he unfolded on the rock.

"A balloon!" I exclaimed. "But how are you going to inflate it?"

For reply Hall showed me a receptacle which, he said, contained liquid hydrogen.

"This balloon I made for our present purpose. It will just suffice to carry up our rope and a small but practically unbreakable grapple of hardened gold. I calculate to send the grapple to the top of the precipice with the balloon, and when it has obtained a firm hold in the riven rock there we can ascend, sailor fashion. You see the rope has knots, and I know your muscles are perfectly trustworthy in such work.

There was a slight breeze from the eastward, and the current of air slanting up the face of the peak assisted the balloon in mounting with its burden and favored us by promptly swinging the little airship, with the grapple swaying beneath it, over the brow of the cliff into the atmospheric eddy above. As soon as we saw that the grapple was well over the edge we pulled upon the rope. The balloon instantly shot into view with the anchor dancing, but, under the influence of the wind, quickly returned to its former position behind the projecting brink. The grapple had failed to take hold.

" 'Try, try again' must be our motto now," muttered Hall.

We tried several times with the same result, although each time we slightly shifted our position. At last the grapple caught.

"Now, all together!" cried my companion, and simultaneously we threw our weight upon the slender rope. The anchor apparently did not give an inch.

"Let me go first," said Hall, pushing me aside as I caught the first knot above my head. "It's my device, and it's only fair that I should have the first try."

In a minute he was many feet up the wall, climbing swiftly hand over hand, but occasionally stopping and twisting his leg around the rope while he took breath.

"It's easier than I expected," he called down, when he had ascended about one hundred feet. "Here and there the rock offers a little hold for the knees."

I watched him, breathless with anxiety, and, as he got higher, my imagination pictured the little gold grapple, invisible above the brow of the precipice, with perhaps a single thin prong wedged into a crevice, and slowly ploughing its way toward the edge with each impulse of the climber, until but another pull was needed to set it flying! So vivid was my fancy that I tried to banish it by noticing that a certain knot in the rope remained just at the level of my eyes, where it had been from the start. Hall was now fully two hundred feet above the ledge on which I stood, and was rapidly nearing the top of the precipice. In a minute more he would be safe.

Suddenly he shouted, and, glancing up with a leap of the heart, I saw that he was falling! He kept his face to the rock, and came down feet foremost. It would be useless to attempt any description of my feelings; I would not go through that experience again for the price of a battleship. Yet it lasted less than a second. He had dropped not more than ten feet when the fall was arrested.

"All right!" he called cheerily. "No harm done! It was only a slip."

But what a slip! If the balloon had not carried the anchor several yards back from the edge it would have had no opportunity to catch another hold as it shot forward. And how could we know that the second hold would prove more secure than the first? Hall did not hesitate, however, for one instant. Up he went again. But, in fact, his best chance was in going up, for he was within four yards of the top when the mishap occurred. With a sigh of relief I saw him at last throw his arm over the verge and then wriggle his body upon the ledge. A few seconds later he was lying on his stomach, with his face over the edge, looking down at me.

"Come on!" he shouted. "It's all right."

WHEN I had pulled myself over the brink at his side I grasped his hand and pressed it without a word. We understood each other.

"It was pretty close to a miracle," he remarked at last. "Look at this."

The rock over which the grapple had slipped was deeply scored by the unyielding point of the metal, and exactly at the verge of the precipice the prong had wedged itself into a narrow crack so firmly that we had to chip away the stone in order to release it. If it had slipped a single inch farther before taking hold it would have been all over with my friend.

Such experiences shake the strongest nerves, and we sat on the shelf we had attained for fully a quarter of an hour before we ventured to attack the next precipice, which hung beetling directly above us. It was not as lofty as the one we had just ascended, but it impended to such a degree that we saw we should have to climb our rope while it swung free in the air!

Luckily we had little difficulty in getting a grip for the prongs, and we took every precaution to test the security of the anchorage, not only putting our combined weight repeatedly upon the rope, but flipping and jerking it with all our strength. The grapple resisted every effort to dislodge it, and finally I started up, insisting on my turn as leader.

The height I had to ascend did not exceed one hundred feet, but that is a very great distance to climb on a swinging rope, without a wall within reach to assist by its friction and occasional friendly projections. In a little while my movements, together with the effect of the slight wind, had imparted a most distressing oscillation to the rope. This sometimes carried me with a nerve-shaking bang against a prominent point of the precipice, where I would dislodge loose fragments that kept Hall dodging for his life, and then I would swing out, apparently beyond the brow of the cliff below, so that, as I involuntarily glanced downward, I seemed to be hanging in free space, while the steep mountainside, looking ten times steeper than it really was, resembled the vertical wall of an absolutely bottomless abyss, as if I were suspended over the edge of the world.

I avoided thinking of what the grapple might be about, and in my haste to get through with the awful experience I worked myself fairly out of breath, so that when at last I reached the rounded brow of the cliff I had to stop and cling there for fully a minute before I could summon strength enough to lift myself over it.

When I was assured that the grapple was still securely fastened I signalled to Hall, and he soon stood at my side, exclaiming as he wiped the perspiration from his face:

"I think I'll try wings next time!"

But our difficulties had only begun. As we had foreseen, it was a case of Alp above Alp, to the very limit of human strength and patience. However, it would have been impossible to go back. In order to descend the two precipices we had surmounted it would have been necessary to leave our lifelines clinging to the rocks, and we had not rope enough to do that. If we could not reach the top we were lost.

HAVING refreshed ourselves with a bite to eat and a little stimulant, we resumed the climb. After several hours of the most exhausting work I have ever performed we pulled our weary limbs upon the narrow ridge, but a few square yards in area, which constitutes the apex of the Grand Teton. A little below, on the opposite side of a steep-walled gap which divides the top of the mountain into two parts, we saw the singular inclosure of stones which the early white explorers found there, and which they ascribed to the Indians, although nobody has ever known who built it or what purpose it served.

The view was, of course, superb, but while I was admiring it in all its wonderful extent and variety, Hall, who had immediately pulled out his binocular, was busy inspecting the Syx works, the top of whose great tufted smoke column was thousands of feet beneath our level.

"There!" suddenly exclaimed Hall, "I thought I should find it."

"What?"

"Take a look through my glass at the roof of Syx's mill. Look just in the center."

"Why, it's open in the middle!" I cried as soon as I had put the glass to my eyes. "There's a big circular hole in the center of the roof."

"Look inside! Look inside!" repeated Hall impatiently.

"I see something bright."

"You've been in the Syx works many times, haven't you?"

"Yes."

"Did you ever see the opening in the roof?"

"Never."

"Did you ever hear of it?"

"Never."

"Then Dr. Syx doesn't show his visitors everything that is to be seen."

"Evidently not, since, as we know, he concealed the double tunnel and the room under the furnace."

"Dr. Syx has concealed a bigger secret than that," Hall responded, "and the Grand Teton has helped me to a glimpse of it."

For several minutes my friend was absorbed in thought. Then he broke out:

"I tell you he's the most wonderful man in the world!"

"Who? Dr. Syx? Well, I've long thought that."

"Well, now," said Hall, rubbing his hands with a satisfied air, while his eyes glanced keen and bright with the reflection of some passing thought, "Max Syx is greater than any alchemist that ever lived. If those old fellows in the dark ages

had accomplished everything they set out to do, they would have been of no more consequence in comparison with our black-browed friend down yonder than—than my head is of consequence in comparison with the moon."

"I fear you flatter the man in the moon," was my laughing reply.

"No, I don't," returned Hall, "and some day you'll admit it."

"Well, what about that something that shines down there? You seem to see more in it than I can."

But my companion had fallen into a reverie and didn't hear my question. He was gazing abstractedly at the faint image of the waning moon, now nearing the distant mountain-top over in Idaho. Presently his mind seemed to return to the old magnet, and he whirled about and glanced down at the Syx mill. The column of smoke was diminishing in volume, an indication that the engine was about to enjoy one of its periodical rests. The irregularity of these stoppages had always been a subject of remark among practical engineers. The hours of labor were exceedingly erratic, but the engine had never been known to work at night, except on one occasion, and then only for a few minutes, when it was suddenly stopped on account of a fire.

Just as Hall resumed his inspection, two huge quarter spheres, which had been resting wide apart on the roof, moved toward one another until their arched sections met over the circular aperture which they covered like the dome of an observatory.

"I expected it," Hall remarked. "But come, it is mid-afternoon, and we shall need all of our time to get safely down before the light fades."

Letting ourselves down with the rope into the hollow way that divides the summit of the Teton into two pinnacles, we had no difficulty in descending by the route followed by all previous climbers. The weather was fine, and, having found good shelter among the rocks, we passed the night in comfort. The next day we succeeded in swinging round upon the eastern flank of the Teton, below the more formidable cliffs, and, just at nightfall, we arrived at the station. As we passed the Syx mine the doctor himself confronted us. There was a very displeasing look on his countenance, and his sneer was strongly marked.

"So you have been on top of the Teton?" he said.

"Yes," replied Hall very blandly; "and if you have a taste for that sort of thing I should advise you to go up. The view is immense—as fine as the best in the Alps."

"Pretty ingenious plan, that balloon of yours," continued the doctor, still looking black.

"Thank you," Hall replied more suavely than ever. "I've been planning that a long time. You probably don't know that mountaineering used to be my chief amusement."

The doctor turned away without pursuing the conversation.

"I could kick myself," Hall muttered as soon as Dr. Syx was out of earshot. "If my absurd wish to outdo others had not blinded me, I should have known that he would see us going up this side of the peak, particularly with the balloon to give us away. However, what's done can't be undone. He may not really suspect the truth, and if he does he can't help himself, even though he is the richest man in the world."

CHAPTER XI

STRANGE FATE OF A KITE

"ARE you ready for another tramp?" was Andrew Hall's greeting when we met early on the morning following our return from the peak.

"Certainly I am. What is your program for today?"

"I wish to test the flying qualities of a kite which I have constructed since our return last night."

"You don't allow the calls of sleep to interfere very much with your activity."

"I haven't much time for sleep just now," replied Hall, without smiling. "The kite test will carry us up the flanks of the Teton, but I am not going to try for the top this time. If you will come along, I'll ask you to help me by carrying and operating a light transit. I shall carry another myself. I am desirous to get the elevation that the kite attains, and certain other data that will be of use to me. We will make a detour toward the south, for I don't want old Syx's suspicions to be prodded any more."

"What interest can he have in your kite-flying?"

"The same interest that a burglar has in the rap of a policeman's night-stick."

In a few hours we were clambering over the broken rocks on the southeastern flank of the Teton at an elevation of about three thousand feet above the level of Jackson's Hole. Finally Hall paused and began to put his kite together.

"In order to diminish the chances of Dr. Syx noticing what we are about," he said, as he worked away, "I have covered the kite with sky-blue paper. This, together with distance, will probably insure us against his notice."

Having ascertained the direction of the wind with much attention, he stationed me with my transit on a commanding rock, and sought another post for himself at a distance of two hundred yards, which he carefully measured with a gold tape. My instructions were to keep the telescope on the kite as soon as it had attained a considerable height, and to note the angle of elevation and the horizontal angle with the base line joining our points of observation.

"Be particularly careful," was Hall's injunction, "and if anything happens to the kite, note the angles at that instant."

As soon as we had fixed our stations Hall began to pay out the string, and the kite rose very swiftly. As it sped away into the blue it was soon practically invisible to the naked eye, although the telescope of the transit enabled me to follow it with ease.

"Don't lose sight of it now for an instant!" he shouted.

For at least half an hour he continued to manipulate the string, sending the kite now high toward the zenith with a sudden pull, and then letting it drift off. It seemed at last to become almost a fixed point. Very slowly the angles changed, when suddenly there was a flash, and to my amazement I saw the paper of the kite shrivel and disappear in a momentary flame, and then the bare sticks came tumbling out of the sky.

"Did you get the angles?" yelled Hall excitedly.

"Yes; the telescope is yet pointed on the spot where the kite disappeared."

"Read them off," he called, "and then get your angle with the Syx works."

"All right," I replied, doing as he had requested, and noticing at the same time that he was in the act of putting his watch in his pocket. "Is there anything else?" I asked.

"No; that will do, thank you."

Hall came running over, his face beaming, and with the air of a man who has just hooked a particularly cunning old trout.

"Ah," he exclaimed, "this has been a great success! I could almost dispense with the calculation, but it is best to be sure."

"What are you about, anyhow?" I asked, "and what was it that happened to the kite?"

"Don't interrupt me just now, please," was the only reply I received.

Thereupon my friend sat down on a rock, pulled out a pad of paper, noted the angles which I had read on the transit, and fell to figuring with feverish haste. In the course of his work he consulted a pocket almanac, then glanced up at the sky, muttered approvingly, and finally leaped to his feet with a half-suppressed "Hurrah!"

"Will you kindly tell me," I asked, "how you managed to set the kite afire?"

Hall laughed heartily. "You thought it was a trick, did you?" said he. "Well, it was no trick, but a very beautiful demonstration. You surely haven't forgotten the bird that gave you such a surprise the day before yesterday?"

"Do you mean," I exclaimed, startled at the suggestion, "that the fate of the bird had any connection with the accident to your kite?"

"Accident isn't precisely the right word," replied Hall. "The two things are as intimately related as own brothers. If you should care to hunt up the kite sticks, you would find that they, too, are now artemisium plated."

"What do you propose to do next?"

"To shake the dust of the Grand Teton from my shoes and go to San Francisco, where I have an extensive laboratory."

"So you are going to try a little alchemy yourself, are you?"

"Perhaps; who knows? At any rate, my good friend, I am forever indebted to you for your assistance, and even more for your discretion, and if I succeed you shall be the first person in the world to hear the news."

CHAPTER XII

BETTER THAN ALCHEMY

FOR six months after Hall's departure for San Francisco I heard nothing from him. In the meantime, things ran on as usual in the world, only a ripple being caused by renewed discoveries of small nuggets of artemisium on the Tetons, a fact which recalled to my mind the remark of my friend when he dislodged a flake of the metal from a crevice during our ascent of the peak. At last one day I received this telegram at my office in New York:

San Francisco, May 16, 1949.
Come at once. The mystery is solved.
(Signed) Hall.

As soon as I could pack a grip I was flying westward one hundred miles an hour. On reaching San Francisco, I hastened to Hall's laboratory. He was there expecting me, and, after a hearty greeting, during which his elation over his success was manifest, he said:

"I am compelled to ask you to make a little journey. I found it impossible to secure the necessary privacy here, and before opening my experiments, I selected a site for a new laboratory in an unfrequented spot among the mountains this side of Lake Tahoe. You will be the first man, with the exception of my two devoted assistants, to see my apparatus, and you shall share the sensation of the critical experiment."

From the nearest railway station we took horses to the laboratory, which occupied a secluded but most beautiful site at an elevation of about six thousand feet above sea-level. With considerable surprise I noticed a building surmounted with a dome, recalling what we had seen from the Grand Teton on the roof of Dr. Syx's mill. Hall, observing my look, smiled significantly, but said nothing. The laboratory proper occupied a smaller building adjoining the domed structure. Hall led the way into an apartment having but a single door and illuminated by a skylight.

Near one end of the room, which was about thirty feet in length, was a table on which lay a glass tube about two inches in diameter and thirty inches long. In the farther end of the tube gleamed a lump of yellow metal, which I took to be gold. Hall and I were seated near another table about twenty-five feet distant from the tube, and on this table was an apparatus furnished with a concave mirror, whose optical axis was directed toward the tube. It occurred to me at once that this apparatus would be suitable for experimenting with electric waves. Wires ran from it to the floor, and in the cellar beneath was audible the beating of an engine. My companion made an adjustment or two, and then remarked:

"Now, keep your eyes on the lump of gold in the farther end of the tube yonder. The tube is exhausted of air, and I am about to concentrate upon the gold an intense electric influence, which will have the effect of making it a kind of kathode pole. I only use this term for the sake of illustration. You will recall that as long

ago as the days of Crookes it was known that a kathode in an exhausted tube would project particles, or atoms, of its substance away in straight lines. Now watch!"

I fixed my attention upon the gold, and presently saw it enveloped in a most beautiful violet light. This grew more intense, until, at times, it was blinding, while, at the same moment, the interior of the tube seemed to have become charged with a luminous vapor of a delicate pinkish hue.

"Watch! Watch!" said Hall. "Look at the nearer end of the tube!"

"Why, it is becoming coated with gold!" I exclaimed.

He smiled, but made no reply. Still the strange process continued. The pink vapor became so dense that the lump of gold was no longer visible, although the eye of violet light glared piercingly through the colored fog. Every second the deposit of metal, shining like a mirror, increased, until suddenly there came a curious whistling sound. Hall, who had been adjusting the mirror, jerked away his hand and gave it a flip, as if hot water had spattered it, and then the light in the tube quickly died away, the vapor escaped, filling the room with a peculiar stimulating odor, and I perceived that the end of the glass tube had been melted through, and the molten gold was slowly dripping from it.

"I carried it a little too far," said Hall, ruefully rubbing the back of his hand, "and when the glass gave way under the atomic bombardment a few atoms of gold visited my bones. But there is no harm done. You observe that the instant the air reached the kathode, as I for convenience call the electrified mass of gold, the action ceased."

"But your anode, to continue your simile," I said, "is constantly exposed to the air."

"True," he replied, "but in the first place, of course, this is not really an anode, just as the other is not actually a kathode. As science advances we are compelled, for a time, to use old terms in a new sense until a fresh nomenclature can be invented. But we are now dealing with a form of electric action more subtle in its effects than any at present described in the text-books and the transactions of learned societies. I have not yet even attempted to work out the theory of it. I am only concerned with its facts."

"But wonderful as the exhibition you have given is, I do not see," I said, "how it concerns Dr. Syx and his artemisium."

"LISTEN," replied Hall, settling back in his chair after disconnecting his apparatus. "You no doubt have been told how one night the Syx engine was heard working for a few minutes, the first and only night work it was ever known to have done, and how, hardly had it started up, when a fire broke out in the mill, and the engine was instantly stopped. Now there is a very remarkable story connected with that, and it will show you how I got my first clue to the mystery, although it was rather a mere suspicion than a clue, for at first I could make nothing out of it. The alleged fire occurred about a fortnight after our discovery of the double tunnel. My mind was then full of suspicions concerning Syx, because I thought that a man who would fool people with one hand was not likely to deal fairly with the other.

"It was a glorious night, with a full moon, whose face was so clear in the limpid air that, having found a snug place at the foot of a yellow-pine tree, where the ground was carpeted with odoriferous needles, I lay on my back and renewed my early acquaintance with the romantically named mountains and 'seas' of the Lunar globe. With my binocular I could trace those long white streaks which radiate from the crater ring, called 'Tycho,' and run hundreds of miles in all directions over the moon. As I gazed at these singular objects I recalled the various theories which astronomers, puzzled by their enigmatical aspect, have offered to a more or less confiding public concerning them.

"In the midst of my meditation and moon-gazing I was startled by hearing the engine in the Syx works suddenly begin to run. Immediately a queer light, shaped like the beam of a ship's searchlight, but reddish in color, rose high in the moonlit heavens above the mill. It did not last more than a minute or two, for almost instantly the engine was stopped, and with its stoppage the light faded and disappeared. The next day Dr. Syx gave it out that on starting up his engine in the night something had caught fire, which compelled him immediately to shut down again. The few who had seen the light, with the exception of your humble servant, accepted the doctor's explanation without a question. But I knew there had been no fire, and Syx's anxiety to spread the lie led me to believe that he had narrowly escaped giving away a vital secret. I said nothing about my suspicions, but upon inquiry I found out that an extra and pressing order for metal had arrived from the government the very day of the pretended fire, and I drew the inference that Syx, in his haste to fill the order—his supply having been drawn low—had started to work, contrary to his custom, at night, and had immediately found reason to repent his rashness. Of course, I connected the strange light with this sudden change of mind.

"My suspicion having been thus stimulated, and having been directed in a certain way, I began from that moment to notice closely the hours during which the engine labored. At night it was always quiet, except on that one brief occasion. Sometimes it began early in the morning and stopped about noon. At other times the work was done entirely in the afternoon, beginning sometimes as late as three or four o'clock, and ceasing invariably at sundown. Then again it would start at sunrise and continue the whole day through.

"For a long time I was unable to account for these eccentricities, and the problem was not rendered much clearer, although a startling suggestiveness was added to it, when, at length, I noticed that the periods of activity of the engine had a definite relation to the age of the moon.

Then I discovered, with the aid of an almanac, that I could predict the hours when the engine would be busy.

"At the time of new moon it worked all day; at full moon it was idle; between full moon and last quarter it labored in the forenoon, the length of its working hours increasing as the quarter was approached; between last quarter and new moon the hours of work lengthened until, as I have said, at new moon they lasted all day; between new moon and first quarter work began later and later in the forenoon as the quarter was approached, and between first quarter and full moon the laboring hours rapidly shortened, being confined to the latter part of the afternoon, until at full moon complete silence reigned in the mill."

"WELL, well!" I broke in, astonished by the singular recital, "you must have thought Dr. Syx was a cross between an alchemist and an astrologer."

"Note this," said Hall, disregarding my interruption, "the hours when the engine worked were invariably the hours during which the moon was above the horizon!"

"What did you infer from that?"

"Of course I inferred that the moon was directly concerned in the mystery. But how? That bothered me for a long time, but a little light broke into my mind when I picked up, on the mountainside, a dead bird, whose scorched feathers were bronzed with artemisium. Then came the attack on the mine and its tragic finish. I have already told you what I observed on that occasion. But, instead of helping to clear up the mystery, it rather complicated it for a time. At length, however, I reasoned my way partly out of the difficulty. Certain things which I had noticed in the Syx mill convinced me that there was a part of the building whose existence no visitor suspected, and, putting one thing with another, I inferred that the roof must be open above that secret part of the structure, and that if I could get upon a sufficiently elevated place I could see something of what was hidden there.

"At this point in the investigation I proposed to you the trip to the top of the Teton, the result of which you remember. I called your attention to a shining object underneath the circular opening in the roof. You could not make out what it was, but I saw enough to convince me that it was a gigantic parabolic mirror. I'll show you a smaller one of the same kind presently.

"Now at last I began to perceive the real truth, but it was so wildly incredible, so infinitely remote from all human experience, that I hardly ventured to formulate it, even in my own secret mind. But I was bound to see the thing through to the end. It occurred to me that I could prove the accuracy of my theory with the aid of a kite. You were kind enough to lend your assistance in that experiment, and it gave me irrefragable evidence of the existence of a shaft of flying atoms extending in a direct line between Dr. Syx's pretended mine and the moon!"

"Hall," I exclaimed, "you are mad!"

My friend smiled good-naturedly, and went on with his story.

"The instant the kite shriveled and disappeared I understood why the works were idle when the moon was not above the horizon, why birds flying across that fatal beam fell dead upon the rocks, and whence the terrible master of that mysterious mill derived the power of destruction that could wither an army as the Assyrian host in Byron's poem:

'Melted like snow in the glance of the Lord.' "

"But how did Dr. Syx turn the flying atoms against his enemies?" I asked.

"In a very simple manner. He had a mirror mounted so that it could be turned in any direction, and would shunt the stream of metallic atoms, heated by their friction with the air, toward any desired point. When the attack came he raised this machine above the level of the roof and swept the mob to a lustrous, if expensive death."

"And the light at night——"

"Was the shining of the heated atoms, not luminous enough to be visible in broad day, for which reason the engine never worked at night, and the stream of volatilized artemisium was never set flowing at full moon, when the lunar globe is above the horizon only during the hours of darkness."

"I see," I said, "whence came the nuggets on the mountain. Some of the atoms, owing to the resistance of the air, fell short and settled in the form of impalpable dust until the winds and rains collected and compacted them in the cracks and crevices of the rocks."

"That was it, of course."

"And now," I added, my amazement at the success of Hall's experiments and the accuracy of his deductions increasing every moment, "do you say that you have also discovered the means employed by Dr. Syx to obtain artemisium from the moon?"

"Not only that," replied my friend, "but within the next few minutes I shall have the pleasure of presenting to you a button of moon metal fresh from the veins of Artemis herself."

CHAPTER XIII

THE LOOTING OF THE MOON

I SHALL spare the reader a recital of the tireless efforts, continuing through many almost sleepless weeks, whereby Andrew Hall obtained his clue to Dr. Syx's method. It was manifest from the beginning that the agent concerned must be some form of etheric, or so-called electric energy; but how to set it in operation was the problem. Finally he hit upon the apparatus for his initial experiments which I have already described.

"Recurring to what had been done a century ago by Hertz, when he concentrated electric waves upon a focal point by means of a concave mirror," said Hall, "I saw that the key I wanted lay in an extension of these experiments. At last I found that I could transform electrical energy into ether waves, which, when they

had been concentrated upon a metallic object, like a chunk of gold, imparted to it an intense charge of an apparently electric nature. Upon thus charging a metallic body enclosed in a vacuum, I observed that the energy imparted to it possessed the remarkable power of disrupting its atoms and projecting them off in straight lines, very much as occurs with a kathode in a Crookes' tube. But—and this was of supreme importance—I found that the line of projection was directly toward the apparatus from which the impulse producing the charge had come. In other words, I could produce two poles between which a marvelous interaction occurred. My transformer, with its concentrating mirror, acted as one pole, from which energy was transferred to the other pole, and that other pole immediately flung off atoms of its own substance in the direction of the transformer. But these atoms were stopped by the glass wall of the vacuum tube; and when I tried the experiment with the metal removed from the vacuum, and surrounded with air, it failed utterly.

"This at first completely discouraged me, until I suddenly remembered that the moon is in a vacuum, the great vacuum of interplanetary space, and that it possesses no perceptible atmosphere of its own. At this a great light broke around me, and I shouted 'Eureka!' Without hesitation I constructed a transformer of great power, furnished with a large parabolic mirror to transmit the waves in parallel lines, erected the machinery and buildings here, and when all was ready for the final experiment I telegraphed for you."

Prepared by these explanations, I was all on fire to see the thing tried. Hall was no less eager, and, calling in his two faithful assistants to make the final adjustments, he led the way into what he facetiously named "the lunar chamber."

"If we fail," he remarked with a smile that had an element of worriment in it, "it will become the 'lunatic chamber'— but no danger of that. You observe this polished silver knob, supported by a metallic rod curved over at the top like a crane. That constitutes the pole from which I propose to transmit the energy to the moon, and upon which I expect the storm of atoms to be centered by reflection from the mirror at whose focus it is placed."

"One moment," I said. "Am I to understand that you think that the moon is a solid mass of artemisium, and that no matter where your radiant force strikes it a 'kathodic pole' will be formed there from which atoms will be projected to the earth?"

"No," said Hall; "I must carefully choose the point on the lunar surface where to operate. But that will present no difficulty. I made up my mind as soon as I had penetrated Syx's secret that he obtained the metal from those mystic white streaks which radiate from Tycho, and which have puzzled the astronomers ever since the invention of telescopes. I now believe those streaks to be composed of immense veins of the metal that Syx has most appropriately named artemisium, which you, of course, recognize as being derived from the name of the Greek goddess of the moon, Artemis, whom the Romans called Diana. But now to work!"

IT WAS less than a day past the time of new moon, and the earth's satellite was too near the sun to be visible in broad daylight. Accordingly, the mirror had to be directed by means of knowledge of the moon's place in the sky. Driven by accurate clockwork, it could be depended upon to retain the proper direction when once set.

With breathless interest I watched the proceedings of my friend and his assistants. When everything had been adjusted to his satisfaction, Hall stepped back, not without betraying his excitement in flushed cheeks and flashing eyes, and pressed a lever. The powerful engine underneath the floor instantly responded. The experiment was begun.

"I have set it upon a point about a hundred miles north of Tycho, where the Yerkes photographs show a great abundance of the white substance," said Hall.

Then we waited. A minute elapsed. A bird, fluttering in the opening above for a second or two, wrenched our strained nerves. Hall's face turned pale.

"They had better keep away from here," he whispered with a ghastly smile.

Two minutes! I could hear the beating of my heart. The engine shook the floor.

Three minutes! Hall's face was wet with perspiration. The bird blundered in and startled us again.

Four minutes! We were like statues, with all eyes fixed on the polished ball of silver, which shone in the brilliant light concentrated upon it by the mirror.

Five minutes! The shining ball had become a confused blue, and I violently winked to clear my vision.

"At last! Thank Heaven! There it is!"

It was Hall who spoke, trembling like an aspen. The silver knob had changed color. What seemed a miniature rainbow surrounded it, with concentric circles of blinding brilliance.

Then something dropped flashing into an earthen dish set beneath the ball! Another glittering drop followed, and, at a shorter interval, another!

Almost before a word could be uttered the drops had coalesced and became a tiny stream, which, as it fell, twisted itself into a bright spiral, gleaming with a hundred shifting hues, and forming on the bottom of the dish a glowing, interlacing maze of viscid rings and circlets, which turned and twined about and over one another, until they had blended and settled into a button-shaped mass of hot metallic jelly. Hall snatched the dish away and placed another in its stead.

"This will be about right for a watch charm when it cools," he said, with a return of his customary self-command. "I promised you the first specimen. I'll catch another for myself."

"But can it be possible that we are not dreaming?" I exclaimed. "Do you really believe that this comes from the moon?"

"Just as surely as rain comes from the clouds," cried Hall, with all his old impatience. "Haven't I just showed you the whole process?"

"Then I congratulate you. You will be as rich as Dr. Syx."

"Perhaps," was the unperturbed reply.

SIX weeks later the financial centers of the earth were shaken by the news that a new supply of artemisium was being marketed from a mill which had been secretly opened in the Sierras of California. For a time there was almost a panic. If Hall had chosen to do so, he might have precipitated serious trouble. But he immediately entered into negotiations with government representatives, and the inevitable result was that, to preserve the monetary system of the world from upheaval, Dr. Syx had to consent that Hall's mill should share equally with his in the production of artemisium. During the negotiations the doctor paid a visit to Hall's establishment. The meeting between them was most dramatic. Syx tried to blast his rival with a glance, but knowledge is power, and my friend faced his mysterious antagonist, whose deepest secrets he had penetrated, with an unflinching eye. It was remarked that Dr. Syx became a changed man from that moment. His masterful air seemed to have deserted him, and it was with something resembling humility that he assented to the arrangement which required him to share his enormous gains with his conqueror.

Of course Hall's success led to an immediate recrudescence of the efforts to extract artemisium from the Syx ore, and equally of course, every such attempt failed. Hall, while keeping his own secret, did all he could to discourage the experiments, but they naturally believed that he must have made the very discovery which was the subject of their dreams, and he could not, without betraying himself and upsetting the finances of the planet, directly undeceive them. The consequence was that fortunes were wasted in hopeless experimentation, and, with Hall's achievement dazzling their eyes, the deluded fortune-seekers kept on in the face of endless disappointments and disaster.

AND presently there came another tragedy. The Syx mill was blown up! The accident—although many people refused to regard it as an accident, and asserted that the doctor himself in his chagrin had applied the match—the explosion, then, occurred about sundown, and its effects were awful. The great works, with everything pertaining to them, and every rail that they contained, were blown to atoms. They disappeared as if they had never existed. Even the twin tunnels were involved in the ruin, a vast cavity being left in the mountainside where Syx's ten acres had been. The force of the explosion was so great that the shattered rock was reduced to dust. To this fact was attributed the escape of the troops. While the mountain was shaken to its core, and enormous parapets of living rock were hurled down the precipices of the Teton, no missiles of appreciable size traversed the air, and not a man at the camp was injured. But Jackson's Hole, filled with red dust, looked for days afterward like the mouth of a tremendous volcano just after an eruption. Dr. Syx had been seen entering the mill a few minutes before the catastrophe by a sentinel who was stationed about a quarter of a mile away, and who, although he was felled like an ox by the shock, and had his eyes, ears, and nostrils filled with flying dust, miraculously escaped with his life.

After this a new arrangement was made whereby Andrew Hall became the sole producer of artemisium, and his wealth began to mount toward the starry heights of the billions.

About a year after the explosion of the Syx mill a strange rumor got about. It came first from Budapest, in Hungary, where it was averred several persons of credibility had seen Dr. Max Syx. Millions had been familiar with his face and his personal peculiarites, through actually meeting him, as well as through photographs and descriptions, and, unless there was an intention to deceive, it did not seem possible that a mistake could be made in identification. There surely never was another man who looked just like Dr. Syx. And yet, was it not demonstrable that he must have perished in the awful destruction of his mill?

Soon after came a report that Dr. Syx had been seen again, this time at Ekaterinburg, in the Urals. Next he was said to have paid a visit to Batang, in the mountainous district of southwestern China; and finally, according to rumor, he was seen in Sicily, at Nicolosi, among the volcanic pimples on the southern slope of Mount Etna.

Next followed something of more curious and even startling interest. A chemist at Budapest, where the first rumors of Syx's reappearance had placed the mysterious doctor, announced that he could produce artemisium, and proved it, although he kept his process secret. Hardly had the sensation caused by this news partially subsided when a similar report arrived from Ekaterinburg; then another from Batang; after that a fourth from Nicolosi!

Nobody could fail to notice the coincidence; wherever the doctor—or was it his ghost?—appeared, there shortly afterward somebody discovered the much-sought secret.

After this Syx's apparitions rapidly increased in frequency, followed in each instance by the announcement of another productive artemisium mill. He appeared in Germany, Italy, France, England, and finally at many places in the United States.

"It is the old doctor's revenge," said Hall to me one day, trying to smile, although the matter was too serious to be taken humorously. "Yes, it is his revenge, and I must admit that it is complete. The price of artemisium has fallen one-half within six months. All the efforts we have made to hold back the flood have proved useless. The secret itself is becoming public property. We shall inev-

itably be overwhelmed with artemisium, just as we were with gold, and the last condition of the financial world will be worse than the first."

My friend's gloomy prognostications came near being fulfilled to the letter. Ten thousand artemisium mills shot their etheric rays upon the moon, and our unfortunate satellite's metal ribs were stripped by atomic force. Some of the great white rays that had been one of the telescopic wonders of the lunar landscapes disappeared, and the face of the moon, which had remained unchanged before the eyes of the children of Adam from the beginning of their race, now looked as if the blast of a furnace had swept it. At night, on the moonward side, the earth was studded with brilliant spikes all pointing at the heart of its child in the sky.

But the looting of the moon brought disaster to the robber planet. So mad were the efforts to get the precious metal that the surface of our globe was fairly showered with it, productive fields were, in some cases, almost smothered under a metallic coating, the air was filled with shining dust, until finally famine and pestilence joined hands with financial disaster to punish the grasping world.

Then at last the various governments took effective measures to protect themselves and their people. Another combined effort resulted in an international agreement whereby the production of the precious moon metal was once more rigidly controlled.

CHAPTER XIV

THE LAST OF DR. SYX

MANY years after the events last recorded, I sat, at the close of a brilliant autumn day, side by side with my old friend Andrew Hall on a broad, vine-shaded piazza which faced the east, where the full moon was just rising above the rim of the Sierra, and replacing the rosy counter-glow of sunset with its silvery radiance. The sight was calculated to carry the minds of both back to the events of former years. But I noticed that Hall quickly changed the position of his chair, and sat down again with his back to the rising moon. He had managed to save some millions from the wreck of his vast fortune when artemisium started to go to the dogs, and I was now paying him one of my annual visits at his palatial home in California.

"Did I ever tell you of my last trip to the Teton?" he asked, as I continued to gaze contemplatively at the broad lunar disk which slowly detached itself from the horizon and began to swim in the clear evening sky.

"No," I replied; "but I'd like to hear."

"Or of my last sight of Dr. Syx?"

"Indeed! I did not suppose that you ever saw him after that conference in your mill when he had to surrender half of the world to you."

"Once only I saw him again," said Hall, with a peculiar intonation.

"It was about seven years ago. I had long felt an unconquerable desire to have another look at the Teton and the scenes amid which so many strange events in my life had occurred. Finally I decided to go alone. I can tell you it was a gloomy place, barren and deserted. The railroad had long ago been abandoned, and the site of the military camp could scarcely be recognized. An immense cavity showed where Dr. Syx's mill used to send up its plume of black smoke.

"As I stared at the gaunt form of the Teton, whose beetling precipices had been smashed and split by the great explosion, I was seized with a resistless impulse to climb it. I thought I should like to peer off again from that pinnacle which had once formed so fateful a watch-tower for me.

"But it took me a long time, and I did not reach the rift in the summit until just before sundown. Knowing that it would be impossible for me to descend at night, I bethought me of the inclosure of rocks, supposed to have been made by Indians, on the western pinnacle, and decided that I could pass the night there.

"The perpendicular buttress forming the easternmost and highest point of the Teton's head would have baffled me but for the fact that I found a long crack, probably an effect of the tremendous explosion, extending from bottom to top of the rock. Driving my toes and fingers into this rift, I managed, with a good deal of trouble and no little peril, to reach the top. As I lifted myself over the edge and rose to my feet, imagine my amazement at seeing Dr. Syx standing within arm's-length of me!

"My breath seemed pent in my lungs, and I could not even utter the exclamation that rose to my lips. It was like meeting a ghost. Notwithstanding the many reports of his having been seen in various parts of the world, it had always been my conviction that he had perished in the explosion.

"Yet there he stood in the twilight, for the sun was hidden by the time I reached the summit, his tall form erect, and his black eyes gleaming under the heavy brows as he fixed them sternly upon my face. You know I never was given to losing my nerve, but I am afraid I lost it on that occasion. Again and again I strove to speak, but it was impossible to move my tongue. So powerless seemed my lungs that I wondered how I could continue breathing.

"THE doctor remained silent, but his curious smile, which, as you know, was a thing of terror to most people, overspread his black-rimmed face and was broad enough to reveal the gleam of his teeth. I felt that he was looking me through and through. The sensation was as if he had transfixed me with an ice-cold blade. There was a gleam of devilish pleasure in his eyes, as though my evident suffering was a delight to him and a gratification of his vengeance. At length I succeeded in overcoming the feeling which oppressed me, and, making a step forward, I shouted in a strained voice:

"'You black Satan!'

"I cannot clearly explain the psychological process which led me to utter those words. I had never entertained any enmity toward Dr. Syx, although I had always regarded him as a heartless person, who had purposely led thousands to their ruin for his selfish gain. But I knew that he could not help hating me, and I felt now that, in some inexplicable manner, a struggle, not physical but spiritual, was taking place between us, and my exclamation, uttered with surprising intensity, produced upon me, and apparently upon him, the effect of a desperate sword thrust which attains its mark.

"Immediately the doctor's form seemed to recede, as if he had passed the verge of the precipice behind him. At the same time it became dim, and then dimmer, until only the dark outlines, and particularly the jet-black eyes, glaring fiercely, remained visible. And still he receded, as though floating in the air, which was now silvered with the evening light, until

he appeared to cross the immense atmospheric gulf over Jackson's Hole and paused on the rim of the horizon in the east.

"Then, suddenly, I became aware that the full moon had risen at the very place on the distant mountain-brow where the specter rested, and as I continued to gaze, as if entranced, the face and figure of the doctor seemed slowly to frame themselves within the lunar disk, until at last he appeared to have quitted the air and the earth and to be frowning at me from the circle of the moon."

While Hall was pronouncing his closing words I had begun to stare at the moon with swiftly increasing interest, until, as his voice stopped, I exclaimed:

"Why, there he is now! Funny I never noticed it before. There's Dr. Syx's face in the moon now, as plain as day."

"Yes," replied Hall without turning round, "and I never like to look at it."

The Man With the Glass Heart

By GEORGE ALLAN ENGLAND
Author of "Darkness and Dawn," "The Flying Legion," etc.

The one man who could mend that heart, wouldn't believe in it

WE HAD just lost our routine bridge game in the smoking room of the *Ferrania*—my traveling companion, Maynard, and I—and had set up the nightly beers for Harrison and Dr. Carmichael, our victors. Tobacco thereafter appeared.

The bright electric lighting, the leather divans and nicotin-scented warmth, contrasting cheerfully with the January bluster of mid-Atlantic, inclined our hearts to narration. All four of us settled down for a good "gam." Men never talk so well, I think, as when the gale is picking at the harp of the rig, the woodwork straining, and the surges slewing thunderously 'longside in the dark.

Thus we spoke of many subjects, and the talk veered at last to the power of mind over matter. Dr. Carmichael was most interesting, and as I recall it, his tale ran somewhat like this:

HARDLY had the intruder opened the door and quietly stepped into the laboratory when Ackroyd glanced round with surprised vexation. For the master mind of electrical science hated interruption above all things. He failed to understand how this tall, stern-featured man, so ominously intense, had managed to slip past the laboratory guard.

So, standing up quickly beside the littered experiment bench that ran along the whole north wall of the room, the wizard crossed his shirt-sleeved arms, clamped his teeth still tighter on the old cob which was his constant solace, and from beneath frowning brows peered with hostility at the newcomer.

For a moment neither spoke. By the light which glowed greenly from the vacuum-tubes about the ceiling of this windowless den, each studied the other. Then the stranger closed the door and came forward.

"Please excuse this rudeness," said he in a deep, courteous voice, which, nevertheless, trembled a bit. "I know how very unwelcome I must be. Still, I am here. I had to come!"

"How the deuce did *you* get in?" snapped the scientist.

"Oh, just a little strategy. Nothing simpler. But let's waste no time on that. I've something far more vital to discuss. And every moment's precious. Now I—I—"

He stammered with sudden emotion. Ackroyd perceived that he was holding unto himself only by a strong effort. Removing the pipe from between his teeth, the scientist stared in wonder, trying to determine what sort of fellow this might be. A professional man, to be sure. Maybe a writer. Ah! Perhaps he wanted an interview.

"Sorry," blurted Ackroyd; "but if you want to write me up, or anything of that sort, I can't see you. Nothing to say. Positively nothing." And he moved to sit down at his work-bench.

The stranger raised an imploring hand. Ackroyd noted how long and fine the fingers were—white, supple, and adorned by a single plain gold ring.

"Pardon me again," said the intruder. "You mistake my errand. It isn't an interview I want. Why, I never wrote a line for publication in my life. I want just a few minutes of your time, at your own price. My errand concerns something far more vital than mere curiosity. It's life or death to me. For Heaven's sake, will you hear me?"

Ackroyd, startled, yet intensely annoyed, thrust out his lower lip and began pulling at it—a way he had when particularly irritated. Time, for him, had no price that could be counted in money.

Just now he was three-quarters through an abstruse calculation. This interruption of his mental process was an outrage, from his point of view—more, a crime. Any appeal to his emotions must be fruitless, for emotions he had none. The cry of sentiment curdled his soul. He hated it. So with raised palm he motioned dismissal.

"Can't see you," he decided. "Good day."

The stranger, paling, clenched both fists. "You must!" cried he.

"So?" sneered the wizard. "That's a new word to me."

He reached quickly for a push-button close beside his chair.

But the stranger, with a sudden gesture, tore open coat and waistcoat, ripped his shirt apart, and on his naked breast exposed a singular object.

Ackroyd, his eyes narrowing slightly, stood still. His finger did not press the little ivory knob.

Thus, for a second, the two men confronted each other.

"Well," cried the scientist at length, "what is it?"

"Listen. If you send me away without hearing me," replied the intruder in eager haste, "you'll miss the greatest—"

"Oh, so you're another crank, eh?" sneered Ackroyd, with a cynical grimace. " 'Greatest scientific marvel of the age,' and all that sort of stuff, eh? That's what they all say—such of 'em as I can't dodge! Why, we turn away, on the average, five or six greatest marvels a day. So I tell you, to begin with—"

"*I've got a glass heart!*" cried the stranger. "Will you listen to me now?"

FOR a moment, Ackroyd stood dumb. Then: "A—*what?*" he exclaimed. As he spoke, the idea "Madman" crossed his brain. But even so, in spite of himself, he was startled. "You mean to say—"

"I do. I repeat it. My heart's made of glass. An artificial heart, mechanical, automatic. Made by Kohler, of Vienna. Put in by Klugermann, of Bonn. And operated by this." He tapped the boxlike affair strapped to his chest. "Do you want proofs? I've got them. Only listen, I tell you. You can at least do that. As a man of science, you're willing at least to hear what other men have done, aren't you?"

Ackroyd replied nothing, but stood studying this singular individual. He noted the high, somewhat wrinkled forehead, the stiff black hair already retreating before the attack of baldness, the aquiline nose, and sharp, intelligent eyes. Then, with a smile, he jibed:

"Not dangerous or violent, are you? Merely harmless, I take it. Because, you see, that's important. I may as well tell you, right now, that I've got a gun in the table drawer, and I can hit a dime, nine shots out of ten, at a hundred feet. Also, there are—well, other devices in this laboratory which might embarrass you in case you tried to start anything. So go slow."

With an expression of intense chagrin the stranger drew from his pocket a neatly folded journal.

"You read German, of course?" asked he, ignoring the insult.

Ackroyd nodded.

"Very well. Look at this."

The scientist, bitterly scornful, accepted the paper. He glanced over a page or two. A one-column article was blue-penciled. As he read the headlines his face became a study.

NEW TRIUMPH OF MODERN SURGERY
Radical Cure of Valvular Degeneration
by Klugermann's New Method
LARGER ASPECTS OF THE
RUSSELL CASE

For almost the first time in his career wholly at a loss, Ackroyd dropped the medical journal on his table, sat down heavily, and leaning forward with a hard, stern look at this astonishing visitor, demanded:

"Well? For Heaven's sake, man, what is it all about? What do you want of me?"

"I'm Russell, to begin with," answered the other. "Francis H. Russell, of Toledo. And, as I said at first, I want just a few minutes of your time."

"All right! All right! Go ahead!" the scientist exclaimed, his voice betraying more emotion than in years. "Let's have it!"

"At your own price?"

"Price? What do *I* want of money?"

"It's useful, at times. Allow me." And Russell, taking from an inner pocket of his disordered clothing a morocco wallet, extracted therefrom a flat stack of bills.

He laid the money on the table. Ackroyd, glancing involuntarily at it, saw that it must total several thousand dollars. He started to sweep it into the wastebasket, but with a sudden change of mind dropped it into the drawer.

"New laboratories," he remarked. "Well?"

The client drew up a plain wooden chair and sat down. Ackroyd noted that he seemed in pain, rather short of breath, and rather pale. But to this he gave no heed. His whole thought now was of the incomprehensible problem before him.

What to think, he knew not. Whether to believe or doubt, he could not tell. He waited. His eyes fixed themselves upon that curious flat box which partly showed through the man's torn clothing. Russell noted the look.

"This," said he more calmly, "is what I came to consult you about—this apparatus here." He tapped the box. "I've *got* to consult you about it. Knowing the futility of trying to make any appointment by letter, I did the next best thing —waited my chance and forced myself on you. Forgive me! A man will do anything almost, even the most distasteful things, to save his life."

"You mean—"

"I'm in great danger. Deadly peril. And only you can save me."

"How so?"

"I'll tell you presently. Just a few words first. Who I am doesn't matter. An American, rich, with children and big business interests. Only fifty-two. Much to live for. Years and years of usefulness still ahead of me, if you help me."

"Yes, yes! Go on!" And Ackroyd, whom not even the keenest interest could long divorce from his tobacco, reached once more for the old pipe.

"Four years ago this spring I developed heart-disease. Had the best specialists—oh, a dozen of them. No results. The dishonest ones exploited me. The others told me the truth—no hope. The most optimistic gave me perhaps three years or so to live.

"Well, I took my death sentence, and tried to bear it as best I could. And for a while things went on, getting worse and worse all the time. No matter about details. I was slowly dying; that's enough to know."

Without comment, the scientist listened. His pipe was going now. Already the air about his head was beginning to grow blue.

"What was it, Providence or mere coincidence, that put Crawford's 'Witch of Prague' into my hands about eighteen months ago? I can't say. At any rate, I read the book. Remember *Keyork Araban's* experiments? One was the keynote of my inspiration. When I read that—"

"Go on, tell me about it!"

"He describes, you recall, substituting a glass heart for the real one in a rabbit. The words branded themselves instantly into my brain. They're all there, still. '*I made,*' says he, '*an artificial heart which worked on a narcotized rabbit, and the rabbit died instantly when I stopped the machine. . . . If one applied it to a man, he might live on indefinitely, grow fat, and flourish so long as the glass heart worked. Where would his soul be then? In the glass heart, which would have become the seat of life?*'"

Russell paused, unduly excited. For a moment Ackroyd peered at him. Then said he:

"So you went to work on that idea, did you, and at great expense of travel, pain, and money had this thing actually done to you? Is that, omitting all minor points, what you're coming at?"

"Exactly. How splendidly you grasp conclusions!"

"I have to, in this business, or quit. Well, then, what do you ask me to believe? That you've actually got a mechanical heart inside there, in place of the old one? And that that's all you keep alive on?"

Russell smiled—an odd, bitter smile.

"I'm not asking you to believe anything," he returned. "I'm merely asking you to examine the evidence and judge it, as you would in any other problem. After that, when you're quite convinced, I want your help."

"How so? What's wrong?"

"The mechanism! Nobody on this side of the Atlantic can set it right except you. There's no time for a journey back to Vienna. You're the only man that can save me. If you refuse—"

"You die?"

"Like *Keyork Araban's* rabbit," assented Russell with quivering lips.

ACKROYD sat frowning for a moment. Keen thinker and clever analyst though he was, this case for a little while seemed to baffle him. How explain it? If the man were only a deluded crank, how account for the article in the German magazine?

The story he told, after all, was not impossible. Though no surgeon, Ackroyd knew something of the marvels of modern medical science—the ingrafting of organs and of bones upon the living body, the stitching up of the wounded yet still pulsing heart, the seeming restoration of life by various processes.

Might it not be true? And if so, how strangely curious a thing to know about! A flash of keen interest passed through his mind. He must have proofs—then he would undertake whatever work this stranger wanted done. But, first of all, proof positive that the thing was as the man declared.

As though reading his thoughts, Russell tapped the flat, boxlike thing upon his breast.

"Here," said he more calmly, "is the apparatus I want you to examine and repair. Put your ear over this way—so—now hear it? Something wrong, you perceive? And you're the only man in America I dare even show it to!"

Ackroyd, all attention, listened hard. From within the box, which was shallow and curved to fit the contour of the man's chest, came a slow, rhythmic sound, dull and almost inaudible, but broken now and then by a slight hitch, as though some delicate cog or gear had stuck, then gone free again. The wizard frowned.

"If what you're telling me is true,"

judged he, "you'd better go to a watch-maker. I'm not the man you want to consult at all!"

"Pardon me," returned the other, "but it isn't a matter of mere clockwork. Here, let me explain."

Taking up a pencil from the work-bench, he hastily, and with considerable skill, drew out a sketch of the apparatus. A strap round the body and two over the shoulders seemed to hold it in place. Within the space which represented the box itself he quickly limned two induction coils, a "U" magnet, and a variety of delicate levers and springs which served to make and break a circuit from six flat storage-batteries inside his coat.

These batteries he showed to Ackroyd.

"Now you readily understand," he elucidated, "my heart can't be operated by direct transmission of power from outside. Magnetism is the only force that can do it, through the body itself.

"The valves of this artificial organ are fitted with disks of steel, capable of being attracted and released by the coils here at 'X' and 'Y.' My batteries, according to directions, I have renewed at regular intervals of one week—two batteries each time, thus always insuring a steady, uniform current.

"But in spite of all this, for ten days past something's been wrong. The mechanism's been out of order. It skipped a few times. Once I thought it was going to stop altogether. You can imagine my state of mind!"

"Well?" interrogated the scientist, reaching for another match. "So, then, you made up your mind to consult me?"

"Just that. And made a record run of it, too, from Toledo! Fancy your own life utterly dependent on—"

"Yes, yes, I know. But what am I to do? Open that box, study out the apparatus, see what's wrong, and make it right! Is that your program?"

"To a 'T'!" replied the client, now visibly excited.

A little color had crept into his face; his hands were working nervously.

"Precisely. And the quicker, the better." He glanced toward the door. "Suppose we should be interrupted! I might lose my—"

"COME, now, calm yourself!" Ackroyd exclaimed. "All I ask is to be quite convinced of the reality of this thing. Then I'll go ahead to the best of my ability."

Turning toward the work-bench, he opened the drawer and began pawing over the disorder to find a small screw-driver such as he would need in opening the long, flat box.

"Convinced?" queried Russell in a strange tone. "How?"

"Well, just show me the scar of the operation, for one thing.. Then let me listen to your cardiac sounds. If they turn out to be, as you claim, purely mechanical, I'll accept that evidence and go ahead. Isn't that fair?" And, still looking for the screw-driver, he bent over the open drawer.

"Isn't that reasonable?" repeated Ackroyd. But his question was never answered. For voices sounded, all at once, outside the laboratory. Then footsteps crunched the gravel.

Russell stood up suddenly, clutching at the box upon his breast. Ackroyd, sensing rather than getting vision of the man's quick rage and terror, whirled round just in time to see him whip an automatic revolver from his pocket.

Outside, a trilling whistle sounded. Steps clumped on the broad wooden piazza.

Russell, livid and trembling with sudden passion, thrust his head forward. With bowed shoulders and disordered dress, revolver balanced in his hand, he crept with stealthy tread toward the door. The grotesque quality of his figure contrasted horribly with its bestial, tigerish, murderous alertness.

Horrified, Ackroyd stood inert. The very suddenness of the transformation numbed him for a second. At the table he remained, staring with wide eyes, his jaw gaping, not yet able to understand, but foreseeing violence.

Came a decisive voice: "I guess he's in there, all right enough."

Another answered: "We'll have him in a minute, now. But be careful. Here, Bray, you keep back. Now, all right?"

But before the door swung open, Russell whirled on Ackroyd as the wizard sprang.

"You hound!" he shrieked, jerking the revolver to position. "You did this! You warned those fiends! You're in this infernal conspiracy, too, to break my glass heart and destroy my soul! But I won't die alone!" The man's face was black with rage, and foam had gathered at the corners of his mouth.

"Die!" he yelled. But as the revolver barked, Ackroyd ducked and, swinging his chair aloft, hurled it full at Russell.

It struck him squarely on the breast and shoulder. His revolver spat again as he fell; the bullet shattered the vacuum-tube overhead. Glass jangled. The light faded. Darkness fell. Ackroyd flung himself upon the man.

In burst the door, and by the glare of day through the opening the rescuers saw Ackroyd slowly getting up, with a dazed, half frightened air. Puzzled for a moment, they held back.

"What's—what's up?" cried a voice. Ackroyd heard the snick of a revolver hammer.

"Wait!" he panted. He found and pressed a button. Instantly a flood of yellow light inundated the laboratory from the reserve incandescents.

By this light they saw Russell lying, distorted, motionless upon the floor. His eyes were open and staring—the hideous eyes of a man who has died in the grip of stark, mad terror.

"He—did he tell you—" began one of the men. They wore blue uniforms and caps. "Tell you he had a glass heart? Want you to repair it for him?"

Ackroyd did not answer. He merely snatched up the big sheet he used to cover his models with and spread it over the corpse.

"Come, get busy!" he commanded. "Take him out. This is no morgue. I'm busy. Too busy for any questions until

the inquest. Then you'll find me on hand, to make an accounting for everything he said and did and gave me. Now, out you all go!"

Thus he dismissed them. Ten minutes later, with the old cob once more cheerfully erupting, he got back to his interrupted calculation, unmindful of the baffled reporters who had already begun to pry about outside.

IN THE smoke-room our little group sat silent for a moment as Dr. Carmichael finished. Then Harrison spoke.

"Just an escaped lunatic? With religious mania, too?"

"Hardly that. If so, extremely high grade. A man of his education, able to write and print a German paper like that just to substantiate his own hallucination can hardly be classed as a mere lunatic. Rather call it a case of acute monomania. Perfectly sane in every other respect. Perfectly hopeless in *that* respect. So firmly convinced of it, in fact, that the shock of the chair against his apparatus dropped him stone-dead. Mind over matter? Well, rather!"

Another pause.

Then, in a satirical tone, up spoke Maynard, my traveling companion and cabin-mate.

"Well," judged he, "it was no more than he deserved for being a plain, infernal fool. Why, if he'd known anything about the subject of glass hearts, or artificial hearts of any kind, for that matter, he'd have been aware that there's only one bona-fide case on record of such a thing actually working. So he stood, a self-convicted faker!"

"One—one case?" hesitated the bewildered doctor.

"Only one. But it's got nothing to do with all that rot about the soul residing in it and so on. Furthermore, it's not all glass, but partly glass and partly aluminum. And it's operated, not by simple magnetism, but—"

"How do you know such a lot of things that aren't so?" snapped the doctor.

Maynard's face grew hard and his eyes narrowed.

"Why oughtn't a man to know about his own heart?" he replied at length.

A dense stillness enveloped our group. Then the doctor coughed nervously, got up, and with a banal word of excuse withdrew down the stairway to the bar below. Harrison also departed. The gale whipped into the room as he shoved out to the heaving deck. Behind him the door banged.

I found myself alone with Maynard.

"The fools!" he laughed. Then he suddenly grew serious, with a strange eager look upon his face.

He drew out pencil and note-book.

"See here!" he whispered, as his nervous fingers began with rapid strokes to form a diagram. "*My* heart is like this—see? I've never explained it yet to a living soul, but—this conversation tonight has decided me. If I should die, the mystery would be lost. I make you my confidant. But remember, if you so much as lisp a syllable of this while I still live, I'll shoot you like a dog."

Then he laughed again, a high-pitched, cackling laugh in which lay no merriment. And while with sudden dread I watched, he began expounding to me, his chosen victim, the secret of the only successful artificial heart now operating in the world.

Coming Next Month:

THE RADIO MAN

RALPH MILNE FARLEY'S

famous masterpiece

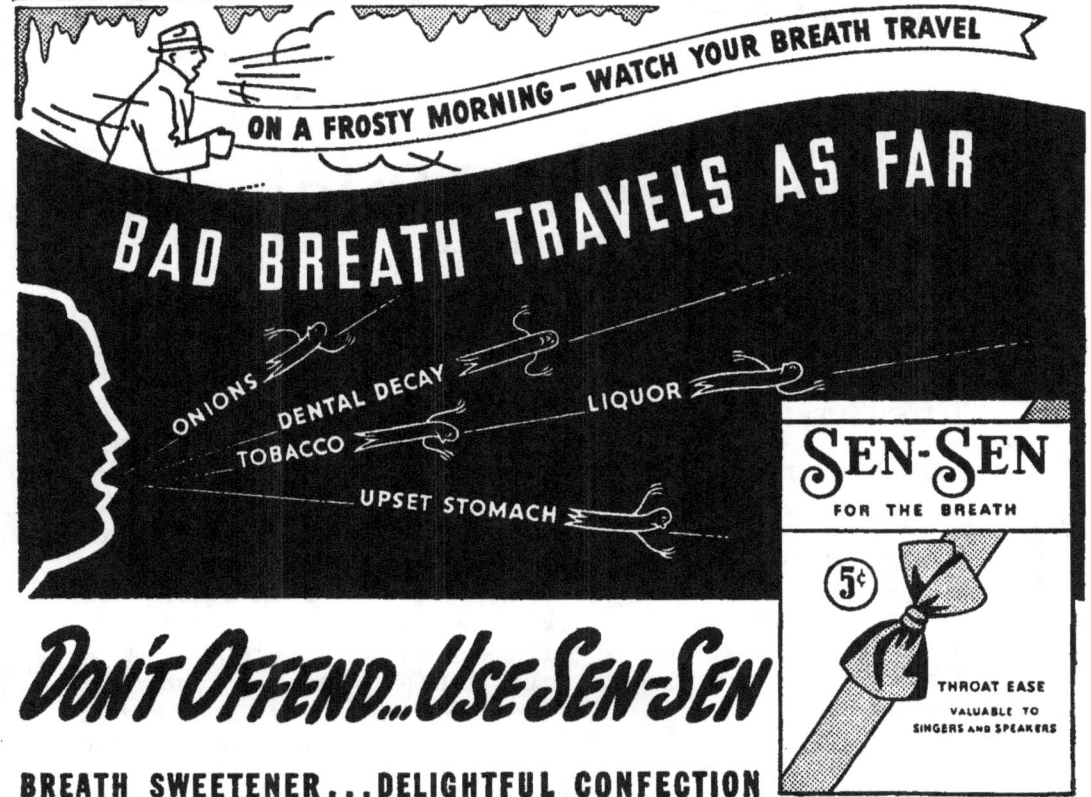

"His eyes grew immense and terrible,
flaming with the most unholy light of ages,
consuming, devouring, unearthly"

Almost Immortal

By AUSTIN HALL

Author of "The Man Who Saved the Earth," etc.; Co-author of "The Blind Spot"

**The snatcher of souls had chosen his
victim. How could he be outwitted?**

CHAPTER I

ROBINSON'S DECISION

THERE were three of us: Robinson,
Hendricks, and myself.

Robinson had had a varied career,
soldier, policeman, lawyer, and several
other professions which he never divulged,
but which kept continually cropping out
in his conversation.

I have an idea he had been a sailor and
had sailed over all the seven seas. There
was no country which he had not visited,
no people nor race nor tribe of which he
knew not the characteristics, nor any insti-
tution with whose history and develop-
ment he had not an intimate knowledge.

Indeed, it was on the historical side that
he was the most remarkable. I have never
seen such a man. The scope of his intellect seemed to embrace everything.
From the Chaldeans down, all was to him
an open book. He appeared to know as
much about Nebuchadnezzar as about me.

All the great lights of history were to
him as men living and present; he would

tell of their foibles and greatness, their manners and personal appearance with as much vividness and distinctness as if they and not I were seated by his side for portrayal. Then he would lapse off into gibbering of a kind which I could not and would not understand, into tongues obsolete and forgotten, which he chose to call Chaldaic, Sanscrit, and what not.

Again he would drift off into anecdote and speak of an incident wherein Caesar and Pompey, and another character I knew not of, were the principals. He knew anecdotes by the million; there seemed to be no limit to the supply with which he amused me from day to day; nor do I ever remember his relating the same one twice.

Big and little, large and small, people and kings, he appeared to have them all at his fingers' ends. I wondered sometimes that he did not write history, he who knew more than all the historians put together. Once I asked him, but he only shrugged his shoulders.

"I have no time," he laughed. "I am a loafer. Besides, I know too much. Were I to tell the truth I would be called a liar."

The other man, Hendricks, was a friend of Robinson's, an attorney who had come up to the mountains to recuperate. It seems that he and Robinson had just been through some terrible ordeal, which had played havoc with them, both mentally and physically.

He had not the wonderfully retentive memory of his friend, nor his marvelous command of language, though he did appear to have a fair smattering of the law, and a very fair education. Most of the time he spent as I did, in loitering about and in listening to the everlasting eloquence of Robinson.

As for myself, I was purely passive.

It was our custom to come out on the veranda at night and to discuss books under the fragrance of a good cigar.

I had on this day been reading a novel of the very cheap and sensational order, one that had to do with a plot of the purely imaginative type, wherein the characters were taken out of the life of ordinary reality and transplanted into the realm of the grotesque and the terrible.

I held that all works of true literary merit should contain, as a basic feature, the elements of real life, and that in their ramifications they should hold by all means to life as it is, and to avoid transgressing the regions of the impossible. For the work at hand I had but little use, and I criticized it severely as a thing absurd and ridiculous.

It was moonlight, and for some moments after I had finished my tirade, we sat watching the shadows among the hills. Robinson was usually loquacious, but tonight he was strangely quiet. Undoubtedly he was thinking. He scarcely noticed my talk at all; but sat there working his cigar at both ends, chewing and smoking, dreaming, and apparently in the land of far away, until the moon, passing behind a cloud, and the flood of mellow light ceasing, he turned to his friend.

"Hendricks," he said, "how long has it been since I escaped from that beast?"

"Third of January, and this is the third of May," answered Hendricks. "Exactly four months. Why?"

"Oh, nothing much. Only our friend here is skeptical, and believes only in the commonplace; he is like all the rest of mankind, only I think we can cure him. I propose that we relate to him our own experience, and prove to him how one man managed to live for ten thousand years in the enjoyment of youth and vigor, and how I came to be devoured alive, and how it happens that I am living tonight to tell the tale."

"Tell him, if you wish," answered Hendricks. "I'll corroborate you as long as you stick by the truth."

Robinson moved his chair closer to mine and sat so that I could get a full and a perfect view of his whole person.

"Do you see any marks on me?" he began; "any tooth marks or anything like that? No? Yet would you believe me were I to tell you that I have been devoured alive. Not only that, but digested and enjoyed."

"I certainly would not," I answered.

"Of course not," he replied, "and really I don't much blame you. Time was, and not so many years ago at that, when I would have said the same thing. Nevertheless, what I am about to tell you is the gospel truth, as you will learn from my friend Hendricks."

And Robinson plunged instantly into the following story.

ABOUT six years ago, after some time spent in the islands, I returned in a practically penniless state to San Francisco. Besides my baggage and wearing apparel I could not have possessed much more than forty dollars.

One day, after I had tramped over a great portion of the city, climbing skyscrapers, invading factories, and I know not what in my never-ceasing search for employment, I struck a crowd surging up Montgomery, and like a chip in the tide, drifted along with it.

In my despair and half-heartedness I little dreamed of the strange and marvelous existence of which I was soon to become a part. Of an existence which was to reward me with a learning which I think has never before been attained by mortal man, and a wealth of such proportions that the human mind can scarce conceive of its vastness.

Both sides of the street on which I walked were lined by office buildings on whose serried windows were hung, painted and gilded, the signs and placards of numerous lawyers, doctors, corporations, and insurance companies. Among them my attention was attracted to a particular attorney's sign, whose reading in gold letters had on me a strange and gladdening effect. It read:

W. E. HENDRICKS

Attorney at Law

I had known a W. E. Hendricks before going to the islands. We had been classmates and roommates while at college, and I remembered now, with a flash of eager hope, that it had always been his desire to build up a practice in some Western State, preferably in California. I can hardly tell you how happy and excited that hope made me.

A MOMENT later I was in the office, all trembling with eagerness over the voice which came from the adjoining room. Sure enough it was Hendricks—Bill Hendricks, the one man whom above all others, under my present indigent circumstances, I would have chosen to meet.

Naturally I moved my belongings to the quarters of Hendricks, where, under the spur of poverty, I lived on his bounty while seeking employment.

One morning, about a month later, I entered the office and found Hendricks, as usual, deep in the intricacies of his profession. Scattered over and about his desk were his everlasting law books, legal papers, and documents, an evening paper, and to one side an early edition of the San Francisco Mercury, which, without looking up, he passed over to me for perusal.

"You will find," he said, "an advertisement in the help-wanted column which it may be to your advantage to look up."

The advertisement was marked with a blue pencil, and I had but little trouble in locating it. It was for a companion, and I must say it was the most peculiar advertisement of its kind that I had ever read. It was worded something like this:

WANTED—A companion for an elderly gentleman; applicant must be about twenty-six years of age, exactly five feet eleven inches in height and must weigh between one hundred and eighty and eighty-five pounds. He must possess a small knowledge of the law; also he must be a good conversationalist and be able to give proofs as to his perfect health and vigor. No applicant with any symptom of disease or any infirmity whatsoever will be considered. Anyone answering these qualifications can procure immediate and lucrative employment by calling, et cetera.

The address of a Dr. Runson on Rubic Avenue followed.

Strange to say, although the conditions were so peculiar and various, and so impossible of filling for the ordinary man, they fitted me to a nicety.

It was almost as if I had received a special order to report for duty. I was exactly five feet eleven inches in height, and had weighed only the day before, one hundred and eighty-three pounds, so that I had a leeway of two pounds in one direction and three in the other. Besides, I possessed a college education and knew considerable about the law. If I had any weakness or infirmity of any kind I had not as yet noticed it. On top of this, I was a very fair conversationalist; at least I had always been considered so by my friends.

The position seemed made for me, and I decided to apply for it immediately.

CHAPTER II

DR. RUNSON

AN hour later I had made my way to Rubic Avenue, where I found the rendezvous to be a most comfortable old two-story house with large, deep, easy-looking verandas, a splendid lawn, and green-shuttered windows.

In response to my knock a neat little woman of some fifty summers—or rather winters, for the quiet, troubled look of her face, and the gray of her hair reminded one more of that season than any other —appeared at the door.

She was trim and neat, and apparently expecting me, for she quietly opened the door and bade me, in a kind, motherly voice which I noticed at once, to enter, and without another word pressed a button beside her and disappeared, leaving me in the hall alone and waiting. In another moment a door opened above and a voice came down the stairs—a musical voice, but masculine and full of vigor.

"Is that you, Mr. Robinson? Just step up this way, please."

Naturally I had expected to meet a stranger, and was not a little surprised at hearing the sound of my own name spoken from above.

"It is," I answered. And I remember wondering how in the world he could know it, and who in the world he could be.

"I am glad to see you, Mr. Robinson," he greeted me when I reached the landing. "Exceedingly glad. I was expecting you. Step right in."

He opened the door and led me into a study, or rather a sitting-room, or still better, a combination of the two.

"Sit down and we will talk business," he said.

A total stranger I was sure. I had never seen him before. Of my own height; but sixty; hair turned gray; of my own features, and might have been my twin brother but for thirty years or so; hands white and immaculate, slender and deft like a gambler's; neat, dressed in black, clean shaved, and a gentleman.

All this I took in at a glance as you would take in a photograph. Nothing uncommon, nothing extraordinary, everything, barring the resemblance to myself which I might have had perfect reason to expect. Then our eyes met.

Someone has said that the eyes are the gateway to the soul. This was an archway. The idea of the common vanished and in its place was the extraordinary, the magnificent. I will condense it all by my own flash of feeling—the eyes of a multitude.

You could not look into his eyes without the feeling, instinctive, but always present, that you were not looking into those of one man, but the eyes of a thousand. However, it was not an unpleasant feeling, more of strength, of power; the impression of an indomitable will which not all the world could change. Nevertheless they were pleasant, with a kindness and a jovialty which danced and fascinated you.

"Now, Mr. Robinson," he began, when we were seated, "let us proceed. I shall talk first, for it is my nature. I am always first. You will be surprised at what I tell you; but do not wonder at that, as I am, I will admit, an extraordinary character. Though you will most likely find me common enough for a few months.

"Now, I decided yesterday to advertise for a companion, and in looking over the available candidates I found you the most desirable. I knew you could easily be reached through the papers, therefore the advertisement. Your name is John Robinson, you are twenty-six years of age. Your height is five feet eleven inches. You weighed yesterday one hundred and eighty-three pounds. You have a smattering of the law and a splendid education; you have a will of your own and are handsome; you are a good conversationalist and enjoy the most perfect health. You have traveled and have but lately returned from the islands; you have but very little money, almost broke, in fact, and you need work. Is not all this true?"

"Most true, doctor," I returned. "I had no idea you knew me, or perhaps—Hendricks?"

"No," he broke in. "Neither. I never dreamed of your existence until yesterday. Didn't know Hendricks was living. Furthermore, just for the fun of it, when you dressed this morning you were minus one sock and did not find it until after you had searched for it for fully ten minutes."

I laughed, for he was telling the truth, though how he came to know I couldn't make out.

"You surely have got me, unless you are another Sherlock Holmes and a past-master of deduction."

The doctor raised his hands imploringly. "Please don't," he said. "Please don't. Not that. It's too puerile, too common. I have read Sherlock and admire the work; but I am, I hope, far above that. I have powers, Mr. Robinson, I will admit; but I am no detective. I never use deduction. Leave that to the mortals."

As he spoke he drew himself up in a proud, isolated sort of way, and I could not help but admire him, though his manner was mystic and his words, to me, rather confusing.

"That is very good flesh, sir. Very good flesh!" He stepped over to my side and to my wonderment began pinching my arm severely. I don't know why, but I drew away with much the same feeling as a fat chicken might have, and was not a little angry.

"It is," I answered, reddening. "Perhaps I had better be going."

"Oh, no! Mr. Robinson. Not at all. Please don't be offended. I meant no harm. I was just wondering how it seemed to be young. You are so vigorous and so full of life that I envied you. But I meant no harm, sir. I assure you I meant no harm."

I sat down again and accepted his apology.

"And about this position?" I asked. "You know that is the object of my visit."

"To be sure!" said the doctor. "To be sure. Well, let me see. How would twenty dollars and your board and room, sound?"

"Sounds all right," I replied; "depending, though, a great deal on how I earn it."

The old man's eyes twinkled and he smiled. "You will earn it, sir, by doing nothing. Absolutely nothing."

"Rather easy," I answered. "But there must be something for me to do. Even sleep is work when you are paid for it and you've got it to do whether or no."

"To be sure! To be sure! Well, we'll amend that. There will be work and it will consist in playing cards, reading, and conversation. You see I'm lonely, I'm getting old. I need a companion and intend to have one. I am wealthy and can afford it. It's merely a whim, sir, merely a whim."

He took an eraser from the table and began tossing it in his hand.

It all looked good to me. He was a character beyond doubt, and his personality attracted me. I foresaw that I would enjoy myself in his company. Here was someone to observe, someone to study; and perhaps a little risk. He was a man with some power, unknown perhaps, and might bear watching. That, however, was an attraction, rather than an obstacle. I would have had it just so. Therefore, we quickly came to an understanding and I agreed to remain.

CHAPTER III

THE CASE OF ALLEN DOREEN

MY POSITION turned out to be an excellent one. There was practically no work, merely to listen to the old gentleman, a task which I found not only interesting but agreeable. In the morning, usually between seven and eight, we had breakfast, after which we read and discussed the newspapers. About ten we would go for a short walk and make a few purchases until noon, when we had lunch.

From that time until three my time was my own, while the doctor retired to his laboratory, or sanctum, into which I was never invited, and none was allowed to go. This was something easily accounted for. I figured that anyone who would willingly devote his life to disease, drugs, and chemicals had all the license in the world to be queer and particular in his habits, and let it go at that.

About three the doctor reappeared, tired and nervous, and ready for a game of cards. Always at this time of day I noticed a hungry, longing look in his eyes; but this I took to be merely the effect of some strain on his mind, some scientific fact sought for but not attained and in no way connected it with myself. From three until dark it was the same thing day after day; cards, conversation, and reading. Rather a snap, don't you think?

So the days went by one after another. Each week my check was in hand and each week my savings mounted higher.

One day during a walk the doctor and I ran across Hendricks. Of course, I had to introduce them. The doctor seemed pleased to meet him and he to meet the doctor.

I noticed when they shook hands that they gazed squarely into each other's eyes and laughed; they seemed to see clear through each other and to take pleasure in the accomplishment. Just before we separated Hendricks took me by the arm.

"Rob," he said, "can you come down to the office? I must see you."

"Certainly," I answered. "This after-noon if you like. What's it about, Hen?"

The doctor had been studying a window display; but just then he happened to turn and once again he and Hendricks gazed full into each other's eyes, and once again they laughed.

"Well!" snapped Hendricks. "Here's my car. I must be going. Glad to have met you, doctor. So long Rob."

And a moment later from the platform of the car he shouted back through his hands: "Important!"

We stood for some moments on the curb watching the car jolting down the street, until the fog settling in, we were left alone in the blanket of mist, gloomy and silent. Somehow I felt like the weather, cold and monotonous and dreary; my life was without sunshine.

"That man," said the doctor at length, "is dangerous."

"What man!" I snapped, turning suddenly on him. He started and eyed me curiously.

"Why, that man, of course, the one we just left. Hendricks, of course. What other could I mean?"

Now I liked the old man immensely; but I could and would not stand there and see him abuse my friend.

"Look here, doctor, you may be a learned man all right and all that, and you may know a good many things unknown to the rest of us poor mortals; but that won't help you one whit, when it comes to judging men. I have known Hendricks practically all my life and I know him almost as well as myself. He is honest and fearless and the best friend that ever trod on two feet. I will not hear a word against him!"

My companion smiled good naturedly.

"Whom are you working for, Mr. Robinson?"

"For you."

"Whose money are you drawing?"

"Yours."

"Well, then, I want you to have nothing to do with Hendricks. He's too analytical, too dangerous. I want you to leave him alone."

I was going to answer him with heat, but just then our eyes met and I subsided. For the life of me, I could not tell why; but a complete change came over me. I instinctively felt that the doctor was right and I was wrong.

Lunch was ready when we reached the house, and after the meal the doctor as usual disappeared in his sanctum. Left to my own resources, I began to come to myself.

"Pish!" I exclaimed. "I'll go see Hendricks!"

In the hall I met the housekeeper. She was dusting some furniture. I had just placed my hand on the door knob when she touched me gently on the shoulder.

"Mr. Robinson."

I noticed that her voice was low and cautious with a sort of appeal in it.

"Well, what is it?"

She lifted her kind old face to mine; her eyes full of tenderness and entreaty and I thought of pity.

"Don't you think you had better go away and stay? It's getting to be that time of the year. You don't know what you are doing or where you are going. I have been watching the doctor. I am sure the time is at hand. You are young; you are handsome, full of life, and strength. Oh! It is not fit to be so! Do say that you will go!"

She seized the lapels of my coat in her hands and looked up into my face.

"Do say it!" she repeated. "He would kill me if he knew I had warned you!"

Just then a door creaked or a window was lowered. I know not what exactly. The woman drew back, her whole form rigid with fear. We both listened. For a moment we stood like two silent statues, alert, but hearing nothing.

"Pshaw!" I said at length. "It is nothing. Now, mother, what is the trouble?"

The sound of my voice restored her and a little color came to her face.

"Go!" she said. "And be sure to remember what I have told you!"

With that a door opened and she disappeared. As for myself, I put on my hat and started for town. A half hour later I was in Hendricks' office.

"WELL, Rob," he said, lighting a cigar, "you got here. Do you know I would have wagered a good five-dollar bill against a single unroasted peanut that you would never have made it! And I'm mighty glad you are stronger than I thought. I suppose you know what you are up against!"

Now this was a line of talk for which I was scarcely prepared, especially from Hendricks. Of course, I was some worked up after the little scene with the housekeeper; but I hardly expected to find my friend in the same humor.

"Oh, say," I cut in, "are you and the old lady in cahoots? Do you want me to lose a good thing? What's the matter?"

He thought a while, went to the window and watched the traffic in the street. Presently he turned about and in his slow, earnest way began to talk.

"Look here, Rob. The gentleman to whom I was introduced today has interested me more than any person I have ever met. He is a character I have dreamed about. I have often pictured myself meeting an individual of this species. I must say it pleases me, though I am sorry to find you in his company. I intend to give you fair warning. I shall tell you what he is, and you can direct your future actions accordingly. But first I want you to tell me all you know about him and what has transpired since you have taken up your position. Go ahead."

Kind of a poser, wasn't it?

But I had confidence in Hendricks. Of all the persons I had ever met, he was the last to take a dramatic posture. I knew him for a deep water man, a man of deep thoughts and few words; but when the words did come they were like chips of steel, sharp and to the point. Therefore, I opened my heart fully. I related to Hendricks all that I knew, also I told him of the old lady's actions and the scene in the hallway.

WHEN I had finished he smiled and began drubbing the desk with his fingers.

"And what do you make of it?" he asked.

I threw up my hands.

"You've got me, Hendricks. There's a rat in a hole somewhere; but I am not cat enough to see it."

"Well," he answered, "I am. The man's a ghoul. Ever hear of a vampire?"

"On the stage."

"Yes, and off. Not the thrilling, entrancing kind that lulls you with a scene of love and beauty and soothingly imbibes while you are in a dream of the seventh heaven; but the real stern, genuine, reality. The kind that measures and weighs every movement of its victim, the kind that watches with the pulsating eyes of a cat every play of the muscles, every flash of emotion until, secure of its prey and sure of the moment, it feeds its greed with the blood of its fellow."

"Pleasant prospect surely," I answered.

"Do you still wish to retain your job?"

"Why, old boy! If that old duffer made an offer to harm me I'd strangle him with my thumb and little finger!"

"You'd do nothing of the sort. That old man has mind. Your strength and muscle don't amount to a row of shucks. When the time comes," he snapped his fingers, "there'll be no Jack Robinson."

"I suppose he will make a sort of salad of me; or serve me up as a soup," I put in.

"Hardly that. Listen, Rob. Did you ever hear of Allen Doreen?"

"The man who walked into a London cottage and disappeared from the face of the earth even though the place was surrounded by watchers? I've heard of him surely. And I believe the story a lie."

"Well, I don't," snapped Hendricks. "The man who had charge of those watchers was my own father. He was Allen Doreen's best friend. Furthermore, when Doreen entered that house, there was a man sitting in plain view of the watchers;

and that man was the exact counterpart of your doctor friend. In half an hour they had both disappeared.

"When they broke open the house it was searched from cellar to attic and from attic to cellar back again; but neither skin nor teeth nor hair was found of either. The place was completely surrounded; yet no one was seen leaving the house. It was as if they had dissolved in air, so completely was it done. That was the last ever seen of Allen Doreen. My father worked on the case for years. The police of London never quite gave it up. Yet it is a mystery today—no evidence whatever, no sign, no clue."

"Perhaps," said I, "a secret passage."

"The place was torn down three weeks afterward," Hendricks returned, "the foundations were torn up for a larger building. Such a thing would have been found. There was none."

"Well," I yawned, "you've got me. Anyhow, I'll hold my job. It's the most exciting way of doing nothing I've yet found. Besides I've started on the serial, and I'm going to see the next chapter."

Hendricks took a fresh cigar.

"Well, that settles it, Rob. You're the same old daredevil. Nothing can frighten you, not even a real, genuine, live bogey man. And I'm glad of it. We'll see the thing through. Between you and me, I think we'll catch the fox and know his game. Likewise there'll be a solution of Allen Doreen.

"So far your cases are parallel; soft snap, nothing to do, pleasant doctor, advertisement, height, weight, and measurement all agree. All we've got to do is change the results. That's up to us. Now I'm going to show you something."

From a drawer in his desk he drew out a small old-fashioned case which he unsnapped and passed over to me. It contained a photograph.

"Perhaps," said he, "you have seen someone who looks like that."

I took the picture and held it to the light. It was the doctor.

"Looks like it, doesn't it," asked my friend. "And perhaps it is. That is the man who did away with Allen Doreen. I am the exact image of my father. He recognized me at once. Now you see why we laughed in each other's faces. It was a challenge. Mine was a laugh of triumph; his, of derision and contempt. We shall see who is the fox. And now, to get down to business what is it that you propose to do?"

"Well," said I, "I see nothing else to do but to return to my work and if anything unusual or threatening occurs—why, I'm the very little boy who will put a stop to it."

"I'm glad," Hendricks smiled, "that you are so confident. However, I am going to take a few precautions, or rather, I have already taken them. Your house is even now under surveillance; there are three detectives of my own hiring on the watch, one each in the houses adjoining and one in the house across the street. They know fully what an important case they are on, and are aware of the consequent glory, if they are successful.

"They are the shiftiest, nerviest, and cleverest of the force and understand perfectly with what a wise old fox they are dealing.

"Now if anything very unusual should happen, and you wish to notify the outside world, all you have to do it to place a piece of paper in a window where it may be seen, and if you need help, two —one in each end of the window. Myself, I shall keep hidden. The old fox is onto me and consequently I shall keep out of sight until such time as I am needed, when I will be there."

"All right, Hendricks," I said, "I'll do as you say. But really, after all, I don't believe the old doc is as bad as you say. There must be some mistake. I have an idea it will all come out right and the only thing to result will be a little foolish feeling for ourselves."

There was an embarrassed pause.

"As you will, Rob," shrugged Hendricks. "Only I wish to take no chances. You have a perfect right to your own opinion."

CHAPTER IV

MRS. GREEN MAKES AN EFFORT

"BACK again?"

It was the doctor; he met me at the door, a smile on his face and his hand extended; he was in his best humor.

"Yes," said I, removing my hat, "I had a little business to transact and thought it was best done before it was too late."

"That's good!" returned the doctor, a twinkle in his eye. "Always keep your affairs in good order. Everybody should do that. Neglect nothing. That's been my motto, always and at all times. We know so little of what is going to happen."

At that moment I would have given I know not what for a more definite knowledge of what the next few days might have in store.

If I was uneasy, I think I carried it off quite well and I don't think the doctor had any suspicion. In a few minutes I was my own self and was dealing out the cards as deftly and easily as ever I had done.

"This is a fine game," said the doctor, who was winning.

"Splendid," I returned inasmuch as I was paid for losing. "Splendid!"

Swish, swish, swish; the cards glided over the table—the doctor's. I dealt myself three. Swish, swish, swish—the doctor's; clip, clip, clip—our hands were dealt. The first trick was the doctor's and his smile grew broader. The next was mine, and the next, and the next; the whole hand in fact. With the turn of luck his good humor vanished.

"A rum hand," he muttered. "Gimme something good!"

However, it was his own deal, and he surely treated himself well. All the trumps were his, likewise the tricks. His good humor returned.

"Do you know, my boy, I always like to win on this night? This, you know is the twentieth of September, the night of all nights. Every twenty years it returns."

He was watching the cards as they glided toward him, picking them up, one by one, with his long tapered fingers, and talking more apparently to himself than to me.

"Every twenty years! I have reduced it to a formula, a science. Twenty years, two minutes, fifty-eight seconds!" He drew out his watch. "Fifteen minutes of eight. Over two hours yet. Two hours and over."

He began playing again—silently—a smile on his lips, anticipating. It was a sort of sensual smile and I noticed an odd look of anticipation in his eyes as he watched the cards. The tricks were all his and he drew back entirely satisfied.

"What's this, doc? Why every twenty years? Why must you win tonight? Experiment or fact?"

"Fact," answered the doctor, "fact. I win for luck; luck always goes with the winner. You lead."

Again we went to playing; but in the intervals of play I began, absently, like one merely passing time, to roll a newspaper which was lying on the table. You may think I was perturbed; but I was not at all; I was merely doing what my friend had advised—playing safe.

If I were going to see the thing through to the end, I calculated that perhaps a little help at the climax would be a thing most convenient. Of course, my mind was working. Hendricks had called the doctor a vampire. I had never seen one; but my imagination had pictured a thing vastly different from this.

During the silent moments I watched him—cool, clear-eyed, and kindly, his every movement an act of grace, his whole manner the embodiment of fascination. When he smiled the very atmosphere seemed to ripple, his clear eyes fairly danced with mirth and you felt a sort of infinite joy in the mere privilege of sharing their pleasure.

I had known him for many days—this man, and during all that time I had found him nothing but kindness and consideration, a companion, jolly at all times. As I studied him and watched him, my mind revolted at its own folly.

What a climax of things ridiculous to classify this man with a species of moral outcast, which mankind in its loathsome horror has refused a classification with either man or beast. Can you blame me for laying the paper back on the table? I had only folded it.

THE game continued, the doctor winning regularly and deriving an infinite joy therefrom; and I, with all I had on my mind, watching him intently for ever so small a sign that might signify or prove him to be anything but that to which he pretended.

The clock struck nine. It came all at once as clocks have a habit of doing when, in the silent hours, a clashing that seems to step right out of the wall seizes you by the throat, and startles you out of your marrow. We both started; but the doctor, I was sure, was really frightened.

He half rose in his chair, seized his watch in his left hand, and stood gazing from it to the clock in a sort of palsy. A look such as I never saw in a mortal came into his eyes; they fairly danced and glittered, and as he gazed at me bewildered, I would have sworn that they dissolved, and that I looked not into the eyes of one, but into those of a hundred.

Snap. The doctor closed his watch.

"My!" he sighed. "How that did startle me! I thought it was ten and I was too late. Let us have some wine."

He reached for the bell and pressed it energetically, almost savagely.

"Do you know, Mr. Robinson," he asked while we were waiting, "do you know what it means to me?"

"Naturally I do not," I replied. "You having never told me."

"Well, I'll tell you"—leaning back in his chair—"it means this: In an hour's time I shall be either alive or dead. If my experiment or fact, as I have called it, is a success you will see me a miracle, alive, young, strong, handsome, a being to marvel at and admire. If it should fail, you will witness the most abject and miserable death that ever has been or ever will be seen on this earth.

"In a few moments from that time I

shall begin to dwindle, to tumble, to struggle, to cry out; my pleading will ring in your ears for years to come; when you are dreaming and when you are waking you will see my fearful image; I shall be a horror and an abomination to you. In a few moments I shall be no larger than this inkstand, and I shall be growing smaller and smaller until at last I disappear—a mere speck of nothing forever and forever.

"But you, who are standing here—you will have seen an army, a strange fantom host, jabbering, incoherent, indistinct, a confusion of the ungodly with the godly —a babel of conflicting tongues, a struggling of opposing nationalities, a maelstrom of fantom hatred, with myself the center of it all, reviled, execrated, loathed, and despised. Their curses will ring in your ears for a lifetime.

"I will stand here alone; they will vanish; one by one they will step into a grave of shadows and disappear, and you will be left alone with nothing but a problem, the solution of which will baffle not only you, but your friends and assistants for all time."

He was quite cool now, and I could see that he was perfectly sane, although my firm faith in his manhood—the good old gentleman kind—began to flicker perceptibly.

"And it was for this," I asked, "that you employed me?"

"Exactly."

"You wished to make use of me?"

"Naturally. For what does one man hire another if it is not his services? You will help me in this crisis. It will be a triumph, a great one, for one or the other of us. In any case you will have beheld something to witness which there are many who would willingly pay a fortune."

The door opened and the housekeper brought in the wine and the glasses. I bowed to her and took the occasion to nonchalantly place the roll of paper in the window; the curtain was up and I was fairly sure that it could be seen from across the street. My action I was sure

was not noticed, for the doctor was pouring out the wine, while the woman was standing alongside the table watching him.

Evidently she was greatly excited, for I noticed that her hands trembled violently, while her face, so calm and healthy usually was ashy white, to which her lips drawn down at the corners as if from some load of anguish, gave that troubled and stricken look of one standing under an impending disaster.

"Mrs. Green"—it was the doctor who spoke—"do you know the day of the month?"

It was said in a cool, steady tone, but there was mockery in it indescribably; an indefinite taunting, tinctured with hatred and self-superiority.

The woman started and her hands clenched; a very storm of fury broke upon her. If the doctor had wished to goad her to madness, he had done it well and with but a sentence. Anyway, it seemed to please him, for he smiled sweetly while she broke upon him.

"You!" she shouted as she leveled her trembling, accusing finger. "You! You liar! You murderer! You dog! You know I know! And you dare ask me! What day is it! What day of the month is it! Yes, ask, when you know so well! It is the twentieth of September, that it is! Your anniversary! Your celebration of crime—of murder!

"Where is Allen Doreen? Down in your black, black, dirty, warped, crime-bespattered soul you are gloating over a murder this very night! Where is Allen Doreen? Was I not with you twenty years ago when you murdered that poor, innocent lad? And because I did not witness the actual deed, do you suppose for an instant that I doubted your guilt?

"I am your housekeeper now and I was your housekepeer then, though you little knew it when you engaged me six months ago! Why did you hire Allen Doreen? Why did you pay him fabulous sums to do merely nothing? What became of him? What did you do with him? Answer me that! Why have you this man here? Sir," she continued, turning to me, "unless you take my advice and leave this house at once, you will never see daylight again."

"Mrs. Green! This is enough! Enough!"

And before I could interfere he had seized her by the arms and ejected her from the room, turning the key in the door as he did so!

CHAPTER V

THE VAMPIRE

HE WAS a man of quick action, and it was done in a twinkling, almost before I could think.

But the scene had decided me.

The picture of the old woman standing there in the lamplight, her face ashen, her eyes flashing, and her accusing finger speaking as loudly as her tongue, will ever live in my memory.

And I can see the doctor still, sitting there with the wine-filled glasses, smiling cynically, egging her on with his mocking, taunting laugh.

I would have rolled a second paper and brought Hendricks and his men thundering through the door, but for a thought. I was morally sure that this man was a murderer, and I was just as certain that he was contemplating another crime this night, with myself for the victim.

But what was the proof?

I had none; only an old woman's word, and that had all been before the law already. I could not call Hendricks yet. If I were afraid, I could walk out of the door. The doctor could not stop me. But I was not afraid. No, there was but one thing to do—to wait. When the time came I would throttle him with my thumb and finger just to show Hendricks; and then call in my friends.

The doctor was in an apologetic mood, though I noticed that he put the key in his pocket. Not that I cared, for I considered myself enough of his master to take it away from him whenever needed, only I noticed it.

"You mustn't mind her," he said. "Mrs. Green is a good old soul, only a little erratic, that's all." He pointed to his fore-head to signify her fault. "She has them once in a while. She lost a dear friend once; but the poor old soul has a haunting idea, of which I can never rid her, that I was the cause of his disappearance. She has been my housekeeper for years. She is splendid. Let us get back to our game."

Once again we sat down, sipping the wine and playing cards. The clock above was slowly ticking toward the fatal ten, and the doctor was having all the luck. I was very curious and expectant; but kept a cool head, watching every movement of my companion.

What were his plans? What his treachery? What his preparations? I could see none, only his everlasting playing.

He seemed superbly confident, humming a low tune, and smiling as buoyantly as a boy of twelve. There was surely something in the air; but try as I might, I could make nothing out of it. I waited.

It was half past nine—twenty minutes of the hour; the room was hot and stuffy, and I began to feel nervous. I had no fear, and, having none, I tried to laugh at myself for giving way to nerves. In spite of all my efforts, I felt myself slipping, a great lump came in my throat which I could not down, and I could hear my heart thumping against my ribs, pulsating so loudly that I was rather surprised that the doctor did not notice it.

Fifteen minutes to ten. I was watching keenly.

"At your first move, old man, I will strangle you," I said to myself.

But the doctor did not move. Instead he kept on playing, calm, happy, and in perfect good humor. His very coolness nettled me; from dislike I was rapidly running into hatred. My hands shook with desire for action. If he were a vampire, I wanted to know it, and to know it quickly!

Why this everlasting delay and these infernal cards?

I was cutting, when the first sign came, and I shall never forget it.

It was a sensation, a feeling I wish

never again to experience. For the first time I knew that I was playing with a power behind the conception of man; that I was eating with the devil and was using a short spoon. It was like a wave; my courage vanished and my confidence was gone. When I looked up the doctor was peering at me.

Lord, what eyes! Cavernous, flaming with the most unholy light of ages! With a cry of horror I dropped the cards.

The doctor said not a word; his whole body seemed to shrivel and become head and that in turn to transform and disintegrate and to slowly reform and grow into eyes, immense and terrible, two great green fires, consuming, devouring, unearthly.

What was it! What was it! A scream!

The eyes vanished; the doctor was sitting there before me. Yes, it was a scream; a woman's scream. How good it seemed! A door slammed across the street; there was a scurrying of feet. I was myself. I seized the second roll and started for the window.

"Put down that paper!"

It was the doctor who spoke. The clock stood two minutes to ten.

"Put down that paper!"

I laughed.

"I'll do nothing of the sort! Stop me if you can!"

In a flash he was at me. Here I knew myself his master. Arms outstretched he made for me and I could not help laughing at his awkwardness. Timing him to a dot, I let drive my left. It was a well-directed blow, and I knew it for a knockout. He was coming head on when my blow landed.

Landed! Say, rather, entered, for my fist entered his jaw like so much mist, passed through his head and out the other side.

Unable to believe my senses, I shot out my right. It passed clean through him. I could see my fist out of his back.

With a cry of horror I sprang out of his reach. I could hear voices; someone was forcing the front door.

"Hendricks! Hendricks!" I screamed.

The old man was after me like a demon.

"Aye, Hendricks!" he mocked. "Hendricks! I fooled the father and I'll fool the son! Every twenty years I eat a man, and I'll eat you as I have the others! Give me that paper!"

He made a lunge, and before I could sidestep he had me. I struggled, but it was useless. It was like fighting with smoke. I knew I was gone; I was helpless. My friend was outside.

But he was too late.

HERE Robinson lit a cigar.

"Well," I asked, "what happened?"

He puffed for a moment.

"Hendricks will have to tell you the rest; my part is done. Go ahead, Hen, and give him the other part."

Hendricks took up the narrative as follows:

CHAPTER VI

WHAT HENDRICKS FOUND

WHEN Robinson left my office I was extremely puzzled.

My friend would do his best, and if the old fox caught him unawares, well, then, he was a slyer fox than I imagined.

Of the man himself I was morally certain. I returned to my desk and studied the picture over and over again. They were the same, barring only the difference in the style of the clothes, which, of course, counted for nothing.

There was one thing, and one thing only, which bothered me.

These two men were of the same age; yet this picture had been taken over twenty years before. Surely the living picture—the man himself—should have aged some in that length of time, or was he one of those upon whom years had no effect and whom advancing age always finds at middle age, stationary, healthy, and belying their own looks?

The telephone rang.

"Hello! Hello! Who is it?"

"Is this Mr. Hendricks?"

"It is. Who is this?"

"Brooks, at Rubic Avenue. We have had the house under surveillance ever since you detailed us. Mr. Robinson has just returned. The old lady—the housekeeper, the woman you mentioned—was just here. You are right, all right. She was mixed up with the Allen Doreen affair, and I think she will be our main witness. I want you to get out here and have a talk with her.

"And, by the way, the old lady says that this is the day, and we want to take no chances.

"She has gone back to the house just at present; she is mortally afraid of the doc, says that if he rang and found her gone he would surely kill her. When can you come?"

"Right away. I will be out there immediately."

In a few minutes I was on a car bound for Rubic Avenue.

My men I found in the house across the street, which they seemed to be making their headquarters. It was now five-thirty.

"Well," said I, "what news?"

"Not much of anything," said Smythe. "But we are awaiting the woman; she promised she would return as soon as you arrived, so we could settle all our plans. She says there is no danger until some time after nine, absolutely none, because the doctor, as she calls him, never works at his trade, or whatever you may call it, in the daytime.

"Brooks, who is on the watch, reports that Robinson and the doctor have just entered one of the front rooms upstairs, and, from the looks, are playing cards."

"Very likely," I answered. "Robinson, who has just left me, says that is their chief pastime."

Then I told them about my interview with Robinson and the plans we had laid.

"So, you see, our best tactics will be to wait and watch."

Well, sir, we waited.

About six came the old lady. She was terribly excited and very much worried; but beyond a recital of her former experience and the fact that she had heard the doctor mumbling, "The twentieth, the twentieth," several times during the past few days, I can't say that she had much information to impart. But on this one thing she was very sure and very much worked up.

"Oh, how glad I am that you men are here to help Mr. Robinson!" she said. "Only I'm afraid, terribly afraid. Perhaps you are not smart enough. Oh, he's clever; it will be just like him to do his work right in front of you, and you not be able to do a thing."

"He would have to be a devil to do that," said Smythe. "I suppose you know that the house is surrounded, and that nobody can leave it nor enter without at least ten eyes upon him."

"I know it, I know it," said the old lady. "But what's been done before can be done again. I tell you for myself I ain't afraid, he won't harm me; but I do care for this young man. He won't listen to me. Says he's not afraid and all that. But I tell you all quite frankly, the doctor's not human. No, sir, he's something else; when a man can do what he does, he's something, and that ain't man either." With that she left us.

There was a good deal in what she said, and I told them so; but Smythe shook his head.

"I've heard of this Doreen case before, Mr. Hendricks, read of it, and I have always said I would have liked to have been there. Now, here's our chance. We have Robinson over there, big and strong, athletic, no fool and no coward, and we have a bunch of men around us, all of them trained, all alert; and we have Mrs. Green there in the house with them, and a code of signals. Everything is in our favor. We can catch the old fox red-handed, save Robinson, and clear up the Doreen mystery, and all at the same time."

WE ALL of us settled down now to our vigil. From our vantage ground of an upper room we could look across into the room where, sure enough, sat Robinson and the doctor, both apparently enjoying a friendly game of cards. It was not too close nor yet so far but that we could make them out quite plainly; the curtains were open and, of course, a great deal of the room was in our plain view.

Well, nothing happened. The minutes drew into hours, and as the first excitement wore away the time began to grow lazy. I began to get sleepy. I think it was some time after nine when Brooks nudged me.

"Look! Look! What's Robinson doing?"

Across the street I could see Rob. He was rolling up a paper.

"Was it one or two?"

I got up; but he seemed to laugh and lay it down again, and to resume his playing. Nothing more happened for about a quarter of an hour; then suddenly the old man started from his chair, pressed his hand to his forehead, and in a startled way began to talk to his companion. A few moments later, after he had resumed his seat, the door opened, and we could see the old man and the old woman shaking their fists angrily at each other—at least the old woman shook hers. Then it was that Rob put the paper in the window.

"Ah!" exclaimed Brooks. "Now there is something doing over yonder! What'll we do?"

"Beginning to be interesting," I answered, getting up. "You stay here, Brooks, while I get the men together. Keep a close lookout. If Bob gives the other signal or if you see anything suspicious, be sure and signal to us, and we will break in immediately."

Below I gathered up the men, placed two at the back, two at the sides, and kept with me two others. Every inch of the house was to be watched. The light was at the window, and the house was silent. For some time we waited; but there was only the thumping of our hearts and the everlasting pulsating throb of the city night. After a little a window was raised, and I heard Brooks' voice.

"Hendricks," he said coolly, "now is your time. Enter quietly and make your way up to the room. You'll have your man easy enough."

I had just reached the steps when a woman screamed, and a frightened, fearful cry it was, to be sure. And then, running and almost falling, I could hear someone coming down the stairs.

With a cry we made for the door; but at the same instant the housekeeper opened it, slammed it, and stood before us. She was white and trembling.

"Oh," she cried, "for goodness sake, hurry! Hurry! It's the devil! Sure, sure it's the devil!"

"Woman," I almost shrieked, "look what you have done! We are locked out!"

"Burst it! Burst it open!" came an order behind.

It was Brooks.

"Hendricks! Get in there! Get in there!"

With the force of two hundred pounds he landed against the door, and in a minute we rolled, men, door, locks, and all, a heap on the floor. The woman screamed again, and above everything I could hear a voice familiar and distinct. It was Rob.

At a bound I threw myself to my feet and dashed up the stairs. A light was streaming beneath the door, and there was a peculiar noise coming from the inside, a sort of chuckle. Brooks passed me, and both together we landed against the door. It was locked; we knew that, so we sent it crashing to the floor.

The room was empty!

CHAPTER VII

VISITOR OR VISITATION

WE WERE baffled, defeated! I had been laughed at to my face! My best friend was gone!

A sort of haze came over me, and for the next few minutes I remember almost nothing. Then I noticed the blaze of light, the cards about the table, the empty wine glasses and bottles, and the soft green carpet, while I could see Brooks dashing about the room, stamping on the floor, pounding the walls, and swearing a great, copious string of heavy oaths.

"You below, there!" he shouted. "Are those men here yet? Well, hold tight! Don't let an inch of this house escape you! I'm going to comb over it with a fine-tooth comb! And if we don't get him, I'll know he's the devil!"

"And that's what I think he is," said I. "I could have sworn I heard him when I reached this door!"

"And I, too," returned Brooks. "Yet here we are, and there is neither hide nor hair of him!"

But however much my detective friend agreed with me, he would not, as he said, allow superstition and mystic fear to get the better of him; and now, while he had a hand in the game and the thing was warm, he was going to see the house from top to bottom, attic, cellar, and sideways.

Keen over our lost prey, we set to work, and I do not believe there was a house searched as this one. With the help from headquarters, we went at it from every corner.

Everything was ransacked, rummaged, burst open, examined; walls were thumped, floors pounded, ceilings tested, and carpets torn up. But it all ended as I had foreseen.

When gray dawn struck, it found a house much like one stricken by an earthquake or a whirlwind, but never a clue that would lead us anywhere at all. Of course, I was heart-broken over Rob, and I swore by everything that I knew that I would never leave off the trail until I had either rescued or avenged him. Nor was I alone.

Brooks, with all his great confidence and splendid nonchalance of a few hours before, was a thing to look at. Truly he reminded me of a bloodhound chasing his tail. With all his skill and technique he was getting nowhere. When daylight came he threw up his hands.

"I tell you, Hendricks, this is not a case; it is a study, and I must have time to think. Likewise"—remembering himself —"I must eat. But I tell you one thing; I will never leave this case until either I or the doctor get each other."

Anyway, we ate. And afterward we re-turned and began our search all over again. And we kept it up day in and day out, and to be doubly sure, we rented the place and moved into it. And we watched and waited, while the days grew into months, and the months into years, until I found myself five years older with a great practice and a greater mystery.

I HAD attained by hard, grinding work, I think, a very credible place in the legal world. I was not married, and was living with Brooks in the House of Mystery, as he chose to call it.

We kept a housekeeper—none other than the old Mrs. Green, who had held the same position under our spooky friend the notorious Dr. Runson, for whom the police of every city of the world were looking and not finding.

There was one great, permeating idea in the house; find the doctor, avenge Robinson, and clear up the Doreen mystery.

Brooks worked on the case as one who would work on a puzzle. He was always ready; had had the police oiled and ready, prepared at any moment to reach out and grasp its victim.

Then one night we received a sign.

At the time we had moved into the house I had chosen a nice cozy room to the rear, and would have made that my sleeping quarters had it not been for Brooks, who expostulated in the loudest manner.

"There is but one room in the whole house, Hendricks," he said, "in which we can sleep, and that is the little room up yonder to the front, where this little scene took place a few weeks back, and there we'll stay."

I remember plainly. It was in September. I had been out to a social affair, and did not get in until about eleven o'clock. When I turned on the light, Brooks was snoring loudly, his head back and his mouth wide open, as though he were enjoying it. I crawled into bed with him.

How long I slept I do not know; but when I awoke some time after with a start, it was to find Brooks, or at least I thought it was he, sitting on my feet. Like any sleepy person, I became angry.

"Hey, you! Gee whiz! Brooks, get off my feet!"

Someone at my side turned, and I saw it was Brooks.

"What's the matter with you?" he said. "I'm not on your feet. Got a nightmare?"

But I was not asleep, and I knew it. There was surely something on my feet, so I raised up and looked. Sure enough, seated there in the moonlight was the form of a man.

It was Robinson!

For a moment I was dazed, my heart jumping and my throat swollen.

"Don't you know me, old boy?" it said.

Hardly believing my own eyes, nor my ears either, I dropped back on the pillow and lay thinking. Finally I reached over and pinched Brooks, who was almost awake.

"What's the matter?"

"Do you see anything?"

"Where?"

"At the foot of the bed. On my feet."

"Pooh!"

With an air of disgust and distrust, my bedfellow raised himself and immediately dropped back on the pillow.

"Who—who is it?" he whispered.

The sound of his voice, and the fact that he, as well as I, could see some one, reassured me; for, though I am hardly afraid of flesh and blood in the real personal form, I, like most other people, have only a creepy sympathy with an apparition. That Brooks had seen and recognized was an assurance I needed, for I must say I was in a cold sweat of fear and apprehension. I raised myself to a sitting posture.

"Well?"

It was Rob who spoke, and it was the old voice.

"Is this really you, Rob," I asked doubtfully, "or just something else?"

He laughed.

"You think me a ghost, don't you, Hen? Well, to tell you the truth, I am, almost; at least, as near one as a man could get."

"Then—then you are not dead, Rob?"

"No," he answered, "I'm not dead, nor alive either, for that matter."

He got up and walked about the room, and I noticed that his walk was ghostlike, no noise, absolute silence, and he nearly six feet and one hundred and eighty pounds.

"Look here, Hendricks." He stopped to look at the clock. "I've got but a few moments to spare. It was only by superhuman struggle that I am here; only by a terrific battle of the will that I am with you; and at any moment, any second, I may leave you. I came to help you, to encourage you. Keep up your search, and some day you will be rewarded.

"I will help you. I am not dead. Far from it; I may live forever. Keep your eyes open at all times and watch personalities. I will try to lead them your way. Only be prepared when the time comes. You were right about the doctor. He was a vampire. I found out when it was too late. If you watch and work hard enough, I will have a chance to die even yet."

He stopped beside the bed and looked at me longingly, his eyes filled with a yearning that was piteous. My mind was in a whirl, and my heart was beating like a trip-hammer; but in the midst of it all I had presence enough to analyze his features. The eyes were the same; the hair, the jaw, and the peculiar expression of the mouth were all his; beyond a doubt it was Robinson.

I remember the wild joy that surged through me at the certainty. I reached up to grasp him, but he drew back.

"Don't, Hen! Don't! Not now!"

He drew back; for, not to be denied, I had sprung out of the bed and was pursuing him with outstretched hands.

"Stop!"

But I would not. Instead, I followed him across the room with my hands reaching out for him.

"Well, then, if you must have it! Goodby!"

There was a good deal of the defiant in the words, and yet a world of misery. And with that he disappeared, vanished through the solid wall as though it were the open air.

CHAPTER VIII

PANDORA'S BOX

OF COURSE, we dressed and began a most thorough examination. The doors were locked, the windows fastened, and everything was found in its accustomed place. We could get no satisfaction; there was no solution but one; and as I was no believer in ghosts or their workings, I was loath to accept it.

Still, what other solution could we give? It was either that, or we had, both of us, been the victims of a huge hallucination, and we were, both of us, too much awake, and had altogether too much pride and confidence in our own intelligence to admit that we could drift off into a state so bordering on the insane as that. How, then, were we to account for it? I admit I tossed up my hands. It was too much for me.

If Rob was not dead, and he said he wasn't, how had he gained entrance to our room? Surely none but a fantom could have done that, and no one mortal could have vanished in such a complete and marvelous manner. Furthermore, if alive, what reason had he for keeping himself hidden, especially from his best friend, myself, whose help he needed, and from whom he had just now sought assistance?

I could see none. But one thing I did do. I cursed the impatient haste and unreason with which I had just acted. Had it not been for my own foolishness and lack of tact, we might have had a few good practical clues on which to work. Rob must have had something to impart, or he would never have paid us this visit, and so I reasoned with Brooks.

"Pshaw!" said my friend. "The man was murdered. That's plain as day. Who did it is the goal. The case has just begun, but I'm going to solve it, believe me. Meantime, I'm going back to bed."

Going to bed and going to sleep were two different things; so we spent the rest of the night in argument and in the consuming of innumerable cigars. And when the morning broke and the gray light of dawn streamed through the windows, it found two men with two different views. I for the living, and he for the dead.

Which of us was right you shall see for yourself.

I WAS engaged on the Huxly case, with which you and everybody else who reads the papers must be familiar. As I have said, I had risen not a little in my profession; my practice was large, my reputation established, and, best of all, I had the name of getting most anything I went after.

At the same time, I was on a dead level with myself, and knew my limitations, even though I did not let others into the secret.

The Huxley case, you will remember, was one of those paradises for attorneys, a sea of legal entanglements wherein they could swim about to their hearts' content, breathing law, living law, sleeping law, with no way out, no exit, no escape.

I was working night and day. It was the climax of my legal career. If I won I was made, and I was going to win.

One day, while deep in the Huxly case, I had ordered my lunch and was looking over a local paper; there was not much in it, so I was running over the market reports. I don't know how to account for it, but I have always said that the great and important changes of life are prone to come upon us suddenly and unexpectedly.

And although I have always made it a habit to watch the turning up of things, as it were, it has ever been my fortune to be caught like a drowsy sentinel, asleep at the post. How little was I aware at this moment. Everything was in the routine. The world was running smoothly; so much so, in fact, that I had to satisfy my craving for excitement with market reports.

It may have been the print, or it may have been anything. I'm sure I don't know exactly. But, anyway, when I was half through the page my eyes failed me and the whole thing blurred.

"Merely a case of nerves," you say. Perhaps so. That's what I thought. I closed my eyes and pressed my fingers against the eyballs. The pressure brought relief for an instant, and I began rubbing them. A flickering and flashing of lights clamored with myriad tattoo across my brain, and my head swam. I opened my eyes again and reached for a glass of water. The paper was still in my hand; but it was an inky black, the light of absolute nothingness, and clean across it, in plain white letters, was the word:

R O B I N S O N

"Premonition," you say. Perhaps it was. Anyway, it startled me. The moment those letters were indelible in my mind, the room cleared and my vision returned. Half startled, I looked about me.

Everything was as before; if anything had happened, nobody had noticed it. It was the same prosaic, hungry crowd, and there was the usual sound of eating, of dishes and spoons, and the quiet, soft step, step, step of flitting waiters.

Nevertheless, I was a perfect tingle of excitement; my hands shook and my heart seemed to swell up within me, to fill my throat and choke me with anticipation. Something was surely going to happen. Carefully I studied everybody in the room. Then I turned clear about and looked at the door. There it was.

It was Rob!

He was standing just inside of the door, his soft hat slouched over his eye and his empty pipe in his hand. I could see the cashier speaking to him, but he shook his head. Evidently he was looking for someone. I had half risen from my seat when our eyes met; he smiled and came quickly down the aisle. How I watched him!

"Rob, Rob, Rob," I said to myself, keeping time with his step as he came toward me. Then hesitation. The resemblance began to glimmer and fade away. The nearer he approached the less he looked like Rob. Could it really be he? How my wild hope rose and fell! When he was quite up to me I saw I was mistaken, and that he was an absolute stranger.

"Pardon me," he said, "but were you expecting me? If you don't mind, I will sit opposite you. You seemed to know me."

Know him! On closer view he seemed strangely familiar, very much like another; there was a difference and a resemblance which, added together, was indeed a puzzle.

"Your face," said I, "reminded me strangely. I took you for some one—a very old friend. And yet it could not be. I see I am wrong."

"Why?"

He looked up from the table with a strange, querulous smile.

"Why couldn't it be? Who is this person?"

A thought struck me.

"Your name is not Robinson?"

He sobered down in an instant, and began arranging his knife and fork beside his plate.

"No," he said, eying his dish; "just Jones. Ebenezer Jones. Fine name that! But suppose my name were Robinson? What would it signify?"

"What would it signify?" I repeated. "Just this. If your name were Robinson and you were the real person, whom you greatly resemble, there would be a mystery solved."

"Ha!"

My companion dropped his fork and looked up.

"What's this?" he asked. "A mystery— a real, genuine, live mystery! Have you one, sure enough? Let's have it. That's my line exactly. It's food and drink to me."

He waited; and before I knew it I was telling him what you already know. I don't know why I should have told it there in the restaurant; but from the first he seemed to have a power over me, and through it all I had that fluttering sensation and my heart kept beating "something will happen, something will happen."

"Splendid!" he exclaimed when I was through. "And have you this picture of the doctor and a picture of Robinson?"

"In my office. Yes."

"May I see them?"

"Certainly."

"Well, I would be much obliged to you. This interests me deeply. We shall go up after we eat."

In another half hour we were examining the photos.

"So this is Robinson, and this is Dr. Runson? Eh? Might have been twins but for thirty years or so. Eh! Well, I tell you, Mr. Hendricks, you needn't worry. In less than six months you will know all about it. No? You don't believe it? Well, well! Wait and see. I have a strange power, and what I say generally comes true. Even if my name is just plain Ebenezer Jones. Now, Mr. Hendricks, I have a proposition to make. How would you like a business associate?"

He staggered me.

"Well, an assistant if you will. Call me anything you like. I will name my own terms. Salary, nothing, and as much work as you can get out of me."

I was taken back.

"Know anything about the law?"

He laughed and his eyes fairly danced with amusement. The chief justice could not have been more amused at the question.

"Just give me a trial is all I ask. I want to stay in this office until this mystery is solved; and while I'm here I want something to do. You'll find it to your advantage. I know something about law and then some. Even though my name may be just plain Ebenezer Jones."

WELL, to make the matter short, I took him in.

It was a rather sudden and strange thing to do on such a short acquaintance. I was a little surprised at myself at first, but soon found that I had made no mistake. Indeed, before many days I was shaking hands with myself.

Ebenezer settled into my office with an ease and a confidence that could only come from ability and energy; and he tore into cases with a vim that was irresistible. I had asked him whether he knew anything about the law. I was soon laughing at myself.

Was there anything about the law that he didn't know! That fellow was a veritable encyclopedia. He seemed to have it all in his head. He became the brains of the office. I might well enough have burned my books. I began asking questions, and soon quit referring to my library. I found it was useless; all I got was a verification of his statements.

Naturally I prospered. We won the Huxly case hands down, although I knew it was Ebenezer's brain and not mine that did it.

Still, I got the credit, so I had no kick coming. Other cases came our way. We won them all. It was so easy that it was amazing. I congratulated both myself and him.

"Fudge," he said. "It's nothing. There's nothing to the law but the knowing."

And I guess he was right. Anyway I was in high spirits. My reputation was bounding up. I became a boy again. Success breeds dreams; I could see great pictures ahead, if I could keep this genius at work; I would be chief justice!

The mystery?

It had grown so old that I was beginning to despair of it. I had, to be sure, a restless feeling, a sort of nervous certainty that it would be cleared up some day; but I had become so used to waiting that it had become a sort of habit; I was helpless and could do nothing, and there was only hope. Of one thing I was certain—Robinson would show up some day, somehow; a sort of subconscious wisdom seemed to tell me that.

Was it the mystery that held Ebenezer? It must have been; though what he was going to gain by sitting in my office, or how he was going to solve it by doing nothing, I could not make out. There was only one clue, and that was his resemblance to Rob. When I questioned him about it he always laughed.

"If I were Rob, I think you would know it, Hendricks. No, no, boy, you're on the wrong track." Then, after a while, after a good many minutes of silence and thinking: "You'll have to wait, old boy. Only, I tell you, things may happen, and when they do, keep your wits about you."

But nothing happened in spite of his words.

Days wore into weeks and weeks into months, and we dug into the laws. Ebenezer was at it early and late; and I did my best to keep up with him. I offered him a partnership, but he refused it. When I tried to have a moneyed understanding he laughed at me.

"I have so much of that stuff that it nauseates me. I prefer to work for nothing and see what turns up."

He had no bad habits that I could notice, and I watched him closely. He always brought a bottle of port wine with him and drank it all during the day; that is, what I did not help him with. Also he smoked occasionally; only it was an old, seedy pipe, such as you would expect an Ebenezer Jones to smoke.

There was only one thing in his habits or possessions that could arouse my curiosity; that was a small case which he always carried with him; it was not more than three inches square and could be conveniently carried in his pocket. The first thing he did on entering the office was to lock this in his desk. And when he left at night it went with him without fail. Once he opened it quite accidentally, and I noticed with surprise that it contained two small bottles, both of them full of a liquid, and that the color was of port wine.

They say it was Pandora who opened the box. Of a certainty that mythical young lady was an ancestor of mine. I can understand her feelings exactly; they must have been tantalizing. Something told me I must open that box. Of course I revolted against the feeling; I fought it fiercely; all the ethics of my nature and training warned me and pleaded with me.

It was no use. There was still that feeling, perverse and ever there. My fingers itched, and my heart yearned for that case.

Why I should have had it I could not

tell; it was a freak of my own nature or the hand of Fate. My lower self seemed bound to triumph in this one case, although my manhood and integrity kept saying: "No, no; thou shalt not."

"After all, what did it amount to?" I would repeat. "Merely a case and two bottles. Examine them and return them; no one will be harmed, and you will be satisfied."

Well, it went on that way for a good many days, and all the time I felt myself growing weaker. It was a trivial thing in itself; but the fight I put up against it made it, with me, a matter of some magnitude.

At length I came to it. I resolved to examine the case and in this way relieve myself of this everlasting torment. It was a simple thing in itself, and were it not for its strange aftermath I would soon have forgotten it.

CHAPTER IX

TWO DROPS!

EBENEZER had stepped out of the office for a few minutes, leaving his desk unlocked. It was quickly done. I stepped over to his desk, drew out the drawer, and took therefrom the little case of mystery.

A slight pressure and the thing flew open, disclosing the two small bottles I knew it to contain. I remember wondering why the two bottles instead of one inasmuch as they contained the same liquid. But did they?

Perhaps they only looked alike. To satisfy myself I picked up one of the bottles, opened it, and smelled. It had absolutely no odor, and of course I dared not taste it. It was full to the overflowing, and as my hand trembled somewhat, a drop fell on the wine-glass that was resting on the desk. I replaced the cork and was about to open the other bottle when footsteps in the hall—Ebenezer's feet—put a speedy end to my investigation.

In a minute I had closed the case and resumed the seat at my own desk.

"Hello," said Ebenezer.

He placed his hat upon the desk and, taking the wine-glass, poured himself a large drink. Then in horror I recalled the spilled drop.

"Horrors! What is—"

No use for more; it was done.

At first he stood stark still, his hand raising wonderingly to his head and his eyes questioning; then his frame shook and his color began to change, first to a yellow, then to a dark green. He was the most uncanny thing I ever looked at, a being dropped from another planet.

"Mercy!" he exclaimed. "It is done!"

Then with a furious haste he tore open the desk and seized the case and vanished into the dressing-room. I could hear the lock crash as he turned the key. Then he fell; but he must have risen immediately, for I could hear someone walking. Then a voice—no, a cry, and how it rang!

"In the name of Heaven, Hendricks, open the door! It is I—Rob! Oh, before it is too late! Hurry, hurry, break it down!"

With a cry of fury I flung myself at the door. It held.

"Hurry, hurry!" came the despairing call from the other side. Then another voice cut in:

"Shut up and come here; I'm master yet."

Something fell, and then there was the tramping of many feet. A struggle seemed to be going on, and above it all the voice of men—not two nor three, but of a multitude. In the midst of my frantic haste I could hear it. Awful, excited, despairing, the incoherent shoutings of all nationalities. German, Greek, French, Italian. And above it all the voice of a master.

"This way; this way! There now; there now!"

In a perfect frenzy of haste I seized an implement and splintered the door and, as it fell back, sprang into the room.

It was empty.

No, not quite.

Ebenezer Jones was standing at the window watching the street below.

"Why," he smiled, "you must be in a hurry, Mr. Hendricks. Do you always enter a room in this manner?"

Shamefaced and abashed I stood there, puzzled, a fool shown up in the height of his folly. I was about to become a hero; I came crashing through the door ready to grapple with a multitude, and instead I was laughed at. Humbly I drew my handkerchief and mopped my face.

"Excuse me, Mr. Jones," I ventured; "but I—I surely heard strange noises in this room."

"Strange what?"

"Noises."

"Tut, tut, Hendricks." He came over to me and laid his great brawny paw on my shoulder. "What noises did you hear?"

"Why," I said, "I heard, or thought I heard, my dear old friend Robinson. He was calling to me right in this room, begging me to open the door. And there were others—lots of them. You had the door locked, so I smashed it down."

"I see you did," picking it up and placing it against the wall. "But you didn't find Rob, did you? Nor the others? Just plain old Ebenezer Jones!" He laughed and slapped me on the back. "Just plain old Ebenezer Jones. What do you know about that? Isn't it awful?" And he went off into a peal of laughter, and laughed and laughed and laughed. "Hendricks," he said, "you should have seen yourself come through that door. Oh, how funny it was. You should have been a soldier; you'd be a general!"

And that is how it ended; humiliated, shamed, and doubting, laughed at and half laughing at myself, I returned to work. But I had a feeling that after all I was right, and not such a big fool as Ebenezer Jones would have me believe. And the feeling grew. It was not long before it became a conviction, and conviction brought action.

I began to see the light.

EBENEZER went to work as though nothing had happened. So did I. But now, after the peculiar experience through which I had gone, I began to take a new interest in my strange companion. For hours I watched him wondering and figuring. From now on he was an enigma, and open question-mark.

I had taken him at first for a queer character, one of those strange personages of whom we have so many in our midst, who for a mere whim or for love of any kind of adventure will adapt themselves to any place or person in order to watch the course of events and be in on the denouement. That he had more than a curious interest in the disappearance of Rob I had not dreamed hitherto. I had taken him for what he looked, and now I felt myself deceived.

Once on a train of new thoughts I worked fast. Why his resemblance to Rob? Whence this almost uncanny knowledge of the law, this almost unhuman legal mind, which knew everything, and which cared so little for its rewards? Why his total dislike for money, society, and honor? Why, too—and I reasoned it over many, many times—the two small bottles?

And why — yes — the one bottle — one drop, the sudden effect, the noises, the multitude, and Rob?

It was not a nice feeling, to be sure; but just the same, far from being ashamed of what I had done, I was resolved on playing the same trick over again on the first opportunity.

From now on I watched and waited eagerly for the little packet of mystery. Once he took it from his pocket and was about to lay it on his desk when something diverted him, and he gave it a steady, studious look, something akin to wonderment, it seemed to me, and with a sudden strange motion snapped it back into his pocket.

Then he looked over at me. It was a strange look, something I could not understand; there was something of power and yet of a strange, terrible weakness.

Could it be that this man was a fiend? Ah, no! The answer came back with the same thought. Surely not.

Yet all through that day and several more that followed there was a strange feeling between us, and at times I could feel his eyes upon me, a most uncomfortable thing. I had the impression of being feared and watched by a wonderful, superior power; I don't know that there is anything more uncanny than that. With a weaker will you at least know that you are the master; but when a stronger begins to fear, the resultant fear that it engenders in you is so haunting and depressing that it becomes horrible.

Not that he was not the same Ebenezer. He was that, and he wasn't. The outward appearance and actions were the same; it was the psychological that changed. There was a shiftiness, a changing; the eye spoke a lie, and the personality seemed to be fluttering. I don't know of anything that could have moved me more or set me to thinking harder. There was fear, appeal, and terror in those eyes. I felt that I was being called on and that action was needed.

"Hallucination," say you?

So it seemed to me; but it was so real, so earnest, and I was so certain of it that nothing would have diverted me. What would I do, and how would I do it? There was that in those eyes which told me I could do something. I was convinced that the scene in the dressing-room was a reality, not a fantom of my own mind.

There were, there must have been many people in that room. It was Ebenezer's secret, and it should be mine. Show a man that which he can't have; and that he shall have. There was but one way—the bottles. I would try them again.

As I said, to all outward appearances Ebenezer was the same. He had the ability, the jovialness, the personality. It was only in the shifting individuality of the eyes with their appeal, their fear, and the resultant effects that he was at all different from the first Ebenezer that had entered my office.

His manners were the same, his talk and his application; he still drank his bottle of port, and he still went out for walks. Each morning he deposited the little case inside his desk, and every time as regularly as he went out, it went with him.

How I did watch that case! How I did

want to lay my hands on it! But there was no use; I could not take it away from him; I must work in secret.

One morning, a very momentous one to me, Ebenezer was late. He had a right, to be sure; for who has not when he works for nothing? However, he had always been so prompt before that I noticed with surprise this one slip of punctuality; and I was more surprised, nay, almost alarmed, when he jarred open the door.

There was an appearance of one who had been out all night; his eyes were bloodshot and his hair had a sort of stand-up-and-refuse-to-lie-down look, although it had been well flattened with the brush. In one hand he carried a bottle of port; in the other I noted with surprise the case.

Without noticing me—we were always very cordial with our greetings—he walked up to his desk more like a soldier than anything and deposited thereon the bottle and the case.

"There, now," he said, and without another word turned on his heel and marched out of the room.

A few moments later I saw him entering a building on the other side of the street. There was an act of finality about it that startled me; a sort of defiance that unnerved me.

Was it a challenge? Anyway, there was the case.

WITH a feverishness that was a mixture of fear, hope, and eagerness I pressed open the cover. There they were, the two of them. Small, small receptacles of mystery: What did they not contain?

My hand trembled and my mind blurred. Here was one of the mysteries of the world; a secret of many things.

And I—I must see, must hear, and must know. I held them up and examined them.

"Ah," I muttered, as by inspiration, "the dose and the antidote. Ebenezer, this is your Waterloo. See." I almost laughed with glee. "One drop raised hell. Two drops will raise more hell." I poured two drops in his glass. "So. And now, old boy, I'll say checkmate."

With this I took out the other bottle and placed it in my pocket. Then I replaced the first bottle and put the case where I had found it. When all was ready I returned to my desk and took up my work.

What a difference there was. On the former occasion I was all excitement and guilt; I felt I had committed a crime and was ashamed of myself. I had lost all honor and self-respect. And now, although excited, I had a feeling of triumph, of certainty, of right. I was dead sure. I was the instrument of Providence. And I remembered Ebenezer's own words.

"Things may happen; and when they do, keep your wits about you."

Well, I had them about me, now. Also, I had a hammer to batter down the door if necessary.

After what seemed an age, Ebenezer returned.

"Well," he said, "how's things?"

"Fine," I answered.

"That's good. Same here. Was out late last night; first time for a long while."

"Theater?" I asked.

"Oh, no. Just going around. Made me sleep late, though. Actually, I thought this morning I could sleep for a hundred years. Have some?" He produced his bottle and poured himself a good drink.

"Not this morning."

I was hoping he would not insist.

"Well, here goes."

He held it up, eyed it for a moment, and then drank it at a gulp.

"So," I said, and raised from my seat. "So!"

It was just as I expected. He turned sickly and was powerless. The two drops had done the business His eyes were—Heavens, what eyes they were! The most unholy thing I had ever gazed into—cavernous, burning—defiant; the eyes of a lost soul at the bar of judgment. He raised his hands to the sides of his head.

"At last!" he said. "At last!"

And, oh, the finality of those four words; the despair!

Then, with furious haste, he tore open

his desk. Like a fleeting thing his hand went around the drawers. It was not there!

"Good Heavens!" he murmured, drawing back. "This is murder!"

And in a flash of thought he was in the dressing-room.

CHAPTER X

AZEV AVEC!

"HENDRICKS!"

The cry came out. Rob's voice! Something fell.

A terrific struggle was going on; all hell seemed to be breaking loose. I made for the door with the speed of fury. It seemed an age. From inside came the old voice, the master's voice, and it said:

"I'll kill you!"

And, oh, the struggle! There were blows and hate, and above all the screaming staccato of many tongues. Hatred, despair, revenge.

Bang!

I let the door have it right in the center. It shivered and caved, the middle part demolished. Bang! I struck at the hinges. With a crash it fell to the floor, and over it I sprang into the room.

As I live I shall never see it again! The room was full of humanity. Naked and struggling they were rolled into an inextricable mass. There was hissing and gnashing of teeth. And in the center in the midst of it all was a horrible thing. It was battling the multitude. Such a struggle I had never seen before. It heaved, fought, shoved, and struck, and still they came on. If it were not master it was giving a good account of itself.

Suddenly, by a gigantic effort, it raised itself up, flung back its assailants like so many flies, and made straight for me. Two eyes—a monstrous thing.

"You!" it hissed.

With a cry of horror I backed against the wall. Its hand touched me and I felt my body grow cold as ice.

"Not yet!"

A form flashed between us and a hand grasped its throat. It was Robinson.

"Back, Hen! Back! As you value your life, back!"

Then he sailed into it. Their forms buckled together, heaved and tossed into the air. They passed in and out of each other like mist. The others came to help, but their actions were slow and aged.

Such a struggle I shall never see again. I can see myself yet, crouched against the wall watching that battle of fantoms. I was too bewildered to be afraid, too horrified to analyze. Like a dream I was passive, unable even to think.

Suddenly there was a heaving and tossing, and the form of Rob shot into the air. He and the thing were locked together. When they came down Rob was on top. The battle was over. The thing lay still, Rob backed away.

"Behold the end of Azev Avec."

It shuddered and rolled over and lifted up its head. I saw it was akin to a man, only black and terribly aged. It seemed to be shriveling. From its ghastly mouth came a sound.

"Robinson," it said.

Rob stepped closer and then knelt down.

"What is it, Azev?" And his face grew kind and pitiful. One could see that if he had any resentment it was buried in pity for what had to be done.

"Goodby, Robinson. You win. You were too strong. All's yours now. I should have picked someone with a weaker will. It was a great fight. No resentment, no hard feeling. Live ten thousand years! Almost immortal!"

All the time his form was shriveling and his voice growing fainter.

"There now," said Rob, drawing away. "Doreen, come on."

From out of the mass of shadows stepped a form.

"Now then, Hen, open the door and into your office. There, now."

We were alone. The three of us.

"Now, take that other bottle, pour two drops for me in port wine. There, now. Give it to me."

I held it to his lips and he drank it at a gulp. The effect was immediate and astonishing. His appearance lost its fantom shadowness, and he became real and human, a man of flesh and blood.

I almost danced with joy. I seized him by the hand and fairly blubbered with my happiness.

"And now give me the bottle."

He took it from me, and with a steady hand prepared a dose for his shadow friend.

"Behold us," said Rob, standing by the side of Doreen. "The two mysteries. The two solutions. Now let's look at the others."

He stepped to the dressing-room door and beckoned me. The room was empty.

"Where are they?" I asked.

"They were dead long ago," he answered. "Their minds and souls were alive. They were imprisoned and feeding on the body of Doreen and myself. Come into the office and I will tell you all.

"THERE, now," he said, when he had rested himself, "I will make it as short as I can, as Doreen and I both want clothes, and we both want to go out into the freedom of the street. Do you remember what you said about the doctor? You were right. He was a vampire. For ten thousand years he had been feeding on human flesh. His real name was Azev Avec. Dr. Runson was merely a composite—so was Ebenezer Jones.

"About ten thousand years ago, somewhere south of the Himalayas, Azev was born, the son of a high priest and an Indian princess his wife. His father was a man deeply immersed in magic or mysticism, or whatever you choose to call it, and held, in addition an almost uncanny knowledge of the natural laws. Among other things, he acquired a knowledge of solids; he early discovered, what we all know now, that no solid is really what the name implies; but a mass of infinitesimal particles held together in a single mass by two forces of nature, cohesion and adhesion.

"Knowledge like this was to a man of his nature and profession only an incentive for tremendous endeavor. The remainder of his life was spent with one object—the control of the particles of a solid, or to be precise, some means by which man might control and manipulate the forces of cohesion. He himself did not succeed; but on his death passed his work and knowledge on to his son Azev.

"Now, Azev added to his father's knowledge, a poetic foresight. He saw that, with this power, simply by increasing the

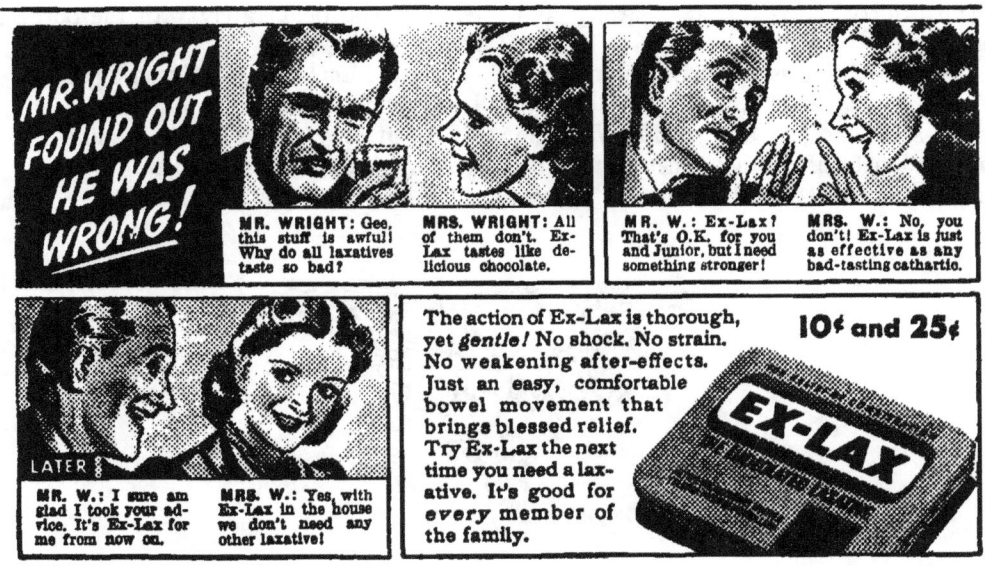

space between the particles, a solid would become a mist and that one could pass through fire, stone, or water without danger and with the same ease with which one swarm of gnats passes through another.

"He worked hard, and he succeeded; but when success came he found that he was an old man, and that life had passed without his enjoying any of its pleasures. The thought terrified him; he hated to die without at least one great splurge of pleasure. But to enjoy pleasure he must have youth, and that had passed long, long before. Then the devil spoke:

"If you have no youth, you can get it. Steal it. Of what use is all this learning and knowledge if you are going to die?"

"The idea appealed, and Azev looked around him. He selected a young man about twenty years of age, beautiful, strong and athletic, and invited him to supper. At a favorable moment he passed him the draft, and while his body was in the misty state entered and took possession. After taking the antidote their bodies became one.

"There were two minds; but Azev's was so much the stronger that the other soon became a negligible thing, a mere occasional whim. Thus was Faust antedated by about nine thousand eight hundred years. Azev found himself a young man again, thirty years of age, strong and healthy.

"A career of dissipation followed. In a few years the body was soft and flabby, so he stole another, and so on. When he was in danger of death he merely took on another form. It worked like a charm.

Sometimes he went in for dissipation, sometimes for learning, sometimes for wealth. He became probably the richest and most learned man on earth.

"He hobnobbed with kings and emperors. Alexander the Great sent for him on his death bed; and had he arrived in time the great Macedonian would never have died at thirty-three. Caesar was his friend: Virgil his confidant. He witnessed the birth of Christianity. He chummed with Nero, and by the lurid light of burning Christians saw the religion of Europe spring into its youth.

"Down through the ages he went, always enjoying himself, and always in someone else's body. He was the Merlin of King Arthur. He was the body servant of Barbarossa, and he alone of all the earth knew the sleeping-place of him of the long red beard.

"He stood a fair chance of living forever. There were but two chances against him, fatal accidents and the absorption of a will stronger than his own. So long as his will was the strongest he ruled the body. Allen Doreen was nearly his equal; I was slightly his superior. It took me five years of terrific struggle to gain any advantage at all. Then I warned you.

"Another struggle and I associated with you, placed opportunities in your way, tempted you deliberately with the bottles, and you fell.

"Here I am. I am Robinson again; but I am much more.

"All of Azev Avec's wealth is mine, likewise his learning and wisdom.

"Now get us some clothes."

Fruit of the Forbidden Tree

By LESLIE BURTON BLADES

Into the infinite they hurled their brains, to solve the ultimate mystery

I READ the scrawled note attached to a bulky manuscript that I had just received, with a sudden sense of disaster, vague and terrifying, for I knew these men well and I could not but accept the half-mad note as reality.

Carry has gone out, vanished utterly, and in a moment's time. I am alone in the laboratory among all the psychological apparatus with which we have experimented so long.

Would to Heaven we had never attempted this last mad project. But it is too late to regret, for he is gone. In the room a vibrant, unseen force, like an unbodied will, is forcing me to complete what I began.

When you receive this it will probably be over, but I want you to come to the laboratory, do what must be done, and give this report to the world. It is our last great contribution to science, and both Carry and myself desire it to be published.

As ever,

Davis.

Something had happened at the laboratory of my two friends, the great experimental psychologists, which had resulted in tragedy.

Hastily collecting the report, I called my car and drove at once to the laboratory as Davis had requested.

Save for the vast collection of experimental appliances for testing brain force, the books on the mind, a few disordered papers and its usual furniture, the place was empty.

I submit the report mailed me, without explanation. Nothing I can say will be of value and the document must speak for itself. What it declares is true. I knew both men and I have seen the laboratory where they ended their work. For the rest, psychologists must attempt explanations which a mere novice like myself could only clumsily propose. It follows:

REPORT OF EXPERIMENTS IN ANALYSIS OF THE COMPOSITION OF THE HUMAN SOUL
Experimental Psychologists, Davis and Carry
A. and S. Laboratory, February 3, 1939

The laboratory was heavy with cigar smoke and the big incandescent in the center of the table flared through the gloom, lighting Carry's face oddly as he sat opposite me.

"Davis," he said slowly through his veil of smoke, "we have succeeded in telepathy, we are skilled in hypnosis, and we have demonstrated the ability of consciousness to turn into itself and observe its own inner workings. Why not go on to an analysis of the human soul? We might discover its composition—the soul stuff."

I stared at him in amazement for I knew that his entire scientific career had been that of a materialistic psychologist who denied soul, asserting that the mind was a mere cooperation of living nerve and muscle cells.

"Of course you are surprised," he remarked casually for I had allowed him to read my thought telepathically. "I don't believe in the soul any more today than I ever did, but I am a scientist and therefore willing to assume its existence till we can test it."

"We can never do that," I asserted positively. I was always opposed to Carry's wild hypotheses. "That is the mystery which science cannot explain."

He smoked in silence for a moment, then I was allowed to see his mind. We rarely talked aloud at such times, preferring to communicate telepathically as a quicker and clearer method of understanding.

"You know," he was thinking, his lips closed around his cigar, "we have made larger leaps in our work before. This seems simple. We can go at it from our separate points of view. You believe that mind is an ethereal pure spirit in touch with the body by some non-material attachment. I don't; but we can accept your belief as a starter. I will go at it my way, you by yours."

"I do not see the method," I answered though my voice was silent.

"I will take the evolutionary view and go down into the remnant nerves of my spine and sympathetic system. They are after all the heritage of man from his beast ancestry and if I could get my consciousness into them I might discover what this life energy—soul if you like—really is."

"But to get down into them is not possible."

"I think it is. We could do this: You hypnotize me and direct my mind into them. I will report back telepathically what I find. I might descend clear into protozoan life, and if the mystery still operated I would go back of organic life, to the unknown—the beginning of life, God—and report findings through my body which would still be under your control."

THE proposal was stupendous with possibilities. If he succeeded, we would have discovered the origin and essence of life itself. With that knowledge man could mold soul in the future as easily as a present day biologist works with organic matter, bacteria and their activities, or as a chemist with material elements.

There was an obvious danger, however. If Carry got so far from his body he might be unable to return.

"I know," he said aloud, "I might go under, but it's worth risking."

"I don't believe that is the direction one would have to go. If the soul is analyzed it must be done by going up into forms of consciousness beyond—above the human."

"That is your part of the experiment," he replied. "You can attempt it and one of us will succeed. Which will it be?"

"Neither," I said shortly. "The risk is too great and I won't attempt it. There is my wife, you know."

He nodded appreciation, for single though he was, he was not without tenderness though one rarely saw it in his cold manner.

We dropped the subject there but it kept recurring over a period of two years; then my wife died.

Such a shock as her death was, can only be appreciated by those who have buried their life's love and are left childless to go on through desolate years.

For months I suffered in silence and during that time Carry's proposal kept recurring more and more vividly. I came to feel that should I succeed I might penetrate the spirit world and find her.

One night I became aware of her presence in my room. I could almost see her brown eyes looking at me and I was sure I heard her voice urging me to attempt the experiment Carry had proposed. Again and again that feeling came to me until at last I told Carry we would make the experiment he desired. That was a month ago. Tonight we have undertaken it and as dawn comes this report will end. With it our story will be completed and I will follow Carry.

Even as I write, here in this silent laboratory I am driven by mad emotion, a translated longing which is thrust into my very soul-center by some terrific force that makes the air quiver about me.

Dawn, and will I see it? Yes, but from what sphere I know not. While strength lasts I must write, however, for in that alone is there peace. In this report alone can either of us live henceforward. May the world find our work good.

At eight o'clock we locked the laboratory doors, drew the blinds and faced each other. I shall never forget the expression on Carry's face. His piercing eyes seemed already penetrating the veil that shrouds the spirit world. Above that bulging forehead that always suggested clifflike ruggedness of mind, his shock of black hair tipped with silver looked unusually rumpled. The firm thin lips upon which a smile so seldom appeared now curved in boyish anticipation as though he were in expectation of some great happiness.

"Davis," he said in a tone of eager delight, "tonight will go down in history and be forever memorable as the great time of scientific discovery."

"Yes," I answered, "and we will go with it if we live."

"What matter if we live or die? Man, we will be the same to the future. Come now, are you ready?"

He crossed to the large divan we had arranged in one corner, and sat down. Then, as if moved by a premonition, he looked around taking in every detail of the room that had framed his life work. Something in his eyes stirred me for I fancied I read a vague but certain knowledge in them that he was seeing it all for the last time; his books, the charts, our many instruments, and me.

"For Heaven's sake, Carry, don't look at me that way!" I realized as I spoke that I was nervous and agitated.

"Come on, Davis, let's begin," his even voice soothed me and he lay full length upon the divan.

"Before I hypnotize you"—I paused beside him—"what is it exactly you want me to do with your mind? I must be sure of what I am doing."

"Direct it into the unused nerve ganglia, set it to work there reliving the life in which that nerve was operative. Get its telepathic report of the experience. Keep it going down, down—till it passes out of nerve cells and is in cooperation with mere living protoplasm; and if need be, send it back of all life."

I met his unperturbed gaze. "Carry, old man, I'm afraid," I faltered brokenly. "There are things not even science in the interest of mankind dares touch, and the source of being—the origin of life, heretofore closed to our vision—is one. God is jealous of his mysteries."

"I am waiting, Davis."

Without a word we clasped hands and I sent him to sleep with the directions driven into his sleeping mind like a sharp wedge of my will. It was as though an invisible arm of my soul reached into his and held it fast that it might be drawn back from its wandering—but alas, the figure is sad. The sense of security it created is now a flaming reproach, yet I went on with the work and shall go on with it still, till I have found my friend again.

THERE was a moment of tense silence and my straining mind caught no word from the soul of that daring explorer. Then my name flashed before my consciousness. We had finally established telepathic communication.

"Davis," a long pause; then in a swift short thought, "We can do it! I am deep in my own spinal cord. Is my face altering? Look closely and tell me. I must know at once."

"No, why?" I studied his calm features so reposed.

"I am occupying what is left in my nerve organism of the first biped life of my ancestry. I felt that I must be taking on his—their squat forehead and pointed brute nose."

I took a pen and began to make notes as he went on. It might be of some little value to submit a few of his reporting phrases verbatim.

I shall do so, hoping that they may aid future psychologists.

NOTES

I have not time left before I follow Carry, to revise these notes, therefore I shall merely submit them as taken. Before his statements in italics I have placed his initials. All else is comment of my own upon my feelings as I listened.

C. I find I can roar like a gorilla. Not one, but some gigantic beast like it, you know. No soul as such. Abounding energy. Ha-ha-ha! Laugh for sheer joy in life. Life, a great swell of impulses, mainly interpreted as—love of blood, hunger, passion, fighting.

As I received this I was suddenly gripped by a terror, for in that thought-message a new guttural quality of speech-

form had appeared, slightly blurring the words. I felt in some way chilled as though I confronted a hairy savage thing that reached for me with great muscular arms, eyes bloodshot and merciless.

C. "That's it."

Carry's own thought answered my feeling.

C. You've got the picture. Good. No soul, only great strength of muscle flooded with life. Don't know what life means as such. Going on now.

I waited, pen in hand beside the still form of my friend. My heart beat regularly. I was taken with tendencies to shiver, and then out of the silence a terrific roar burst upon my brain. It was so vivid I started, thinking it actual sound but Carry's lips were closed and no sound had escaped them. I gripped the pen and waited. After a moment I got his thought. It came from what seemed infinite distance, fainter than usual, and more confused.

C. Davis—greatest feeling of power. Big as a house. Must be deep in old life-forms like Ichthysaurus, you know. Scaly and brutal, raging all over like a shivering savage. Blood mad but no soul. Not much sensitivity. Mere raging life-stirred flesh.

There was a silence here, then again:

C. Great heavens, feel as if I could crush your whole petty civilization under one hand—no, not hand, flipper, Davis—big steel-clawed flipper. No soul, though. Brain mighty small and coarse. Not much spinal cord but lot of energy. Energy seems to be the essence of life, not soul. Motion, that's it—lust for movement.

For fifteen minutes I waited spellbound in that laboratory. When I was almost in despair and reached to touch Carry's face that I might bring him to himself, I fancied that he called, or rather felt his thought as it reached me.

C. Pterodactyl. Flying on wide, feather-less wings. Immense heights. Teeth that clash together. Almost no brain and what a lust for extension of movement! Being itself becomes mere elaboration of motion. Flying, flying!

Of course I was familiar with these forms of which he spoke for it was necessarily part of my knowledge to understand the life history as geology reveals it, but that in no way reduced the sudden agony that sent my blood cold.

I became aware of a slight palpitation of the air in the laboratory as though unseen electric currents moved around me. A dim sensation of pain attacked my head, and vague impressions of a ruthless will opposing mine made me afraid. Was a stronger will, an unknown mind-force attempting to break my hold on Carry's mind far down in the dead past? I gritted my teeth and sent his name out with all brain power.

C. Here, I don't understand things. Mere glutinous mass of stuff, no nerves—life, yes, but vague, groping and not limited to organism. Mere life force everywhere among great masses of rolling protoplasm, water and blazing, burning heat. No eyes. No individuality—no thought. Not even instincts.

For Heaven's sake, tell me my body is real, alive and with you!

The last was a cry of anguish and I answered but my thought seemed blocked by that increasing force about me. I was not sure that he got it. If so, he made no reply.

His body was now stiff and cold yet his heart acted, and his respiration was even, though shortened.

I laid a hand on his breast to keep close watch of his heart, then I became aware that his flesh was changed—different in some inexplicable way, and I shouted aloud to him in terror.

JUST one more of these noted statements it seems advisable to include. The two or three others I have destroyed. It came to me after an interminable wait. All the tense nervous fear of a lost man had flooded me. I sat oppressed and white, for that unknown power had swelled in the room until it crowded me. The lights went out and yet I could see. There was no defined light such as we of the modern world know, yet the room was not dark.

Every article in it seemed held, crowded by light whose essence was substance that could form itself around an object. I was shrouded in it and found movement difficult. My chest was heavy, and I gasped. While invisible, more terrible, was that gigantic throbbing will that seemed tearing at my own as I sought to hold to that of my friend much as a fighter seeks to separate an antagonist's grip from his throat.

C. Davis, unable to think. Lost beyond matter in the preworld time. Great swirling vortex of fire-mist, brilliant, light, awful, and charged with will, savage. Trying to drown me in fire. Can never reach body again. Going under. Goodby. If my soulless body still breathes, kill it, Carry.

As he ceased I was shaken as though some vicious hand had laid hold of my shoulder. I started to my feet. A ghastly pallor was spreading over Carry's face. His skin was hard, seamed and scaly.

I caught up an electric galvanizer and applied it to his chest. It sputtered, snapped into silence and was useless.

In despair I reached for a revolver we kept in the table drawer, while that dominating force seemed to be throbbing a rhythmic agony through me.

"Wait!"

I turned to meet the open eyes of the body on the divan. They were not Carry's eyes, for no intellect shone in their red fire depths. Only a rending fear was there looking out at me with eager hunger for aid, and his thickened blue lips moved clumsily as he spoke blotched, uncertain words without precision, as though an animal suddenly found tongue.

"I got back but not for long. Consciousness burned to nothing. Mere cinder of a soul, but I know what we want to know. The soul is a spark of Divine God—and God is, is—"

He ceased speaking, and his body jerked spasmodically. Before I could move, it twisted, writhed, became horrible—while over the features a series of changes passed in a flash. I saw them change from human to beast features, ugly, misshapen, grim with hanging lips and great teeth, then onto the floor rolled what had been a man. I swear it was the long thick body of a serpent, red-eyed, terrible, with great rough scales that gave out a grating noise on the floor.

I could not move. That vibrating agony of power held me as though I were bound. Before my eyes it danced in a whirl of gleaming points, violet, red and white.

Through the glare of them I saw that serpent, then as I started, a wild laugh, Carry's laugh as it might have been had he gone mad, sounded through the laboratory. The thing on the floor grew dim; its outline grew less distinct, a film of gray shrouded it, and the whole became vaguely transparent. It spread, moved, and in a sudden small cloud was gone.

I was alone with that force in the room and a thunder of thought reverberated in my head:

In the day that ye eat of the tree of knowledge ye shall surely die.

I sank upon a chair and covered my eyes to shut out those swirling lights. My face was wet with perspiration.

I am alone in the laboratory, yet I know that I am not alone. With me is that power, and in it I know Carry still lives. I feel him beside me and he urges me to go up, up—as we agreed I should into the higher realms of spirit life.

I must obey for the force drives me. Is it a mockery? Am I, too, being deceived by the imagined spirit of Carry that I may be destroyed? I cannot tell, yet I must try the experiment as planned.

One thing comforts me. I feel my wife near and I am assured that she will be waiting. More than that, I am a man of will. I shall arrange things so that if possible my hand will act unconsciously to my will and write what I discover though I, Davis, the soul, am separate from it.

I fear the terrible end Carry knew. I cannot, will not become the ghastly thing I saw last. To avoid it I have tied myself in this chair before the table. A rope is securely fastened under my arms and about

the chair. So long as I have arms I cannot fall.

Should they vanish I have prepared live wires from the attachments we have, and however I fall from this chair I will strike them.

At least I shall be burned away before that awful end overtakes me. I am ready now and will go by self-hypnosis.

It is made easy by the presence of Carry —if it is Carry who helps me. In my hand is a pen. I hope it writes on as I think.

I am going now, going, going—going to sleep.

HERE there was a break in the report as I found it and read it in the empty laboratory that morning after Davis had summoned me.

A large blot spread over the lower part of the page and below it a few uncertain lines ran slantwise down the page.

I could make nothing of them. On the next page letters appeared again, faint shaken letters, misshapen and uneven, but legible. I read on. In giving the report to the world I have thought best to rewrite this latter part keeping to Davis's own words but copying for the sake of legibility.

What he wrote seems to me more startling, more strange and possibly more terrible than the discovery made by Carry.

Certainly it is less encouraging; yet in it are paragraphs of great hope, bits of inspired beauty, as though the writer sang of glorious things, sublime truths and marvelous places.

CONTINUATION OF REPORT

AS I stand beside my own body here I can see the heavy blot where my pen fell as I went to sleep. Looking into my own face is a strange experience and suggests something to me which I have always suspected but now feel sure must be true.

For years I have entertained the idea that a man's appearance is directly related to his soul. It seems to me clear now, for

I am an unbodied spirit and a new power is mine. I can observe my unfleshed self as easily and as truly as I see my body tied in the chair. We resemble each other only dimly, yet there is something in the transparent skin, the even features, and the calm of that face that is due to my soul and to nothing else.

The truth becomes more definite as I recall Carry's face. I see now that he looked in the flesh quite as the structure of his soul compelled, but where is he? I cannot see him, although I was sure that I should do so as soon as I was freed from my material person.

Another strange fact here deserves comment before I state my exact position in the realm of the super-conscious. I can control my body even though I am separate from it. The delicate psychic fibers with which I operate that hand are clear to me and there is something exalting in the sense of power; yet I am not happy. Too much of mystery still shrouds the activities of this night. Still pulsing like a flaming artery through me is that dread force that lights the laboratory with such a weird glow.

Worst of all the thoughts that I see pass in my own head like shadows of flame is the sudden realization that I am alone.

Where is the great world of spirit? I stand here free, unbodied—yet I am alone and the four walls of the laboratory hold me. I must go on and up, for rest is impossible while I am without the secret of space that will enable me to find my wife and Carry.

I am moving now, going slowly toward the farthest wall and I find that those invisible soul tendons which manipulate my writing hand stretch as I move. They will reach across all the space of the universe, and I am able to go where I will among the stars—conscious that my body awaits me, alive, under my control, and well.

A great feeling of exhilaration swells within me, and I pass through the wall easily. I am master of the fourth dimension.

Below me the sleeping city spreads an infinite pattern of dark squares edged in long lines of gleaming lights. Above the star-filled sky smiles blue and calm. I am soaring into it.

Since writing that preceding sentence a long lapse of time has occurred. To me it seems eternal, though I know it was but a few seconds. I am now in a form of consciousness superior to man. Where I am, I do not know, nor by what means I came, save that my will aided by that ever burning vital force has brought me here.

I hesitate to describe it, fearful lest the utter incredibility of the truth strikes whoever reads and causes denial.

Above all things let me warn against negations. They are the tragic soul crises into which one goes to destruction as Carry went. He denied the soul, and I know now that he is gone. Wiped out by the great will—and even his spirit is extinct, a waste cinder floating somewhere in bottomless chaos.

As for myself, I am alive with a joy that thrills me madly. I shall succeed, and my gain will reward the world with truth.

I am a dancing, whirling, conscious flame, hotter than fire, more brilliant than light, beautiful beyond words—and I leap up from nothing to nothing like a great burning tongue that lives without fuel. Not even space or time contains me. They lie below me there in that petty universe where my unsouled body writes at my command.

All the rare colors of the rainbow, summer sunsets, and the light-refracting dew are thrown off by my dancing soul of heat, and gleam around me in an iridescent sheen.

Vague harmonies stir in the center of my columned fire, and I am stirred to infinite yearnings. Now I am going higher, higher —and I change again. The raging heat diminishes, my colors fade. Dear Heaven, am I going out? Am I to end in nothing, like a fuelless spark?

No! I am in a glory of extreme exalted life. I am the essence of music, singing great arias of pure melody.

I know not how to explain my being,

save to say that I am the very soul of harmony, and everywhere about me tumultuous chords in crashing volumes not audible to the human ear ring vibrant through the worlds and stir the stars to action. Fine fabricated melodies weave in and out among the thundrous bass and I am part of it—conscious and alive, like the very inspiration of the universal hymn.

I must resort to figurative speech, for no words live that can portray the vital essence of the music that is a spirit.

I am a moving sound, glittering with rare beauty, and about me stars of chords and planets of melody swing through a sea of motion like dancing agonies of ecstasy. This is the bliss of far-extended soul, and ahead of me I know God waits to reveal—Himself. The knowledge comes in notes like cosmic flute tones and I swirl on and on. Motion, always motion and energy, are the very deeps that guide even as they were with Carry—but how different! One thing is sure. All things center about movement, and all things that are conscious move. I am motion that expresses itself in pure unmaterial sound.

Were I in the compass of the universe we know, I could say that I had gone millions upon millions of miles during the time I described these two states of being, but I am outside time and space moving toward God. I am more definitely aware of Him now, and there is a swift leap of yearning that changes ever and again to movement.

Movement grows more and more important. It is the essence of all things. I have left the realm of sound and am movement, energy—conscious and swirling. I am force itself.

A dreadful fear has crept into my mind as I sweep on. I have ceased to exist as a form at all and am mere motion tearing on and on while I swirl in a circle like a tornado. It is ghastly, for I am not certain of things now. Try as I may to attain the ecstasy of a few minutes ago, I fail. Despair grows in larger and larger blackness while I am diminishing. That is tragic, for I have become a mere vortex ring, a swirling circle of force that gyrates about a vacuum. I want to return to the laboratory where I know my hand still moves at the dictation of my will, but it may stop soon.

I feel that giant-will trying to tear me from my body. It strikes at my will in an attempt to paralyze me into destruction. I am mad with motion, and—Heaven help me, I am nearing that same dread feeling Carry knew. I am mere fire mist, consciousness, swimming in fire, and a fire that shivers with savage will, rage, and desire.

If you could imagine all the energy of the world, all the yearning of the human race, all the savagery of life from the beginning become strong, leaping, dancing sparks of anger-conscious fire, then you will know what has occurred to me. I swim in it desperately, and there is no rest—no salvation. I shall go down in it and be lost. My body will be there or—I am mad; it will follow Carry. I see it all now. I, too, am lost to all!

Oh, the supreme folly of man! We are

a race of dreaming fools. All the high imaginative forces we have aspired to master are our very mockeries. I thought I was attaining God, my wife, and the peace of freed spirit. Instead I am battling agonizingly for life in my body. Imagination has been the curse of my days. I laughed at the glory of human life. I aspired to conquer soul.

There was Carry who denied, and I saw that he was gone as though he had never been. In my supreme egotism I warned against negation. I am wiser now, for like Carry I have crossed the last great rim of life and am beyond it at the heart of God.

I am sinking, sinking to death of mind in this fire, and I pray only that my body fall upon the electric wires in the laboratory soon, that it too may vanish from the world.

Agonies are endured in a moment and still I fight against the accursed savagery of will that beats me down. Wait!

I am back in my body staring at the sheets of written words. I know, remembering Carry, that my eyes are not the blue orbs of Davis but ghastly fear-driven flames. Soon I shall go out and the vibrating agony that beats in this room so wildly will be avenged.

Before that time I have one word to write. Luckily I write instead of talk, for my words would be blundering and bestial.

I have been to the heart and I know the soul is a part of God.

My arms are growing shorter! Heaven have mercy—my skin is heavy, coarse and snakelike!

HERE the report ended in a spreading black smudge. I studied it closely and I found the top of three letters dimly visible above the blot, while the lower part of two others showed. The letters were: Q, H, Z, R, F.

I need add very little for the purpose of complete clarity. The laboratory was, as I stated at the beginning, empty when I arrived, and the door was locked, the key being on the inside. I burst open the door.

These later sheets lay on the table in a disordered pile, while a pen had fallen to the floor where I found it beneath the table.

Not a trace of either man was discoverable save their hats which hung in a small closet against one wall. Around a chair before the table wires were carefully arranged and I found by testing that they were alive with great voltages of electricity.

Upon the back of the chair a rope hung. It was tied in a circle passing between the round pieces in the chair back.

A minute charred fragment of something not organic lay beside the chair.

I have investigated thoroughly and am able to assert that since my two friends left their apartment on the evening of February third and entered the laboratory, they have not been seen nor heard of.

Personally I have accepted their report, weirdly improbable as it seems, for one thing more supports their combined testimony. I examined the laboratory furniture minutely as well as its walls, floor and ceiling. All of them looked as though they had been edged in a flame of unusual quality such as an unknown light might be, for all were marked with slight char that was in odd ripples evenly rhythmic, as though the flame had leaped and throbbed as it burned.

Davis rails at imagination rather forcefully in one brief sentence. From my knowledge of him it seems probable that he intended to imply that Carry was right in denying the existence of the soul, and that his own experience was a mystical prolongation of imagination in fields where art operates.

I may be mistaken, for it is equally true that he was incapable by temperament of disbelief in spiritual things. Perhaps his statement means something never to be understood unless some other inquirer repeats his experience with more success.

What value this report may be to science is not clear to me, for I am an artist and not scientific. I submit it with the hope that the lives of my friends may not have ended in vain.

The Radiant Enemies

By R. F. STARZL

**Tons of radium on a comet—guarded
by weird creatures of space**

"Look! Nuggets of It!
I'm rich!"

INGRAHAM shifted the broad restrain-
ing belt around his waist a little with
awkward hands, for the terrific decel-
eration of the ship made his arms seem

almost too heavy to lift. Held in place
before the astrogation panel, the man
fought against dizziness, for at this critical time even the slightest mistake might

easily dash them in ruins upon the jagged nucleus of the comet.

Radiant Comet, Ingraham had named it, for the spectroscope had shown it to be rich in radium, the universally used "starter" for all atomic disintegration processes. A tiny speck of radium activated the atomic motors of this very ship, and without radium the slender silver rods which slowly fed into the bulky power domes about them, and above and below them, were inert and useless.

Ingraham permitted himself a backward glance, to where Durphee's gross form gasped for breath.

"Be there in fifteen minutes," he said jerkily, struggling against the weight of his own diaphragm.

Durphee did not answer, except to moan, and Ingraham turned to his panel. As the image of the nucleus slowly enlarged on the teletab, crossing the graduations marked thereon, he plied the levers and dials, until their speed was well under control.

He breathed a sigh of relief and unclasped the safety belt.

Skillfully he permitted the ship to settle, until a slight jar proclaimed that they had landed.

Durphee lurched to his feet. He was a trifle taller than Ingraham's five feet ten, and thicker about the waist. Durphee looked older than his indulgence-sated forty years, and Ingraham younger than his thirty.

Ingraham was the scientist who had discovered the true nature of Radiant Comet, looping in a vast parabola around the sun, and already well on its way to the outer spaces again.

It was situated well beyond the orbit of Saturn, because of the delay in adapting an ordinary Earth-to-Moon ship for this mad adventure.

But Durphee had raised the money, in a last desperate gamble to recoup a wasted fortune.

"How much radium is there?" Durphee asked, staring out of one of the thick ports.

THE other man did not answer immediately. He also stared over the strange landscape. He saw a desolate inferno. They had landed on the side away from the small, brightly yellow sun, and looked upon night. But not a true night. Everywhere the rocks gave forth a light, faint and spectral, a light too weak to dim the unwinking stars. But light enough, it would seem, to allow a man to walk over the sandy plain.

"Millions of tons of radium," Ingraham said at last. "My spectroscopic analysis—"

"Millions of tons?" exclaimed Durphee in a loud voice. "What are we waiting for? Let's get going!" He made as if to turn the handwheel that locked the oblong door.

"Wait!" Ingraham commanded sharply. "Open that door, and you're a dead man. And I am, too. Put on this suit."

He opened a locker and brought out a single garment, which included a helmet and boots shod with lead. It was a typical space suit, and Durphee knew how to put it on. Ingraham got one for himself.

"Notice the fine metal mesh, almost like chain mail," Ingraham explained, "over the outside of the regular fabric. That is, you might say, a radiation screen, activated by a small oscillator in your pack, along with the respirator tank. It will protect you from the emanations, which would otherwise burn you up. You see—"

"Let's get going!" Durphee insisted. "Millions of tons—"

"Don't be a hog!" Ingraham cut in coolly. "We've only room for a couple hundred pounds of the stuff in our insulated cases. Some of the stuff is pretty thinly distributed. We have to look for the richest—say—for metallic radium, if we can find it."

"All right, come!" Durphee begged. He slipped on the helmet, sliding up the sealing wedge. His eyes glittered greedily back of the vitrine face-plate.

Ingraham slipped on his own helmet.

"All in good time," he said levelly, speaking into the inductance phone.

"This atmosphere is mostly helium, given off by the disintegration of the radium. Sure that your respirator is working?"

They opened the lock, and the door flung outward from the pressure of the air within, and their suits instantly inflated, standing out firmly. Valving off a little air they stepped out upon the surface of the Radiant Comet. They carried their tools and instruments, and a cylindrical container for the radium.

Although the possibility of meeting hostile inhabitants was remote, they carried at their belts light little deionizer tubes, those deadly modern weapons that destroy life by inducing a chemical change within the body.

"Look back once in a while," Ingraham cautioned. "Keep an eye on the ship. We don't want to be marooned here on a comet."

"Let's start picking the stuff up," Durphee proposed, staring about him.

"Richer ahead, where those rocks crop out."

They arrived at the designated place after a long walk, and here the levelness of the sands was broken by a mad confusion of splintered rock, huge upended masses, and giant crystalline forms. It was a scene of malefic fairyland, lighted by radiance that streamed silently out from every side. Overhead was the foggy luminescence of the comet's tail, stretching out into infinity, but it was cold and unreal compared to the living light that came from the rocks.

Durphee gave a hoarse cry.

"Look! Look! Veins of it! Nuggets! I'm rich! I'm rich!"

"Not till we get it back to earth!" Ingraham reminded him.

Durphee fell to his knees and snatched up fragments of the dangerous heavy metal, fondling it, holding it to the faceplate of his helmet.

"Don't do that, you fool!" Ingraham said. "Do you want to go blind or crazy? Drop it into the canister. We're going to fill that, and leave as fast as we can."

BOTH fell to work, filling the can with their incredible hoard, Durphee almost tearful at the thought of leaving so much of it, Ingraham sharply reminding him that no man could use so much wealth.

They nearly had enough when overhead appeared a light. At first it might have been merely another star, but soon it resolved itself as some object that was rapidly approaching them. Other lights appeared, fast growing.

In a few minutes the Earthmen were gazing up at the strangely beautiful beings slowly circling about them at a distance of a few feet from their heads. One may imagine a multiplicity of diaphanous ruffles, like crumpled cellophane, all aglow with prismatic light of their own.

They were not wings, those thin, radiant processes, and yet they might have served as fourth-dimensional models of butterflies. They did not move at all, and appeared to have no part in sustaining themselves in the air. They might have been merely large absorption surfaces, to absorb and hold the radiant energy pulsating everywhere on that comet.

A fittingly strange form of life in strange surroundings, thought Ingraham, looking at them wonderingly, and with appreciation of their beauty. Looking through them, he saw no body, no nucleus; merely thin, shimmering, membranous matter.

"Hey, listen!" came Durphee's sharp voice in the receiver. "Are those things dangerous?"

"They don't seem to be unfriendly."

"Well, I don't like the looks of them!"

Suddenly one of the radiant beings ceased its movements, hung, as it were, helplessly. In its shimmering membranes a hole had appeared, a hole through which the cold stars showed. Quickly, like a fire eating through cloth, the hole widened, spread through the complex ramifications of its being. It reached the tips of the ruffles, and went out. The prismatic light disappeared.

"You fool!" Ingraham tried to knock the deionizer from Durphee's hand, but the heavy space suit hindered him, and another of the radiant creatures died. And yet another, before Ingraham wrenched the tube from the other's grasp. Like glowing bubbles before a gale, the visitors swept upward and away, and in a few seconds there was no sign of them.

"What's the matter with you?" Durphee growled, stooping and resuming his excited mining operations.

"Those beautiful things; why kill them?"

"They're no good."

"As I may have mentioned before, Durphee, you're a hog. Men like you blasted the ancient Moon dwellings, out of pure cussedness. If you didn't care what you destroyed, you might have considered that it's dangerous to antagonize them—"

"Get busy with this stuff," Durphee snapped crossly. "As for them, we're well rid of 'em."

"Don't be too sure. I think they're coming back."

They were coming back. Sweeping up on a long arc from some place a mile or two across the plain, they were sweeping back like avenging fireflies, hundreds of them.

"Now we're in for it," Ingraham said angrily, handing Durphee his deionizer. "Wait till they attack."

"Will they attack?" Durphee asked, with growing anxiety.

"They've got plenty of reason to," Ingraham reminded him. "Stand still."

THE radiant beings flung themselves upon the Earthmen in a frenzy of movement. It seemed that they must be annihilated beneath the weight of that attack. But when it was over, and they recoiled, the puzzled men realized that they had hardly felt as much as a touch. The radiants hovered about uncertainly, as if undecided, and made no further hostile move.

"Thank goodness!" Ingraham exclaimed. "We're immune to their offense. It's some form of radiant discharge, and our suits protected us. See, they're sluggish now.

It may take them some time to regenerate enough energy to attack us again."

The colors of the diaphanous multiple ruffles were in fact dim, lacking the living fire they had owned before.

"You mean they can't hurt us?" asked Durphee with returning courage.

"It seems not."

"Then let 'em have it!"

This time the weakened Radiants winked out in death almost instantly before Durphee's deionizer, and the survivors fled precipitately.

"You murdering fool!" Ingraham raged, grabbing for the tube.

"No, you don't!" Durphee replied, backing away warily. "Not with me owning half of a few billion dollars' worth of radium. I'm taking no chances."

"Keep it, then!" Ingraham yielded with disgust. "When there's plenty for both of us, why should I rob you?"

They fell to work, and in a few minutes the canister was full. Despite the slight gravity on that comet, it was all the two of them could do to carry their treasure. When they arrived at the ship they were both weary.

Once inside they prepared to lock the door and leave at once, for the comet was steadily carrying them away from the Earth. With a word of warning to Durphee about handling radium unprotected, Ingraham started to lock up and set the air machine to working. Suddenly he gave a cry:

"They've stolen our fuel rods!"

Through the plate of Durphee's helmet his face was ashen as he looked up. The slender silver rods were indeed missing.

"It's them unholy what-you-call-'ems!" he gritted. "The thieving—" He wallowed in foul language.

"Keep your suit on!" Ingraham warned him briskly. "We've got to find those bars or we're marooned here forever. We'll die here, you understand?"

He added, not without bitterness:

"It seems those things are intelligent. If you hadn't been so quick to murder them, they might have been friendly to us. I think they were friendly at first."

Durphee tottered to the door.

"Wait!" Ingraham called. "I think I know where they come from. They may have taken the rods there."

The low cliffs stretched like the frozen surf of a phosphorescent sea across the plain. Somewhere along that low line must be the dwelling of the Radiants. Ingraham looked back once, regretfully, at the ship. There was no way of locking it from the outside, for the builders had anticipated the danger of being locked out by oversight. Now this precaution stood them in ill stead, but they must risk the chance of having the ship tampered with again.

The cliffs were nearer than they seemed. After a walk of about two miles the Earthmen arrived and skirted along their base until they came to an opening in the rock. The interior was illuminated with the same milky-white light, and Ingraham went in.

"Follow me," he instructed Durphee, "and don't use the tube unless you have to."

They passed through a corridor for several hundred feet, and, traveling downward, came to a lofty chamber three or four hundred feet in diameter. Until then they had seen none of the Radiants, but now, as if by signal, thousands of them appeared, floating in the air over their heads. Durphee pointed the deionizer at them defensively, but did not discharge the weapon, and the Radiants hovered, apparently waiting for something.

Ingraham called excitedly:

"Look, Durphee! In the center of the room! See, on that round thing?"

A ROUND boss, like the stump of an enormous tree, but crystalline in character, was in the center of the great room. Through the transparent mineral, liquid, flowing fires, in all the colors of the rainbow, could be seen, slowly ebbing and flowing, sending out streams of silent color that bathed the lofty vaults and arches like the long slow surges of a ground swell. But Ingraham was looking at the little bundle of silver rods lying on the table-like rock—the stolen fuel bars.

Swiftly he strode toward them, Durphee following, and as the Earthmen approached the light seemed to ebb, while the Radiants retreated to the farthest extremities of the room.

But as Ingraham extended his hand and took the silver rods, a light as dazzling as lightning and as overwhelming as a geyser burst from the boss, blinding him. Nevertheless he took the rods, and, turning, groped for Durphee.

The latter was shielding his eyes with his forearm.

"What is it? What's that light?" he asked, in alarm.

"Some powerful form of radiant energy," Ingraham replied. "I'll bet those things are wondering why we weren't killed. Our radiation screens saved us Let's get out and get back!"

The great light ebbed, and as the Earthmen turned to go the Radiants reappeared, seemingly imbued with the greatest excitement. They whirled about their heads with the fury of a tornado, and Durphee laughed.

"That for you, firebugs! Wish I had time, I'd take your god, or whatever that thing is, with me."

"Keep your tube in its clip," Ingraham warned.

"Who in the devil are you—" Durphee flared. But he got no further. A rock as big as a man's fist toppled out of some niche or cranny high overhead, struck his shoulder, ripping out a triangular rent in the mesh of the radiation screen covering his space suit. Instantly one of the Radiants flung itself on the vulnerable spot and clung there, limpet-like. A cry of desperate agony rung in Ingraham's induction phone:

"Help! It's burning me to death!"

As Durphee fell, Ingraham leaped forward and caught the Radiant in his clumsy gauntlets. He crumpled the gauzy ruffles of its being as easily as paper, and saw its shimmering light go black under his hands. Then, before another of the creatures could fasten itself on the place, he lifted back the torn flap and twisted the thin wire ends together as well as he could.

"Can you stand now?" he asked.

Durphee scrambled to his feet, cursing and groaning.

"It burned the liver out of me," he muttered.

Rocks were still raining about them, as if the Radiants had just discovered by accident this primitive method of fighting and were making the most of it.

Suddenly, Ingraham, struck on the head, fell to the ground.

He must have been unconscious only for an instant, for when he got to his knees he could see Durphee walking away, scarcely ten feet from him.

"Durphee!" he called. But his partner paid him no heed. He had already entered the corridor.

Ingraham saw that his body was literally covered with the Radiants, but the rock had torn none of the protective screen, and he was impervious to their attack. Reeling, he rose to his feet, brushing the fragile beings from him, and so followed Durphee, raging with anger.

Too cowardly to murder him, the avaricious Durphee nevertheless was willing to abandon him to death, he thought. Durphee was running, and Ingraham ran after him. The Radiants did not follow.

JUST then Durphee turned and saw him. In that uncertain light, with the handicap of the clumsy space suits, Ingraham was not sure, but he thought he saw his partner start. Durphee spoke first:

"Close squeak!" he congratulated thickly.

"Durphee," Ingraham asked coldly, "did you see what happened to me?"

"I didn't see anything," was Durphee's sullen reply.

"You didn't see me fall, and keep going?"

"You had the fuel rods," the other man retorted. "What good would it do me to leave you?"

Ingraham felt a sense of shame.

"We're both unstrung. This unholy place! Lead on, Durphee; let's be on our way."

Their tracks in the luminous sand were clear and pointed unmistakably to the ship. In less than an hour they were close to the shiny ovoid. Durphee was the first to reach it. At the door he stopped and waited for his partner to come up.

Ingraham stepped beside him unsuspectingly. In an instant Durphee had snatched the weapon out of the clip at Ingraham's belt, and delivered a staggering blow to the solar plexus. Ingraham went down, and Durphee fell on top of him. His weight, on that small world, was not great, but the shock of the fall paralyzed Ingraham's breathing.

Something was thudding on the vitrine face-plate of his helmet; repeated blows from the heel of Durphee's hand, trying to break the glass.

Blind anger gave the under man strength, and in a fury of despair he struck back at the muffled body of his betrayer. He clamped an arm around the other's neck, only to have it painfully wrenched free. He took hold of the folds of Durphee's space suit. There was a metallic rip as the insulating screen tore away, but Durphee rolled free and staggered to his feet.

Ingraham tried to rise also, but as he did the glowing sand came up to meet him. He sprawled, and the thud of a kick in the ribs came to him only impersonally. He gave himself up for dead, and before his eyes the sand under the face-plate glowed mockingly.

But Ingraham was not dead. With faint surprise he came to that realization some time later, and immediately afterward the freezing horror of his fate bore in upon him. Marooned! Marooned on a comet and speeding away from the sun—already far beyond all past limits of human travel and drifting remorselessly into the void. Betrayed by the greed of a man to whom he had unhesitatingly entrusted his life.

He lifted his body, supporting it on his hands, and stared ahead of him, wondering if he had overestimated the passage of time, for the ship was still there, just as it had been, and the tracks in the sand showed where Durphee had stepped in, letting the door fall shut, but a narrow line showed that it had not yet been drawn tight and locked from within. The silver fuel rods were gone.

With wild hope Ingraham tottered to the ship. Had Durphee relented, or was he battening the cruel streak in him on his victim's despairing efforts?

Ingraham felt for his deionizer. It was gone, and was nowhere on the ground. He was still at Durphee's mercy, then!

After many clumsy failures he managed to insert the thick fingers of his space gloves into the crack of the door. Quickly he flung it open and stepped inside, ready to fight again for his life.

His first glance showed him that he would not have to fight Durphee. His partner lay at full length on the floor, and as Ingraham came in, ten or more Radiants rose from the prostrate body and hovered in the air, as if expectantly, projecting, one might imagine, a question.

There was no need to examine the charred fabric of Durphee's space suit where the Radiants had fastened, undeterred because the radiation screen was torn. Durphee had paid, in full.

Fear lifted from the soul of Ingraham, and shrouded it again as he saw the slender bars suspended, by some invisible force, beneath the bodies of the hovering Radiants—the silver fuel rods—the key to his escape into a normal world.

A quick glance out of the corner of his face-plate showed him that he had left the door open, and he knew beyond doubt that before he could take one step his visitors would be gone, taking the rods with them.

But even as that appalling truth sank into him, Ingraham was thinking of the prismatic beauty of these exquisite creatures, and as he did so something passed between the Earthman and the Radiants, and something like a benediction and a sense of understanding flowed from them to him. They drew together, and light streamed from one to another. The silver rods fell to the floor of the ship about Ingraham, and swiftly the radiant beings flew out of the door and were gone.

The Readers' Viewpoint

The Editors,

Famous Fantastic Mysteries:

Congratulations! At last you've published the magazine I have been waiting for, and you've done a mighty fine job at that. My greatest criticism is that you issue it only every other month. That's hardly being fair to your readers. However, I feel sure the success you no doubt will have will make it possible for you to give us FAMOUS FANTASTIC MYSTERIES every month in a short time. The title is well chosen.

I hesitated to clip the coupon on the last page because I want to save the magazine intact—and I save very few magazines. Besides, the coupon hardly gave me space to say the things I wanted to say.

It's hard to select my favorite story, almost every one being far above the average. "The Moon Pool", "Karpen the Jew", "The Girl in the Golden Atom", and "The Witch-Makers" all run a close race for first place, "The Moon Pool" having, perhaps, a slight edge on the others. All of these seem to follow closely the suggestion implied by the magazine's title, although the quality of mystery is somewhat lacking in "The Girl in the Golden Atom."

"Space Station No. 1" seemed just another science fiction story.

"The Whimpus" and "Blind Man's Buff", also struck me as not being in strict keeping with the title of FAMOUS FANTASTIC MYSTERIES although the latter story was quite amusing. However, I rather resented the humorous touch in a magazine of this type. If you must include humor, please hold it down to a single story each month.

In regard to the type of story I'd like to see in future issues, I suggest that you stick to ones like "The Witch-Makers", "The Moon Pool", and "Karpen the Jew". These tales are definitely unusual and well in keeping with the magazine's title. Exclude stories the likes of which we can find in a dozen or more other publications. In short, give us the stuff that's hard to find elsewhere.

Whatever you do, don't change the cover. As it is now it adds a great deal of character to the appearance of the magazine, character that would be considerably lessened should you resort to a pictorial cover; then the magazine would become just another fantastic fiction publication instead of something new and refreshingly different.

As you see, my criticisms are few. FAMOUS FANTASTIC MYSTERIES give me exactly what I've been waiting for. I think you've done a grand job. Keep your magazine on the same high level of quality and I'll remain a most devoted reader.

L. ROBERT TSCHIRKY

ROSEMONT, PA.

Not to Kill Time

Although I am not given to writing to magazine editors usually, I feel strongly moved to give my two-cents worth concerning your new magazine FAMOUS FANTASTIC MYSTERIES.

It is my opinion that you are doing us science-fiction readers a real service, and answering a long felt need, in producing this magazine. Certainly, although science-fiction stories are new, compared to the art of story-telling, as old as man, there are, by now, a number of real classics in this field. And what could be better than that we readers may read the select material?

I do not read them "just to kill time," but to supply the mental diversion from cold realism. Therefore, I am constantly searching for higher type stories. I believe your new magazine will fill this need, and you may count upon me as a permanent reader.

Good luck to you!

GEORGE E. STEWART

PENSACOLA, FLORIDA

Suggestion for Future Series

I have just seen a copy of your publication and wish to congratulate you upon your achievement. It has been needed for a long time. As to the stories, Merritt's "Moon Pool" takes first place, of course. Next come "Karpen the Jew," "The Whimpus" and "Blind Man's Buff," closely followed by the others. All were good and you are to be commended for your selection.

As a suggestion for future issues, please print the following:

Merritt—Metal Monster, Conquest of the Moon Pool, Face in the Abyss, Through the Dragon Glass.

England—Darkness and Dawn trilogy.

Stilson—Polaris of the Snows, Minos of Sardanes, Polaris and the Goddess Glorian.

Giesy—Palos of the Dog-Star Pack, Mouthpiece of Zitu, Jason, Son of Jason.

WILLIAM EVANS

SALEM, ORE.

Print One Complete Novel

After reading your new magazine, FAMOUS FANTASTIC MYSTERIES, I cannot describe how thoroughly I endorse it. To find a magazine printing just one story like "The Moon Pool," I would consider a stroke of luck, but to have "The Moon Pool" amongst stories like Cumming's "The Girl in the Golden Atom" (which I waited for many years) and others just as good—well, it was a stroke of genius.

Couldn't you print one complete long novel, or if that is impossible print the longer novels in parts? Need I say that we want the sequel to both, "The Moon Pool" (Conquest of the Moon Pool), by Merritt and "The Girl in the Golden Atom" (The Princess of the Atom), by Cummings and please print "Brand New World," also by Ray Cummings.

Again I say, well done and in the same breath —give us more of the same.

LUCILLE GALES

LIVERMORE, IOWA

Wants Farley's Radio Series

GREETINGS AND CONGRATULATIONS!

I enjoyed every one of the stories in your first issue.

"The Moon Pool" is easily tops, but have you abridged it or is there a sequel to this famous story? Second place goes to "The Girl in the Golden Atom" and the third to "Karpen the Jew."

I'd like to have "The Blind Spot" and its sequel published and also some of Ralph Milne Farley's stories of the ant people of Venus.

Once again congratulations and may this new Argosy of yours be as laden with success as the original of that name.

HERBERT S. SCHOFIELD

PHILADELPHIA, PA.

Something I Hoped For

Congratulations. And I mean it. This magazine is something I had hoped for, for a long time. Let's see, it was about 1935, I think, that I gave up reading science fiction (while still keeping my collection intact). But then I happened to pick up a copy of George Allan England's "Darkness and Dawn." Well! Here was real stuff. No, I wasn't jaded but only tired of mass-production science fiction. Therefore I welcome the new magazine with wide open arms.

I hope you won't confine the stories to shorts, since some of the best tales have been serial length. And please do not use (for the present) those that are still available in book form. My suggestions follow:

Of course the sequels to "The Moon Pool" and "Golden Atom." Ralph Milne Farley's

trilogy, "The Radio Man," "Radio Beasts," "Radio Planet." J. U. Giesy's triology, "Palos, of the Dog Star Pack," "Mouthpiece of Zitu," "Jason, Son of Jason." Merritt's "Metal Monster," "Three Lines of Old French," "Through the Dragon Glass." Garrett P. Serviss: "Moon Maiden," "Conquest of Mars," "Conquest of the Moon." George Allan England's "Darkness and Dawn." H. E. Flint: "The Planeteer," "Queen of Life," "Man in the Moon," etc. Austin Hall's "Into the Infinite," "Rebel Soul," "Almost Immortal." Flint and Hall's "Blind Spot." Garret Smith's "After a Million Years."

LESTER ANDERSON

SAN FRANCISCO, CAL.

Knows His "Fantastics"

I have just purchased the first issue of FAMOUS FANTASTIC MYSTERIES. I have not read it, for it happens that I have already read, and have in my possession every story in the magazine. You see, I am a fantasy fan and collector.

I'll buy every issue of FFM you put out.

I think your selection of stories for the first issue is excellent. Some readers will be disappointed (as I was), to discover that "The Moon Pool" is only the novelette which precedes the real story. Obviously, you'll have to publish "The Conquest of the Moon Pool". The same thought applies to "The Girl in the Golden Atom", and its sequel, "The People of the Golden Atom". These are serials, long ones— yet they are the classics which the fantasy readers have been so anxious to read. More of that a bit later.

The other stories are well chosen. "Karpen the Jew" by Leath and "The Whimpus" by Robbins are striking stories. Giesy's "Blind Man's Buff" is a humorous note which might well round out every issue. Wandrei's and Wellman's yarns, I think, are too new but they are good stories, nevertheless.

As for future issues, you have an almost inexhaustible source of material from which to draw. But—the long stories are the stories you should feature! "The Blind Spot" by Austin Hall and Homer Eon Flint, and its sequel, "The Spot of Life" . . . J. U. Giesy's triology, "Palos of the Dog Star Pack", "The Mouthpiece of Zitu" and "Jason, Son of Jason" . . . George Allan England's novels: "The Empire in the Air", "Darkness and Dawn", "Beyond the Great Oblivion", "The Afterglow", "The Golden Blight", "The Fatal Gift", etc. . . . Homer Eon Flint's yarns: "The Planeteer", "The King of Conserve Island", "The Lord of Death", "The Queen of Life", "The Devolutionist", "The Emancipatrix", "The Man in the Moon", and "Out of the Moon" . . . Charles B. Stilson's "Polaris—of the Snows", "Minos of Sardanes", and "Polaris and the Goddess Glorian" . . .

Garret Smith's "After a Million Years", "Between Worlds", "On the Brink of 2000", and "Treasures of Tantalus" . . . Merritt's "The Metal Monster" (though you should use the shortened version titled "The Metal Emperor") and his other famous fantasies . . . Ray Cummings' "The Fire People", "The Man Who Mastered Time", and a dozen others. . . .

Lots of luck!

L. A. E.

READING, PA.

Wants Cover Illustrated

I want to thank you for making these great fantasies available in your new magazine.

I was always under the impression that Merritt's "The Moon Pool", was a book-length novel instead of a novelette. The ending seemed to suggest that there is more than you published. How about it? Otherwise the story was all I heard about it. Other prize winners, Robbin's "The Whimpus" and Cummings' "The Girl in the Golden Atom".

Suggested for future publication, "The Blind Spot", "The Planet of Peril", "The Radio Man" (and the rest of Farley's "radio" series), "The Queen of Life" and "The Lord of Death", both by Homer Eon Flint.

I would also like to see the cover illustrated.

HAROLD F. BENSON

WEST WARWICK, R. I.

"Golden Atom" Best

I think you have an excellent magazine here. The first issue was perfect and it hit upon all my weaknesses with its variety of stories.

"The Girl in the Golden Atom" by Ray Cummings, was the best I have ever read. Personally I think you should use many more like it and occasionally change off to stories like "The Whimpus" by Todd Robbins.

LOU MILLER

ALBANY, N. Y.

All Right Mr. Frank, Smooth Edges

As editor of a fan series of publications, and as a fantasy fan I want to laud your new publication, FAMOUS FANTASTIC MYSTERIES.

You have a swell line-up of real classics in this first issue; the make-up is neat, attractive. As for the stories, you can't rate tales when they are all the best.

Suggestions for improvements: Give us smooth edges. Get Virgil Finlay for one of your artists.

And give us serials.

I hope that the magazine becomes a monthly real soon.

RICHARD FRANK

MILLHEIM, PA.

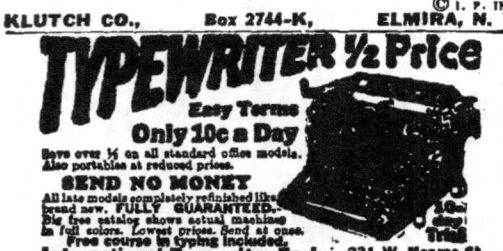

Wants Very Old Classics

Congratulations on a fine magazine! The idea behind FAMOUS FANTASTIC MYSTERIES is splendid—even if the title is not. The stories in the Sept.-Oct. issue were all excellent reading. As a science fiction enthusiast, I would naturally like to see the classic type of story predominate—though whether it is a Merritt type, with plenty of imagination, or a story like Wellman's, more rigidly scientific, I do not care. The supernatural stories are o.k., but only in small doses.

All in all, the magazine is a very good one; but I have a few criticisms and suggestions to offer. In the first place, stories as recent as 1936 should not be used. Why not make 1934 the limit?

Secondly, I'd like to see the magazine published monthly.

Thirdly, and this is most important, please use some serials. Titles like "The Metal Monster," the "Radio" series.

In any event, I'm looking forward to the next issue.
PAUL H. SPENCER
WEST HARTFORD, CONN.

Shows a Nice Balance

I have just read the first issue of FAMOUS FANTASTIC MYSTERIES, and I like it. I approve of its aim. And I approve of the make-up of the magazine, which seems to be à la ARGOSY. The make-up is an important factor in my estimation; if you had made the magazine look like a Sunday supplement, I would have been repulsed. As it is, FAMOUS FANTASTIC MYSTERIES shows a nice balance between sprightliness and decorum. Keep it the way it is.
A. H. L.
HOLLIS, N. Y.

More of the Same

Here is what I think of the stories in your first issue:
The Moon Pool—a good fantastic.
Space Station No. 1—a good space story.
The Whimpus—good.
Karpen the Jew—very good.
The Girl in the Golden Atom—the best story I have ever read.
The Witch Makers—good.
Blind Man's Buff—a really funny story.
I want to read stories like "The Girl in the Golden Atom."
I have enjoyed this book more than any other magazine I have ever read except the Argosy.
I want to read more of this kind of stories.
FRANK BROOKS.
ASHLAND, KY.